Possums Sing

For Shari,
All the Best
Marlina

Marlina Claire

Wild Winds Publishing Mount Sterling, Illinois

Published by
Wild Winds Publishing
Post Office Box 83
Mount Sterling, IL 62353

www.wildwindspublishing.com

This is a work of fiction. Any references to events, to real people, living or dead; or to real locales are intended only to give the fiction a setting in reality. Other names, characters, and incidents either are the product of the author's imagination or are used fictitiously, and their resemblance, if any, to real-life counterparts is entirely coincidental.

First Printing November 2000

10 9 8 7 6 5 4 3 2 1

Printed in the United States of America by Morris Publishing
3212 East Highway 30, Kearney, NE 68847

ISBN 0-9703726-0-4

Prairie Winds is an imprint of Wild Winds Publishing

Acknowledgments

There are many students too numerous to mention who have provided stories of events from which the author based this novel. Both the horrors and joys represent the reality of those events. It is the author's hope that by this fictional encounter between good and evil, others may pause to consider their own lives and place in humanity.

Dr. David Deamer, one of the original authors of DNA to music; Dr. Clyde Snow, a forensic anthropologist; Debbie Marcum, wildlife rehabilitator specializing in opossums; Steven N. Austad, Harvard University Biology Department; Kevin Kackley, D.V.M. for taking care of all animals and for generously loaning his books; and Ingrid Newkirk whose book *Save the Animals* was always part of my biology classroom curriculum.

Opossum tracks provided for the back cover by Beartracker, AKA Kim A. Cabrera whose authentic tracks are only a part of the fascinating subjects exhibited at:
www.geocities.com/wind_tracker/

Author's photo by Nozawa Photography, Quincy, Illinois

The front cover of the book is taken from an actual picture of the author's JoJo who is gone but not forgotten.

Dedication

To JoAnne Edwards,
my mentor, my friend.

This was a beautiful spring day, a day that swirled it's fragrances on a gentle wind all around the big old farm. John Rossi came out on the porch to watch his wife. She frowned and sighed as she went from flowerbed to flowerbed assessing winter damage to edgings. She planted new seeds for the warm and wonderful days expected in the summer. John pushed white hair back from his high forehead and made his way down the old board steps. His work was piled high on his desk, but he wasn't about to let these precious moments with Clara pass him by. He didn't speak to her or her to him, and he eventually walked back to the porch. He fingered the frail-looking chain on the porch swing as he did every time he sat down, and pulled his pipe from his pocket. He filled it from an old fashioned leather pouch, and then reached in another pocket for matches. A whisper of noise made him turn and look down between the porch slats. A tiny calico kitten was walking up and down the drainpipe, slipping now and again, as she practiced her balance. A triangle of an abandoned web clung to the bush and the drainpipe. It sucked in and out with each breathy breeze, almost mimicking John's attempt to light his pipe. The kitten tired of her game and ran off to play with her littermates while John went back to watching Clara. He held the still warm match until it cooled, before throwing it over the porch rail.

Laddie had gone over to Clara, his big paws squashing in several feet of her carefully planted flowers, but she didn't seem to notice. He nosed around some small pots of snapdragons and she began to tell him things about her garden.

"I don't know what to plant here this year, but I think I'll go with the 4 o'clocks." The dog's tail moved slightly as he sat next to her. "And over there should be the straw flowers."

She sat back on her heels and looked at the area already planted. Laddie gazed in her direction for a second and then got to his feet. A figure passing in the distance made the hairs along his neck stand up. He bunched up slightly and lowered his beautifully shaped head emitting a low growl. John Rossi squinted into the direction the dog faced, but couldn't see anything. He puffed nonchalantly on his pipe. The sound of short footfalls behind him made him turn slightly towards the slender young woman he and his wife had come to love dearly.

"John, can I get you a cold drink?"

"Rachel, our friend is back," he nodded his head in the direction of the light colored dog.

"He's come fairly close this time," Rachel replied.

John let his eyes trail around what he could see of the farm. First one, and then another, of the men working in the yards and gardens looked his way and tipped their hat slightly, indicating they were aware of the man's presence. John Rossi went back to Rachel's question. "I would love some lemonade with a bit of orange added," he said.

Rachel left as quietly as she had come, light on her feet in spite of the heavy heels she always wore.

The brassy ring of a telephone in the airy recesses of the house ended abruptly as someone answered it. Shortly after, Rachel appeared with his lemonade. He gave her a sigh as he took the metal glass from her and raised it to his lips. "Can't I possibly have this in a regular glass when Clara isn't looking?" Rachel didn't answer, she just smiled, and he continued to drink, letting the condensation run down his forearm.

"Simon phoned and wants you to call him back when you can."

Rachel absently fingered the light chain that was holding her benefactor. "Shall I go and help Clara?"

"No, she loves to plant her gardens just so; our help would not be appreciated. When she tires, she will probably want something cool to drink and then will take a nap. I'll call Simon back then."

Rachel went over to the far end of the porch where a heavy red couch had been placed. The thick old brocade often left marks on Clara's face, so John had a quilt placed over it. Rachel straightened the soft blanket and fluffed the pillow, smoothing out any wrinkles with her palms. When she straightened up, she looked at Clara again and asked John, "How many acres of flowers do you think we will have this year?"

John knocked the ash from his pipe, "I would have to say about four," he said laughing. "How one little women could do so much planting is a mystery to me."

Rachel smiled as she watched Clara pick up her trowel and empty seed packets and come toward the porch. Her pink flowered dress brushed the nose of the collie at her side and he closed his eyes slightly as the hem fluttered in his face. He left her at the porch to seek his own form of heaven, a big dirt hole just out of sight under the porch.

The prairie wind caught Clara's old straw hat, but her grip was firm, she smiled at her little triumph over nature and then waved to her husband. White flowers dusted to her feet as Clara came up the steps. She paused to push back some branches of white spirea that had come through the railing.

"Papa, wait until you see the garden this year, it will be the best ever." Clara arrived beside him slightly breathless. She laid her things on a near-by table and sat on the porch beside his knee, tucking her heavy white garden shoes up under her dress. "We are going to have the most beautiful garden in the world!"

John Rossi lit his pipe again and let one hand fall lightly on the white hair at his knee. "It's already beautiful Clara, all your early spring flowers are still in bloom and I believe I saw buds on the peony bushes over there. Have you decided what color hollyhocks to put by the back fence yet?"

"Yes, yellow, double yellows." Clara's big blue eyes sparkled as she imagined how her flowers would look against the white fence that had enclosed the clotheslines for over a hundred years.

Rachel waited a few moments to be sure Clara was through talking. Clara's eyes matched her husband's perfectly; it was a pity, she thought, that they had never been able to have children. They would have been very handsome people.

"Clara, I was just about to bring out a pitcher of tea, would you like a glass?"

Clara turned to Rachel, "Oh, yes, thank you very much."

Rachel walked back into the house. Clara waited until even the light scent of her perfume had dissipated and then asked, "who was that Papa?"

"That's Rachel, Clara dear, she takes care of our household and helps me with my paperwork. She will be staying with us from now on." John Rossi tapped his pipe on the bottom of the chair and watched the tobacco blow slowly to the edge of the porch before he turned his attention back to his wife. "What flowers have you planned for the sides of the porches this year Clara?"

Clara went back to her dreams, making small motions with her hands of tucking something imaginary in a sleeve, and smoothing her skirt. "I think Wisteria. I saw pink Wisteria in that big box of seeds you gave me and I think it would be perfect."

Rachel returned with their tea and set the tray on the table nearest the porch swing. She handed each of them a glass and picked up John's empty lemonade glass before she returned to the house with a reminder to John, " Be sure to call Simon as soon as you can."

John nodded, he had forgotten he was to call. His mind had lost itself in the beauty of the day and had secretly made him forget his duties. He held the now sweating metal glass in his hand and removed the matching long plastic spoon after a quick stir. "Don't you like the glasses we have in the cupboard, Clara?" he asked her as he once again sipped his cool drink. The condensation was soaking his shirt in spite of his holding his hand under the bottom of the glass.

"These were Mama's favorite," Clara answered, holding her own deep yellow glass out to examine carefully. Clara never had the condensation problem, John noticed. It had to be because she only held the glass with a thumb and two fingers. John tried to imitate but failed, it didn't suit him. He put his hand around the glass and held it to the side of the swing so he didn't have to endure wet trousers and gave his attention back to what Clara had to say. "I like to think she is here with us, just inside the kitchen." She placed her glass on the table and held her knees.

John Rossi ran his fingers lightly through some of the snowy hair that had fallen from their pins and lay on her neck. Clara's mother had died forty years ago, so, of course, he had never met her. But through Clara, he could almost see the exquisite, fair woman setting tea out on this very porch for her little daughter, quietly combing out little Clara's tangled hair and then disappearing back into the house to bake bread or cookies, singing softly as she worked. Sometimes at night, lying in his big oak bed, John was comfortably positive that the shifting of the old house would release yet another of her songs and lull them all to sleep.

Clara's delicate lids had begun to flutter and her head started to nod. She set her empty yellow glass on the floor and leaned against John's knee. John laid his own glass aside and rose, carefully pulling Clara to her feet. He gently picked her up, carrying her to the old couch where the kindly lady curled up without a word and was soon fast asleep. John pulled the dusty shoes off her tiny feet and set them on the floor. One fell on its side but he didn't move to straighten it. They lay, oh so naturally, on the little round blue rug next to the big old couch. He adjusted her dress so that it covered most of her legs and ignored the little black kitten that had appeared and curled up by her knees. He stepped over Laddie, and the dog took his place on the floor next to the couch, on the rug, next to the shoes. John retrieved his pipe, and walked slowly back into the house filling the brown bowl as he went. The sweet smell of ripe tobacco trailed behind him.

"Simon! You wanted to speak to me?" John leaned back in the leather chair, preparing for a lengthy chat. Holding the telephone beneath his ear and shoulder, he adjusted one of the rolled up sleeves of his white shirt. He smiled at its soggy edge and glanced out the window at his sleeping wife.

"Sir, we have gone over the figures twice and the results are the same, your net worth has doubled again. You Sir, have taken the financial lead!"

"I couldn't have accomplished this without you Simon," John said candidly. "You are a financial genus my boy, I'm proud of you. When are you going to come for a visit, it's been too long!"

"I don't feel it's safe Sir, this is quite the situation you know. Won't you let me send more guards to Stormont?"

"No, no, we are completely safe. No one could possible guess that we are the same Clara and John Rossi of financial fame. The couple you hired as doubles for us are doing a grand job of fooling the press. We get a few jokes around town about having the same name, but nothing more.

"Mr. Rossi," John reminded him dryly, "you pay them a quarter of a million dollars annually, have given them your Island home, and your social status. They *owe* you a grand job.

"Simon the cynic," John chastised with a chuckle. "I only hope for you that one day you love someone as much as I love Clara. I have lived forty beautiful years with her as man and wife; and now, through the grace of God, I am living her childhood with her. Instead of growing old seeing sights we have already seen and visiting people who have already told us everything they know, we have embarked on a new adventure. We are rebuilding Stormont from only her fondest memories of it. When we are finished it will be paradise."

Simon was silent at the other end. He had known Clara and John for nearly fifteen years. He had watched Clara change from a stunning middle-aged socialite to a shy backward child. His comparative youth allowed him to accept, but not to understand John Rossi's feelings and subsequent decisions. So, instead of lying and telling him he understood, he said with heart felt emotion. "I will make plans to sneak a week-long visit with you. I miss you both."

"That *is* good news, Si! We'll see you soon!"

After hearing the click at the other end, Simon called his secretary. "You can take the other phones off scramble now." He hung up and clasped his fingers together lightly. The deep line that extended on the diagonal of his forehead eased as he looked out his office window over the huge city below. Rachel's image appeared to him on the dark glass and he watched the mental hologram for some time. His mind replayed their last encounter slowly. He savored this moment alone with her. His guard was completely down and he let himself watch her and listen to her, as he never would if she were really there. The image faded and he stared at the toe of his shiny expensive shoes. He laughed at himself and dialed his secretary. Maybe he did understand John after all. "Scramble the lines again and get Rachel on the line please." He hung up wondering what reason he would give for his call this time.

Clara woke to the peaceful hum of insects warmed by the spring sunshine. She glanced at the swing and noticed it was empty but she wasn't alarmed. She knew *Papa* was close. The kitten was still asleep beside her, the deep slumber of the young and innocent who have not yet encountered their first cause for fear. Clara looked up at the old ceiling. Paint still peeled slightly from the narrow old boards, a light gray paint with just a hint of blue. The breeze curled and uncurled the tiny hairs around her face as she drifted off to sleep again.

"Papa!" Clara's scream brought John instantly to his feet and with surprising speed and agility he ran through the house and out the back door onto the porch. Laddie was on his feet, his ears rotating between the sounds of Clara's screams and cries and the sound of John's heavy running footsteps. The kitten was gone from the porch, hiding from the unfamiliar and unexpected noise. Clara sat with her face buried into the back of the sofa. The thin shoulders shaking with sobs and fear supported a cascade of white hair that had pulled loose from its pins and tortoise shell combs.

John sat on the edge of the couch and gently pulled his wife into his arms. The quilt came away also, still clutched in her hands. As John held her, he soothed her by saying her name over and over. "Clara, shh, Clara." As he talked, he straightened the quilt and found enough pins and combs to fix her hair back up in a swirl above her crown. Damp little wisps curled against her face as she leaned away from John to accept a drink of cool water from a concerned Rachel. Clara stared over the porch rail towards the peg and board barn. Both John and Rachel knew that it wasn't the barn they would be visiting when Clara regained control. It would be the secret place in the old pasture next to it.

Clara got to her feet and taking John's hand, she went barefoot down the steps as fast as she could. Rachel grabbed up the little white shoes and caught up with them as they continued their grim journey to the pasture. No one spoke when Clara let go of John's hand and half ran down the brick path. She paid no attention to the stones on the path or to the new pier near the edge of the pond. Her focus was complete and absolute and it gave her strength. When John and Rachel caught up, she was already at the little graves.

She was allowed to sob over them without interruption. Clara sat back and looked at the tiny white crosses, or at least what was left of them. She looked at the ground and felt it with her hand. She could see beyond the grass and beyond the dirt to what was truly there. With a sad heart she picked up the vases near the crosses and emptied out the still fairly fresh flowers. Looking around she focused on some lilies that grew near one of the new pasture trees. She rose to get them. Tears streamed down John's face as she picked the flowers. Rachel looked down at the shoes she carried and absently checked the heels for wear, a habit that had carried over from orphanage life. She left John's side and knelt beside the woman, brushing Clara's feet with her hand before she put the shoes on her. "These are the most colorful of all the flowers Clara," she said trying to speak lightly. Rachel helped her fill each vase and then carried them back. Clara let her set them at the head of the two small graves while she stood in John's arms and fiddled with her sleeve.

Clara's mood suddenly changed and she stood up straight, she stopped fidgeting with her sleeve, left John's arms and walked over to the kneeling Rachel. Rachel was startled to see her standing so close and remained on one knee. One small vase waiting to be set down was still in her hand.

"Rachel," Clara said, "I want you to put an end to this. Do you understand me?"

Rachel looked up at the slight woman whose clear blue eyes never left her own dark ones. "Of course, Mrs. Rossi," Rachel answered from habit and heart. She put the other vase down giving her a chance to avert those penetrating eyes, the eyes that were looking for the lie. When she turned again to the older women, she stayed on her knee and looked into Clara's eyes without wavering and without doubt and said, "Clara, I will spend my life doing as you wish."

Clara put out her hand and symbolically helped the taller, younger women to her feet. She then turned and walked back to the house as she had come—alone.

John Rossi looked at Rachel for a long moment. The ritual had changed drastically that afternoon.

"So that's why we have come back to this place and time," he said.

A man appeared with a bucket of water and filled the vases. Neither John nor Rachel looked at him. He was expected. John turned and followed his wife back to the house. Rachel looked down at the little graves and then put her ear into the wind. Was that laughter she heard? She looked at the backs of the old people but they were well ahead of her and out of earshot. She listened again but only heard the wet, guttural noises of the frogs at the edge of the pond. The prairie wind loosened a few well-trained hairs around her face and the sun changed her face to golden. Still she listened, but the prairie noise makes you forget troubling things so Rachel walked back down the path thinking only of the frogs and dragonflies and all such other pond things.

"I heard Clara's spell and came right over," Millie explained as she pulled the screen open with a couple of fingers, balancing a still steaming pie with the remaining digits. Mary, Stormont's permanent cook and housekeeper ran to help with the door, getting there only in time to close it.

"Where is the dear woman?" Millie asked, putting the pie on a hot pad Mary had managed to get to the table before Millie put the bubbling sticky desert on the lace tablecloth.

"She will be here in a moment," Mary told the stout little woman. "Rachel wanted to help Clara change her dress and freshen up a bit. She will be thrilled to see you, Millie. Let me get some plates down and make some coffee."

"Wonderful!" Millie cried to the other woman. "Coffee and warm apple pie to celebrate Clara's new gardens is just what we need to do." Millie began to whistle as she bustled around the kitchen getting the table ready before Clara came in.

"Millie?"

"Dear Clara," Millie hurried to the other woman's side and put her arm around her, leading the way to the table. "Clara, I was just taking this pie out of the oven and I knew I couldn't enjoy a bite of it if you didn't share it with me."

Clara sat at the center of the long table as if expecting a birthday cake. Her recent trauma already part of the past again. "Millie, I'm so glad you could come."

"Of course, I'm here with you, Clara." Millie sat down next to her and poured some coffee. "I'll stay for a while. Nancy won't be back until dark, so I haven't anything to do until then."

Clara ate her pie and drank her coffee in happy silence while Mary, Rachel, and Millie fussed over her and engaged in harmless gossip. Soon Clara began to doze a little and she leaned slightly toward her friend. Millie didn't pause in her conversation about her niece's wedding as she put her arm around Clara and let her lie against her ample figure. Clara's head gave a definite nod.

"Oh dear, look who's tired," she said, lightly kissing Clara's forehead." Let's go to the study and tell John good-night and then off to bed."

"I'll take her," Rachel said getting up. "I didn't realize the time!"

"No, no, no, dear girl, sit with your coffee and enjoy the sunset. I won't be a minute judging from the looks of this poor tired soul." And off she went with her charge.

Rachel heard John get up and saw the study lights go out. He always checked in on his wife and made sure the night-lights were on and the door that adjoined their rooms was open so he could hear her in the night. Winding up her favorite music box, he sometimes would sit with her until the music ran down.

Mary sat across from Rachel. They slowly finished their coffee in the warm kitchen. John and Millie soon joined them and the conversation became serious.

"You know Rachel, John said, no one would hold you to the promise you made to Clara this afternoon. I don't know why she said it; I don't know why she became so lucid for that few minutes. She won't even remember talking to you."

"Now, what's this?" Millie asked.

"Clara asked me to put a stop to cruelty and I promised I would."

"It can't be done," Millie confirmed. "Not while there are people around like old man McNiff and all his kin."

"Why does he hate Clara so?" Rachel asked, reaching for more coffee.

"Who can understand a man like that?" Millie went on, shaking her head. "He can't understand her any more than she can understand him. And besides, the man is pure evil. I've seen snakes with more warmth behind their eyes than he has." She paused to wipe her hands on a napkin, and to look at the thin gold rings, holding her hand out flat as she must have done a million times since that first time they went on her finger.

"I think it has a lot to do with those two little graves out there." Everyone leaned forward and got comfortable. A trip into the past with Millie was always as good as curling up beside the fireplace with a good book. "I'll never forget that day myself, but no one was affected as much as Clara. We must have been about nine when we went up to the pasture that day. Her Daddy had an old workhorse he'd put out to pasture that was just right for us to ride. It was a day like today in fact, spring, all the new little animals were getting about half grown and started wandering around. They were everywhere, and Clara and I couldn't keep track of them all. It was a game to see who could spot and count the most baby animals each spring.

That's how Clara came to be at the place in the pasture before anyone else. She saw two little forms over there in the tall grass by the fence and ran over to see what they were so she could add them to her count. But when she got there, they weren't alive; they just looked alive because of the way they were hanging. We had seen skinned animals before all right, but these were different. Those two little raccoons hadn't been dead when they were skinned and they had crawled to the fence and had tried to get away, to crawl over it and get away. One had one foot on the picket fence and had lifted its head to pull itself up. The other little one was half way up. Both were looking over the fence at a place beyond the farm when they died. The sun dried them in that position as if to tell the world, *Look what you are doing*. Clara took it hard. They smelled and had flies all over them, but Clara freed their little feet from the fence and wrapped them in some purple satin pillowcases her Mother had given her. She dug those little graves and buried them there. The dirt put them out of sight to everyone but Clara.

So then, she went after McNiff. She hounded him every time she saw him. She used to walk down Railroad Street and stand outside his house and yell that she saw what he did and she would get even some day. Well, McNiff always stays just inside the law. What with the crooked Sheriff we got he still gets away with his evil ways. He's just bad to the bone, that's all, and now he likes to show it up to Clara. The only problem with that is, Clara doesn't seem to remember him. It's just as well," she said rising, collecting the rest of her pie, and moving towards the door. "I'll see you all at the picnic on Friday."

John opened the screened door for her and watched as she made her way down the steps. Her whistling started almost as soon as her feet touched the brick sidewalk that led over to Spring Street and Millie's house. It had been added many years ago when the girls were teenagers. They had talked their parents into helping lay bricks if they worked to buy them. By the end of summer, they had met the cost of the bricks that would match the sidewalk to the barn, the pond, and of course LaDue Street. While Stormont house was located on the corner of these two streets, the rest of the farm stretched for miles behind. The land had been allowed to go back to its natural state; very little was cultivated. It was great combination of town life and country life.

John stayed by the door long after the whistling stopped and he was sure Millie was home. Rachel watched his back for a few minutes while she finished her coffee. She would have loved to talk to him, but when he didn't turn, she quietly left the room.

Friday was a glorious day to wake up to. The festivities everyone was looking forward to made it doubly enchanting. The entire town would turn out to eat, visit, and play games in the park. Rachel and Mary went happily about the house filling the baskets with good things to eat and checking the closets for exactly the right dress for Clara to wear. As the sun warmed the front of the house, different choices were made until dresses of all weights and colors were laid on the bed to be chosen from.

"Clara, what would you like to put on?" Rachel asked, holding up two of the choices.

Clara picked a light blue with a white lace collar and eyed Rachel as a complete stranger who toyed with her things and was certainly one who would bear watching.

Rachel had come to accept and ignore Clara's whimsical moods and went on with their plans in complete happiness. She even lightly kissed Clara's cheek after she had made such a good choice and breezed out of the room to attend other matters.

Clara sat on the bed and admired the dress, her good choice, and waited for the stranger to return and help her get into it.

"Have you seen Mr. Rossi?" Rachel asked Mary.

"He is out on the porch, I think," Mary replied as she turned the chicken, then hurried to check on the sun tea.

"John," Rachel approached him, "do you feel up to going to the park?"

John didn't turn, "I have been a little tired lately, it must be the heat. Perhaps you ladies could go ahead and I'll join you later."

"That will be fine," Rachel said sitting across from him. "Are you sure you are all right?"

John finally turned to look at her. "I assure you I am fairly fit for a man my age," he smiled as he spoke to her. "There will be days like this in the future I'm sure. Remember Rachel that every minute is a gift."

Rachel patted his shoulder and went back to helping Clara get ready. Millie would be there shortly and then they would be off.

The park was vast and tree-filled. A brook ran through it making perfect places to watch the cedar-wax-wings play and splash in its rocky shallows. Picnic tables were everyplace and gay colored material flapped in the easy breeze on tables that had already been claimed. Rachel led her group to a big table under a bur oak, sure that such a heavy tree would shade them the whole afternoon. Millie took charge of Clara and off they went to visit the other ladies and see the sights. Clara was especially enamored by the game of horseshoe pitch and Rachel knew they would watch the participants for hours. She checked to make sure that Charlie was aware she was letting Clara go off with Millie. She saw him with his family not far from their table.

He nodded in Clara's direction, then in Rachel's before he kissed his wife on the cheek and moseyed over to play horseshoes.

Rachel felt unusual relief at being assisted momentarily with her charge and after spreading the blue gingham cloth, she set the picnic basket and tea jar down to hold it in place.

"Rachel, what a great surprise!"

Rachel turned away from her task of laying the silver around the table. "Hello, Michael."

"It's nice to see you!"

Rachel's high cheekbones took on a rosy shade and she brushed a few dark strands of hair back from her face before she caught herself.

Michael noticed however, and sat down on the bench with a little smile on his face. On looking back up at her he had managed to wipe it off and went on seriously. "Don't you ever get any time off? They can't be paying you enough to work everyday."

"I don't mind," Rachel said, turning back to the picnic basket and thinking briefly about the apartment she had in New York and the Mercedes in storage. She felt a small pang for the life she had left behind. The shopping trips with Clara and her work in John's office as his private secretary had brought her, not just personal wealth, but prestige—and a little closer to Simon. They weren't dreams that had come true, because she hadn't even known these luxuries existed.

The thought of Simon gave her a warm glow that was pushed aside by the here and now voice of Michael.

"How about a movie, Rachel, just a movie?"

Rachel thought about Clara's unpredictable spells. "It's out of the question, Michael, I really appreciate your kindness but really, it's out of the question."

"Rachel," he persisted, "the cotton-tops can do without you for one evening. What did I say? Rachel, what, what did I say?"

Rachel had turned a cold look at Michael the second the disrespect issued from his mouth.

"It's not a bad word, Rachel," he started to explain. "Cotton-tops is definitely not a bad word."

Rachel ignored his discomfort and was about to go on with another topic when a half taunt came from the table next to them.

"You know Rachel has a thing for old man Rossi."

Rachel stopped mid-way to the table with the glasses and looked at the face that went with the mouth.

"Ignore Grace," Michael said, "she has a very nasty way of looking at things. Let's go for a walk."

Rachel took the opportunity to get away from the giggling group sitting with Grace and took Michael's hand. Thoughts of Simon were out of her mind as she stood beside the big man and he led her away from the unpleasantness.

"I've known Grace since high school," he went on lightly. "I haven't ever known her to think any other way about anything. It's just the side of life she sees, which says more about her than you." He bent over and kissed her on the top of her head. "No one can match your loyalty and integrity, Rachel."

Rachel was glad for the company and the support and tried to think of a way to make amends for her earlier rebuffs. "I wonder if instead of a movie, you might come to Stormont some evening and we could play cards or take a walk or something."

"Done!" He was glad he had been given a chance to be with Rachel. The most he had gotten in the past was a cup of coffee when he chanced across her in town running errands for the Rossis. Michael wanted to love Rachel. He wanted to show her off as his wife because she was a natural born lady and she was refined. Michael was not, he had learned his manners and ways. He was aware they were slowly being lost as his school days passed further and further behind him. Someday he would be ordinary and plodding. His days would be spent watching crops grow and having coffee and donuts with other men just like him. Life with Rachel could change his destiny. He resisted the urge to spit.

"There are a lot of Bar-B-Ques going today," Rachel said, as they wandered around the swing sets and watched the little kids play games.

"I noticed that myself," Michael said, fanning away a sudden burst of smoke that wafted his way. "Let's go down by the creek."

"Too late," Rachel laughed, "Father Kessler has spied us and is on the way over."

"It's good to see you young people out on this lovely day," he greeted them. Father was a thin man about Rachel's height. She looked right into his sincere face, but the only thing she ever noticed was his eyes. His gift of abundant curly lashes was not very fair in her opinion.

"Good to see you, Father," she said. "This picnic is turning out very well."

"It's good for everyone to get together once in a while, especially in the spring. When people mingle after a long winter it puts to rest a lot of gossip. Issues don't seem so big out in the bright sunshine and we all have God's world to enjoy together. It brings us all a lot of peace, don't you think?"

"I agree with you a hundred percent," Michael said squeezing Rachel's hand and moving on as Father said good-by and headed for another table of friends to talk to.

Rachel let go of Michael's hand and said, "I must go now, but I hope we still have a date Saturday night?"

"Saturday night is good for me," and taking full advantage of her change of attitude towards him, he leaned down and kissed her softly on the mouth.

Rachel gave his arm a small squeeze and turned to make her way back to the table under the oak. The leaves on the cottonwoods next to the creek had changed to silver. The wind has changed she thought; it will probably rain. She looked around for Clara and Millie and saw them still watching the men pitch horseshoes. She poured a glass of tea and sat for a while, thankful that Grace and her gaggle of gossipy friends had left. Watch yourself Rachel, she reminded herself. Clara would never talk like that, but then she thought, Clara hadn't been born poor in the Midwest either. She could match these people if they pushed her too far.

The wind had decidedly changed direction and had given Rachel a strange feeling. Maybe it was getting cooler. Somewhere a baby cried and she looked around absently, automatically trying to locate the helpless little sound. She set her glass down and stood up. Clara was still O.K., but there was definitely a child in need of assistance. She looked around but didn't see any frantic mothers or older siblings looking as if anything was amiss. Rachel decided to follow the sound. It seemed to be coming from the other side of the hill farthest away from the picnickers. Michael was talking to someone. It looked like Robert, so she turned in the direction of the sound and began to walk alone. She paused from time to time to listen—nothing—and then there it was again. Rachel walked faster. She was sure beyond doubt this time; a child was in great distress. Going up the hill was difficult in her summer dress and thin little shoes and she paused to catch her breath. There were three little kids at the top of the hill, but they were hiding in the bushes and laughing, not weeping. And yet the crying and horrible distress grew louder.

"What on earth are you laughing at, Lewis," Rachel said as she neared them.

The young boy looked at the ground and didn't say anything. The other boy giggled.

Rachel managed to pull herself to the top of the hill despite finding herself in a bramble patch and put her hand up to shade her eyes from the wind and sun. Below her were makeshift pens and the animals in them were standing still but crying, crying not for help. Crying for themselves, for still being alive. She began to make her way down the hill. Something was terribly wrong here.

She neared the pens and stood stock-still. What was this going on here? The men had deer in the pens. Wild deer and they were leaning over the fences making them scream in the most horrible way. She covered her ears against the unholy sound of animals crying and men laughing.

She heard one laugh and say, "That one screamed so loud I'll be deaf for a week!" Several joined in with laughter. A kind of laughter she wasn't use to hearing.

Now she could see what they were doing. They were cutting semicircles of hide in different places on the flanks and lifting them up like window shades. They would then slice pieces of living flesh from the animals. The cries of agony would end as the animals went into shock and just stood panting and gaping at a place very distant from the bloody little valley. Rachel ran to the nearest pen, surprising the men who hadn't seen her coming. At first, they looked at her with sheer guilt in their eyes, and then defiance.

"You shouldn't be here Rachel, so just go back to the picnic."

"Mr. Welch, what in God's name are you doing here!" Rachel tried to keep herself from screaming as hard as the deer were.

"It's the best way to get fresh meat," the man reasoned—"and we let them go; it's better than killing them. This way, if they die, it's away from here and we don't have the flies."

"Mr. Welch, I demand you let these animals go and put a stop to this."

" Look Rachel, I've got a family to feed . . .." He turned and spit, and when he looked back at her, his eyes were cold and spittle was stuck on the side of his unshaven chin.

Rachel felt herself harden into the survivor she had been forced through circumstances to be. "Don't give me that crap Mr. Welch; you are a fat, pus-laden man who could afford to go hungry for a year. You are not giving anywhere near this much meat to your children, and I might add, that at this very moment both of your children are at the top of this hill watching this sickening display you are putting on here!"

"Go back to the old people, Rachel," Welch leaned toward her from the top of one of the make shift pens. "You ain't welcome here."

Rachel had to take her eyes off the bloody knives and the men squeezing fresh blood out of still living flesh.

She began to run—she unlatched and pulled open all the pen doors as she ran.

"Stop her!" one man yelled over the confusion.

She felt a hand on her arm but it hadn't the strength of a man. Looking into the face beside her, she realized it was Terry Griffin, the altar boy she saw every Sunday. He had the unsure look of the large child he was. Rachel didn't care, he was restraining her movements, and the men were too close. She pushed him as hard as she could and ran to the last pen. The animal inside didn't run when she opened the gate; it stared straight ahead with its chest heaving. Drool, running out of the gaping mouth, ran down Rachel's neck as she pressed into the pen next to the animal.

One of the men landed on the fence above her and grabbed her hair.

"Run! Run!" Rachel pleaded with the motionless animal.

The man was trying to pull her up the fence by her hair. She held his arm with one hand and slapped what used to be the deer's flank with the other. The animal bolted past her catching the man's face with his antlers. As he fell backward off the fence, his hand unclasped her hair. Rachel was pulled out of the pen by the force of the huge animal's bolt for freedom.

She lay in the dust of the pen trying to get her breath, her hair in her face, blood and saliva all over her dress and five angry men yelling names at her.

Arms reached for her again, but they were kind.

"Charlie. Oh Charlie." Rachel put her arms around his neck and cried. "Charlie, we have to have more guards at Stormont! We can't keep this back from Clara's world anymore!"

Charlie felt his eye, the one that was split and turning black. He moved Rachel to the least sore arm but still held her protectively as he faced the retreating men. Charlie was armed but he hadn't pulled out his weapon, still, the men ran away.

"You're right, Rachel, this is too big an area for just the four of us. You and Mary in the house, Jake, and me on the grounds, it's not going to work. It was all right when we just had to watch for reporters, a few nut cases from town, and to keep Clara in our sights, but this, what is this!"

"It's a new enemy, Charlie, to us anyway. Clara has seen it all along." Rachel attempted to stand on her own, bracing herself on a fence rail. "I don't even know its name."

She pointed to a wandering fawn in the distance.

Charlie looked in the direction she indicated. "You go back to Clara," he said.

He began to gather dry brush and grass.

Rachel did as she was told. At the top of the hill, she noticed the children were gone; she smelled smoke but didn't turn around. Charlie was a mean man—dark, hairy, big and strong. Rachel smiled a little smile. In another life, she was sure he had been a junkyard dog.

She made a detour to the creek and tried to clean up. She watched the waxwings flutter in the little pools and the sun turn the water white with its brightness.

"How can this paradox occur," she thought aloud, leaving the creek and heading for her picnic table. Both pictures of what she had just seen overlapped each other in her mind. Confusing her more than the adrenaline drop she was experiencing.

Millie was the first to see her. "Rachel, what on earth have you been up to?"

"Oh, just playing with the children."

Millie knew it was a lie but would talk to her later. "Clara and I have had the best afternoon, didn't we Clara?"

Clara nodded, smiling as Millie added little goodies to her plate and pushed her iced tea closer to her hand.

She was fixing Rachel a plate, but Rachel pulled it roughly from her when she started to add the fried chicken. It was the first contemptuous gesture she had ever seen Rachel make. Millie's eyebrows moved slightly upward, and then she began to whistle a little tune. She covered the chicken and put it away in the basket.

Rachel looked at the other tables, trying to calculate how many people knew about the horror at the bottom of the hill. Charlie, back with his family, was also scanning the group under thick eyebrows. Who was who! Her eyes lighted on Michael, he waved when she looked his way. She waved back but not with any of the enthusiasm she had felt earlier in the day.

The blood on her dress was drawing flies, but she noticed Gib McNiff was watching her, so she didn't look down. He smiled and waved. Rachel sipped her tea and stared at him until her eyes burned. He left laughing.

"Millie, how well do you know these people?"

"Clara and I know most of them, wouldn't you say so, Clara?"

Clara reached for the lace hanky Millie had tucked in her sleeve. She dabbed her mouth and went on picking out small pieces of her apple pie to eat. They waited until she said, "yes."

Rachel looked at Clara; she couldn't ask questions now. "I was just curious. It seems as if it might rain, I wonder if we should start home."

"We surely should," Millie agreed. "It's getting windy and Clara might like a nap." She finished her pie and then gathered up dishes while Clara finished hers. Rachel's head hurt and her arms were beginning to bruise, scratches stood out in black crusted lines. She just wanted to forget what she had witnessed. The crack of a baseball against a bat, the laughter of children, and the women with their chubby bodies and rosy faces were a front. It wasn't the truth; the whole scene was a lie.

Rachel's day was not over. A Hertz car was parked in front of the house.

"Clara, Simon must be here," Millie told her as they got out of the car. Mary ran out to help with the baskets and took care of the picnic dishes. Laddie ran up, adding to the confusion, but he was always allowed to stay. Aside from Millie, he was the only one Clara remembered correctly all of the time. She went off with her faithful dog to check the flowers.

Simon and John came out to greet them; John's step was lighter then it had been that morning. As they got closer to Rachel they saw the blood and dirt on her dress and their expression changed. John looked quickly toward Clara, saw her pull a few weeds, and could see that she was all right. He started to ask Rachel what had happened.

"I suggest you talk to Charlie in private and then we'll all get together after Clara goes to bed," Rachel said, addressing them both as she wearily walked by. "I'm going to shower."

Shower she did. Forty-five minutes later she stepped out on the mat in the bathroom that adjoined her room. She dressed and fixed her hair before taking the newspaper-wrapped parcel containing everything she had been wearing that afternoon out to the trash.

On the way back in, Simon met her on the porch. "What can I do for you?" he asked with concern.

"Nothing. I'm okay. Did you talk to Charlie?"

"I did. So did John." The furrow appeared on his forehead. "He won't hear of more guards because Clara is settled with things the way they are, and he did have a point. Clara will never be in a position again to see anything but smiling faces and apple pies. What will the guards do? We just have to keep her in her own back yard."

"For God's sake Simon, aren't there laws against people who do things like this? And isn't it child abuse to impose this type of thing on minors? Why aren't these people in jail?"

"There aren't any laws that are enforced, Rachel, you know that. A few people are caught, but things like this go on all the time."

"Does that answer mean you aren't going to try to do anything, Simon?"

Simon was taken off guard for a second. Rachel wanted him to exercise his lawyer's expertise to the fullest extent, but after weighing the consequences, he had decided to abandon the idea—and now, he had to tell the lovely woman in front of him.

"Rachel, the animals are gone, the pens have been destroyed, and how many people who were at the picnic do you think would testify?"

"So that's it? I don't see it that way, Si. Those deer are somewhere. I was there. Charlie was there. Five guilty men are at home watching TV or at the tavern right now. What about that side of it?"

"What about Clara and John, Rachel? A story like this will stir up a lot of trouble and the press will get wind of it . . .pictures, interviews with those who attended the picnic. Can we take the chance?"

Rachel looked at him. He only cared about doing his job. She could be dead at this very moment with all her hair pulled out and he probably would not bat an eye as he identified her body on some morgue slab.

Simon saw the hurt in her face, but he did not know how to respond, so he stood there waiting for her to go, which she did.

"Mary, can I help with anything?" she asked, closing the screen door on the outside world that included Simon.

"I just thought we'd have some hot soup and sandwiches," Mary said, smiling. "I think the storm that's coming will bring a lot of cool air."

"Where is Millie?" Rachel asked, taking down some soup bowls. She intentionally did not look at Simon when he walked through the kitchen. But he did not hide from her coldness. He made a point of looking at her. He made a point of looking at her figure.

Mary noticed the situation, but smiled only to herself. The way things were going they really might not realize that they love each other.

"Millie's resting with Clara. You know, Rachel, she has to be over sixty if they were kids together. I worry about her overdoing it sometimes."

"She's a strong woman," Rachel replied, "but you're right. Sometimes though, I think she could run circles around both of us."

They both laughed thinking how tired they were and how rested Millie and Clara would be. They would be looking forward to bedtime while the older women would want to play cards or talk.

Laddie came to the door and scratched, so Rachel opened the screen door to let him in, pausing to look at the darkening sky. "I hope we don't visit the pasture tonight," she whispered to Mary.

Mary nodded her agreement. She didn't always follow them out. She would check out the window and judge the light intensity of the flashlights that John, Rachel and Charlie carried. If she couldn't see them on or if they looked dim, she would take more flashlights to them. If the lights were O.K., she would go back to bed and get up with John at dawn while Rachel and Clara slept.

The evening was cozy and the expected rain fell. Millie and Clara alternated between playing cards, fixing hot chocolate, and talking about their childhood. John and Simon spent a great deal of the evening in the study.

Rachel found herself alone in the kitchen. Hearing some of the kittens near the screen, she took a bowl of milk out to them. Standing on the porch near the railing, she felt very much at peace as she looked out over Stormont. She folded her arms and let the cool breeze fan her face. The lightening still flickered in the distance, but the rain had stopped falling for now. Rachel stood closer to the porch rail; putting both hands on the white curved wood, she leaned slightly forward. What was that in the old pasture? She looked over her shoulder slightly, but no one was curious as to where she was going. She made her way in the half-light along the slightly overgrown brick path. When she neared the barn, another distant flash of lightening lit up the tiny graves. She gasped and stepped backwards. Her hand went to her breast. There in the dim light were two baby raccoons trying to get over the fence. Rachel waited for the next flash to be sure of what she had seen. When it came, they were gone. The damp prairie wind played with her skirt. The thin material wasn't enough cover on this chilly night and she turned to go in.

"Clara!" she jumped in surprise to see the older woman standing silently behind her. "Oh my heavens, dear lady, you gave me such a start."

Clara put her hand out for Rachel to take and they began their walk back to the house.

"Clara your hands are chilled, I'm so sorry I didn't see you coming or I would have gone back to get your sweater."

"I'm not cold, honey," the older women assured her. "Why are you out here?"

"It was such a nice evening. I thought I would get a breath of fresh air, Clara."

Clara turned to Rachel and asked her," You saw them trying to get over the fence, didn't you?"

"Yes, I did," Rachel told her. To lie to Clara would have not only been pointless, it would have ruined the faith and trust they had built in their relationship over the years. Despite Clara's lapse in some memories, the intangible feelings were still intact. A person's aura didn't alter. Where there had been love, there still was love; where there had been trust, there still was trust. The only thing missing really, were the names to these things.

"What can we do to free them, Clara?" It was out. The real reason for rebuilding Stormont. She didn't need to pussyfoot around the issue anymore.

Clara lifted her head into the breeze and closed her eyes for a moment as they walked. A great weight had been taken from her shoulders. " When we have done all that we can do in this lifetime to build compassion and rapport between all living things, then they will be free."

Rachel took small steps to ensure them not getting to the house too soon. "You have done that already, Clara. No one has been as good and kind as yourself."

Clara's brow furrowed, "It hasn't been enough, there is more that has to be done. And I am getting to old to figure out what I am supposed to do."

"I have a feeling that we are very close to some kind of happening here, Clara," Rachel told her, remembering the horror of the afternoon. "I believe you are right in saying that more has to be done. I can also see that good people aren't going to turn their backs on what goes on out there very much longer."

Clara held her hand tightly as they walked.

"Look out, Clara!" Rachel put an arm around the woman's waist and pulled her closer to her, "What on earth is that by your foot?"

It was completely dark by this time. The women had been navigating by watching the yellow lights in the windows and feeling the bricks under their feet. That, combined with familiarity of the farm, seemed to be getting them home, but now, something very unfamiliar was in their way.

Clara reached down and felt with her hand before Rachel could stop her.

"Why look what we have here", she said, "are there any more?" She began to walk slowly in small circles, feeling the grass as she went with the toe of her shoe.

Rachel couldn't see a thing; in fact, she couldn't even see what it was that Clara was holding in her hands. "Clara, wait right here and I'll run in for a flashlight."

Rachel ran the length of the back yard and opened the back door with a little more noise than was usual for her. Mary was in the kitchen washing up a few of the cups of which there seemed to be a constant flow. She looked up with a little controlled alarm.

"Nothing," Rachel assured her. "Just need a couple of flashlights, want to come?"

Mary grabbed a couple more flashlights, glad for the slight disturbance in her day. "What are we doing?" she asked, as they hurried off the porch.

"Clara's found something and wants us to help her," Rachel was back to her old self. An adventure like this with Clara always proved to be a happy occasion.

She waved to Charlie. He was standing in the dark by the fence with its half-grown hollyhocks. She couldn't see him very well, but knew he wasn't waving back. He might have nodded his head in her direction.

The women got nearer to Clara, they slowed so they wouldn't step on whatever it was.

"I'm here," Clara called softly.

Mary and Rachel moved closer to her side, flashlight rays played all over the ground. In the indirect light, Clara held out both hands. Lying in the palms of both hands was a baby opossum. The three ladies stood looking down at the tiny creature, as women do when they see a new life.

"Clara, he's so beautiful, and so tiny," Mary said feeling the little furred creature. "Where can the rest be?"

"This one has dropped off the Mother," said Clara still looking around the ground in the white streams that the flashlights were making. She started towards the house with her little charge. "We will check tomorrow to make sure there aren't any more."

Clara went in to her room the second they got back. John followed, filling his pipe as he went.

"Clara, what have you got there?"

John put the unlit pipe in his pocket to take the little animal Clara held out to him. "Well, this is quite a fine little guy," he said smiling down at him.

Clara was already calling to him from his adjoining room," I need one of your shoe boxes, Papa."

John heard a pair of his shoes hit the floor and soon Clara was back shaking imaginary particles out of the empty box. "Here is one," she said holding up her treasure.

Mary arrived with some clean rags just in time to save his shirts. Quickly, he placed one of the castoff garments under the little opossum. He casually checked his trousers for signs of accidents and, seeing nothing to worry about, he went back to holding him and trying to light his pipe at the same time. He covered the little fellow's face slightly as he blew the smoke to the side. Then he settled down in Clara's bedside chair and watched the women prepare for the new houseguest.

Rachel brought in a large basket and put a sandbox in it at one end. Clara put the shoebox in the other end and Mary brought fresh water. Everyone stepped over Laddie who was lying in the doorway watching Clara.

Clara pushed the big basket to the foot of her bed, "There," she said. "Here Papa, I'll take him."

"What's this!" Millie cried from the door." I leave you for a few minutes to talk to Simon and I miss out on all the excitement!"

Clara proudly held out the tiny bundle wrapped in rags for her friend to see.

"Clara, what a little love." She snuggled the baby opossum, blanket and all, before giving him back to Clara.

"Clara dear, I must run now. Nancy will be back any time and I forgot to leave the light on for her. She has such trouble seeing those steps at night. I will see you tomorrow. Simon has promised to take us to the Shelly's estate auction and it should be an all day affair." She paused, and then added, "I think we may find some more of your Mama's things there."

Clara's face showed recognition at the mention of her Mama. "Do you think we will find some more books?" she asked hopefully.

Millie was on familiar ground here, "I'm positive we will find something, Clara. We always find something, don't we?"

"Yes, we do," Clara said hesitatingly. She wasn't sure.

John took charge, "You are right Clara, we always have in the past." He took the little opossum from her hands and put it in its box. He fussed with it for a moment but the baby opossum crawled under the material by himself. John was pleased about that because he certainly did not want to smother Clara's new pet.

Clara was happy with his approval and hugged him tightly. John held her with all the love he had in his heart.

Rachel stayed to help Clara to bed and John saw Millie to the door. The music from Clara's favorite music box blended with Millie's distant whistling. Rachel partially closed the door on the already sleeping woman, her watchful pet, and the little opossum. She was certain she could also hear a woman singing softly to her daughter.

"Isn't it a beautiful day?" Simon asked the ladies as he sat down to breakfast.

"It is going to be perfect, "Rachel agreed, sipping her coffee.

Clara didn't answer. She sat with her little opossum on her lap and tried to get him to eat as much of her breakfast as she possibly could. The little fellow was glad to oblige her, but stayed in the relative safety of his rag blankets. All anyone could hear was occasional smacking noises and light scuffling.

John sat next to Clara and handed her napkins as needed and secretly picked up any crumbs that happened to drop to the floor on his side. As if anyone couldn't tell what he was doing!

"Mary, do you have any plans now that we are out of your hair all day?" Simon asked.

"Yes, I think I'll spend the day with my family. My folks don't live very far from here and I like to see them when I can."

"Simon, can you stay the rest of the week?" John asked. "Just to sort out a few business details."

"Of course. I've left Everett in charge and you know he is trustworthy. You liked him from the start, John, and your judge of character has always been sterling."

Rachel was not sure, but she thought Si might have been including her in on that compliment. She looked at Simon, but he did not give any indication at all that was the case. In fact, he looked a little bored when he looked in her direction. In reality he was watching her every move. He loved the soft arms that brushed by his shoulder when she reached for the cream. He loved the tasteful little earrings that sparkled just at the end of her ear. He had to turn away, his love for her overwhelmed his emotions.

Rachel began to pick up dishes and put them by the sink. She could get so mad at Simon without one word passing between them. God help them all if they ever actually started talking to each other on a regular basis.

A faint whistle told them Millie was on her way. Rachel looked out the door and then waved.

Millie looked at her ring in the sunlight and then waved back. Laddie ran up to her and she greeted him with much fanfare before she came up the steps to the porch.

"Oh good, you have the little angel out," she said to Clara when she came in. She shook out a couple of receiving blankets to show to her. "Look what I found in the linen closet, dear. I can't remember which one of Nancy's kids they belonged to, but they sure don't need them anymore." She held the blankets to her for a second before she went on. "In fact, their kids don't even need them. Where has the time gone?" She handed them over to a delighted Clara.

Rachel noticed that Mary was staying noticeably away from the whole proceeding. Her enthusiasm of the night before seemed to have waned a bit in the light of day. Rachel shrugged, let the ladies have their fun. The little opossum deserved Clara. He would have a chance to have a nice life if she could get him through his babyhood.

"Let's get the little fellow in his new duds, Clara," John said, taking the old rags away and throwing them in the trash. He pulled the squirming baby animal out of a lock of Clara's hair that trailed down her neck. The second he was exposed, he had gone up her neck and tried to hide his face among the curls she had at the back of her head.

John carried the blanketed baby possum off to his basket so Clara could finish her breakfast and get ready to go to the auction.

"Clara, which dress today?" Rachel asked, pulling out several choices.

"No question," Millie answered for her. "It has to be the yellow one so that we match."

Clara pulled the pale yellow dress over her head, and peeked at Millie's. Her dress would match her friends, how delightful.

Rachel left to answer the knock at the back door. Seeing whom it was, she stepped out and went to the edge of the porch.

"Did you find any others, Charlie?"

"No, but I found the mother. Someone set a trap just the other side of the pond. I looked every place, but the rest are gone. There were two dead ones that stayed with the mother, but they didn't have a chance after that storm the other night. They needed her body heat to stay alive. I'll keep an eye out for any more survivors."

"Charlie, who set the trap on Stormont property?"

"I don't know." Charlie looked at the ground and wiped his forehead with his forearm. He wasn't sweating; he was disgusted. "Stormont is huge and it was easy to get back there because the barn hid them from my window. They could have come from the far corner of the property and kept the barn between them and me the whole time. Jake is making his rounds with the property fences. We have a lot to repair and he will be gone a couple of days yet. Who ever it was didn't leave any clues."

"They should have been in plain view of the house. Why didn't I see them?"

"You are usually busy with Clara and these creeps come and go as if they have rights to everything that walks or crawls. They probably set the traps for the beavers that have taken over the far end of the pond."

"Laddie didn't bark, wouldn't he have heard them?"

Charlie's gypsy eyes met hers, "He wouldn't have barked if he knew them."

Rachel studied the man's face. He had a good point.

Charlie turned to walk back toward Millie's. His house was right next to hers.

"I'll check back with you later, Rachel. Meanwhile, don't say anything to anyone in the house about the traps."

Soon after Charlie left, everyone was ready to leave and enjoy the day ahead. A large estate sale held many surprises and Clara and Millie didn't want to miss a one. Rachel hurried to catch up with the older ladies. She remembered to get a lace hanky for Clara. She gave it to Millie who tucked it in Clara's sleeve. Clara adjusted it until it's edge showed, ever so slightly, out of the buttoned sleeve. Her dress had long sleeves, but they were made of thin material. Clara had an aversion to exposing what she termed *old arms*.

Rachel sat in the back seat with the other ladies. The men were in the front, rather like the days when they attended the theater. Nothing was expected of her, so she had time to concentrate on Simon. He seemed serious today. The line that blazed its way from his temple to the bridge of his nose was very deep. Even when he laughed it was there. But then, he and John had been behind closed doors in that airless study for nearly twenty-four straight hours. Something must be up. Simon handled all John's business for him. John never questioned his decisions on anything. Rachel decided to fish a little.

"Well, Simon, are you sure you have time to go on this little adventure?"

Simon lowered the visor so he could see her in the mirror. It saved his turning around. "We can take a small break for a while, you know how much I enjoyed the last sale." He put the visor back up and watched the scenery for a while.

That suited Rachel just fine. She remembered the last sale also. They had a glorious time, and afterward, they had spent hours storing the things away in the attic. They had also spent a great deal of time in each other's arms. She loved Simon, but the time wasn't right for an intimate relationship. She wanted love and she wasn't sure Simon could love her. The thought of him kissing her was pleasant, very pleasant. She decided to daydream about it all the way to the sale.

"Careful Clara," Millie cautioned as they left the car, "the ground is muddy here." Millie stopped a second to look at her ring, and then, after deciding which end of the estate display looked most inviting, they left to examine the items that would soon come up to bid.

John and Simon wandered off to look at nothing as far as she could tell. That was odd. They were both auction freaks and now they were ignoring a bidder's paradise. Something was up.

Rachel tired after a couple of hours looking at antiques and sat down on a bench to enjoy a glass of lemonade. Clara and Millie were in heaven. Millie was making long lists for John to bid on for Clara. Clara was touching many things with loving hands. Rachel could see her from where she was; holding up a picture that Millie was gushing over. Rachel knew the picture even from the back. It would be a picture of a little child and a big dog. There were many of those beautiful pictures. Rachel used to think the dog in them was the same kind, but that was proven untrue. After careful examination, the dogs weren't the same. The girls in the pictures would all have dresses to the ankles, the boys would have short sailor outfits, and both would have the Buster Brown haircut. Rachel tried to imagine how she would look with one.

"I guess you noticed …I'm an Indian."

Rachel was pulled rapidly back to the here and now of the auction. The rapid-fire bidding had begun. Kids were playing chase around the sale items and women were gathered in groups, talking. And this man she did not know had just asked her a question.

"I can see that, yes, how interesting," Rachel replied looking him up and down.

"I raise horses," he said smiling at her.

"Really, how interesting, I used to have a horse myself." Rachel wondered what tribe he was from. The necklace and headband were probably significant if she could understand their symbols. And besides, how could she not notice he was an Indian. The only thing he lacked was a loincloth over his jeans.

He left her to see how the bids were going. Rachel smiled to herself, but had actually been glad for the unusual interruption on her thoughts.

"Millie!" Rachel called. She hurried to join her friends.

Clara was already happily holding an armload of treasures. Millie was pouring over her list and then hurrying back to John and Simon. Rachel looked at the two men and had to smile. They looked more out of place than the Indian friend she had just met. Both were standing near the hay wagons used to display the goods and they were sweating profusely in the noon sun. Both were dressed in suit pants and white shirts. Simon had abandoned the tie idea, she noticed. It had probably been thrown away in a nearby trash barrel. His shirt was open about three buttons down, and she thought the view was nice. They were completely engrossed in the list Millie flapped in their faces from time to time, and the items on the cart. Rachel thought she would take pity on them and get a cold drink from the hot dog stand Jacobys always provided.

"Hi, Robert" she greeted the owner. "Could I have three medium cokes?"

"Hi, Rachel," he greeted her personally. "Three cokes Diane," he said over his shoulder. "So how are Clara and Millie?"

"Still full from that last lovely lunch they had at your restaurant."

Robert laughed, " They don't eat enough to feed a bird. I even hate to charge them."

"Here's your cokes kid," Diane said, pushing in beside her husband. "Are the girls shopping again?" she smiled.

"Yes, yes, I hope Charlie arrives soon with the truck. I see she has too many items to fit in the car. I think she even bought a bedroom set. That one over there with the marble tops." She pointed near where John and Simon were standing.

"I know that set," Robert said squinting slightly in the sun. Looking at his wife to confirm he said, "That belonged to Mrs. Shelly's grandmother."

Diane nodded, "It's been in that family a lot of generations."

Another customer came up and started to chat with Robert and Di, so Rachel picked up the cokes and headed back toward the men. Clara would never know from those two nice people that it hadn't actually been her mothers.

"Thanks, Rachel." Simon actually looked a little grateful as he took a long drink and then blew on the ice in an attempt to get some cool air on his face. John was just happy it wasn't in a metal glass.

Clara and Millie were sitting in the shade of one of the trees on chairs they may or may not have bought. They were fanning their faces with their lace handkerchiefs and enjoying a cold drink of some kind. They looked cool enough. Both ladies made it a point not to get so warm their face powder was ruined. They were talking to Frank Wakeland. Actually, he was talking. Frank was a true compulsive talker. His sentences didn't even have periods. He was interesting enough; everything he said had merit. The problem was finding a polite pause to go on with your own thoughts. The ladies didn't care, he was close to their age, and they found his attention charming.

Rachel moved down the rows with the auctioneer. The bidders squished her more to the fringe of the crowd, but she didn't mind, it was cooler there.

"How is that crazy old lady getting along?"

Rachel turned and was face to face with Gib McNiff. She had learned not to justify ignorance long ago, so she ignored his comments. She only stared at him with hatred.

Old Gib seemed to thrive on loathsome looks. He smiled at her from an unshaven face.

"Still trying to buy her past, is she?"

Rachel gave a little start. Gib was sharp in his own way. He seemed able to hone in on the most secret things going on at Stormont.

He laughed a gruesome laugh at her discomfort. His teeth were little more than strong yellow pegs.

"So Gib, …I missed you at the picnic."

Gib stopped laughing; he didn't follow her line of thought.

"In the valley over the hill," she whispered.

The light in Gib's dead eyes was brief, "So it was you who ruined the boys' party."

"I thought that information would be all over town by this time," Rachel said. She was enjoying the edge she had taken.

"No one cares, Rachel, you're weak…you're……nothing." He lit up a cigarette and let the smoke curl up around his face.

Rachel eyed him carefully, know your enemy she thought to herself. His face was greasy dirty and his nails were bowed and claw like. He wore filthy rags. The teeth he had were like horse teeth. Big and thick, the color of old straw. He was showing most of them now in what could loosely be described as a smile.

Gib eyed Rachel in turn, but she hadn't any idea what he was thinking. They weren't looking at each other man to woman. They were enemies in the highest personal order. Rachel had Clara, and all she stood for, to protect. And Gib McNiff, well, he had a tradition and a way of life to protect.

Gib watched the people moving past him for a while before he spoke again. "Your kind wouldn't survive if you didn't have your fine stores and food brought practically to your door. Do you think buying wrapped meat makes you any different from us?"

"No, it doesn't Gib, you're right on that point. We aren't talking about food per se; we're talking about cruelty. Which brings me back to my original question, Gib. Where were you when the boys were having their fun at the picnic?"

Gib tossed a cigarette to the ground and lit another before he looked at her. Smiling he said, "Busy, Rachel, I was busy." Then, he walked away laughing.

"Talking to an old friend?"

Rachel jumped slightly before she turned. "Charlie, you have a habit of showing up at the right times."

"You're getting jumpy, Rachel. Is taking care of Clara wearing your nerves down?"

"I don't think so. Millie is with her nearly every day and the rest of us manage to give each other time to do other things. No, it isn't that. Clara is part of the life that I enjoy. It's something else, Gib McNiff for one thing."

"I don't think it's just Gib, Rachel. It's a movement that's taking place all over America to phase out cruelty in all forms. Profiles we've done on serial killers always show a background of cruelty to animals as sort of their launch pad. It starts with the young kids. It's going to take time to change generations of thought patterns."

Charlie was a Pinkerton man, one of their best detectives. Rachel looked at him in his jeans and short sleeved shirt. He blended better than any of them.

"It's going to be like cleaning up litter was in the "60's", there will be a movement toward reform that a lot of people will hate and fight against. Then the government will finally impose large enough fines on offenders that the issue is forced on people who like to ignore majority rule."

"What do you think, Charlie, about these people? Do you think they just learned cruelty or do you think they have it in their genes? Are they just born mean?"

Charlie led Rachel over to a bench that had just come free under a willow. "I don't think all of them are rotten. People like Gib are the extreme of one side and people like Clara are the extreme of the other side." He smiled and looked over at Clara. "I must say that the world would be a nicer place with people like Clara, though. No, I think they are just nice people doing evil things. If they can't be changed, I hope their kids can."

"You know the day of the picnic? Where was Gib?"

Charlie looked at her with interest, then shrugged. "I think he was at Stormont setting traps."

"Laddie hates the man, he would have had a fit if Gib was that close to the house. Remember that Mary was home that day. She wanted to hang the sheets on the line to dry in the sun as I remember. She did . . .she had the sheets out because I helped her fold them and bring them in. Not only that, Laddie always follows us out to the line and lays down on his side of the gate to wait for us. Both of them should have seen anyone setting traps by the pond."

Charlie got up as he saw John and Simon coming their way. Under his breath he said to Rachel, "Watch Mary."

"What a day," John told her as he came up and handed a few books to Charlie to load in the truck. "The rest of the furniture is being watched over by Mary Lee Denehea over there." He pointed to an area occupied by an attractive woman sitting on the top of a dresser, watching the crowd. People watching was a habit everyone had at these gatherings. "Clara and Millie are already in the car, Rachel. How about you taking them home while we help load the truck."

"John," Rachel said with some alarm. "You can't lift those heavy things."

John put an arm around her shoulder and leaned closer. "We don't intend to, my dear. There are young entrepreneurs all over the place ready to assist all those who bought more than they can carry. All I have to do is direct."

Rachel gave his back a pat and then walked over to the car where the women were waiting. Mary Lee called to her from her perch.

"Rachel! Tell the girls I have a new order of lace accessories that have just come in!"

"Thanks, Mary Lee, I'll tell them!"

Rachel got in the car and turned on the air conditioning. She didn't need to tell the ladies about the new shipment, they had overheard and had already made plans to visit her shop on Monday. As she backed out onto the road, she noticed Simon having a chat with Mary Lee. He hasn't talked to me that long in the past year, she thought as she drove away with her charges.

Getting Clara out of the car without her letting go of the things she had bought was a trick.

"Shall I hold one of those statues for you?" she asked Clara.

"No dear, I have a good grip on them."

It was easy to tell she and Millie had spent the afternoon together. They picked up each other's manner of speaking until they became a blend. She had even caught Clara trying to whistle, after a day like today.

Rachel decided to pull Clara's legs around so all she had to do was stand up and get out of the car. It wasn't working, Clara scooted and heaved, but the big heavy statues wouldn't allow her to get out of the car.

Millie had taken a few items into the house and realized there had to be a snag somewhere because no one followed her in, so she went out to help.

"Here, dear." She wedged in between Rachel and the open door. "Let me take those so you can get out more easily. I hear little coughs coming from your room. You know what that means, a little one is waiting to see you."

Laddie squeezed in between the legs of the women, as thrilled to see everyone as if they had been gone days instead of hours.

"Shoo," Millie said lightly to him and took the statues from Clara's hands so that she could finally get out of the car. The idea of a pet that needed her attention had encouraged her to accept help.

With everyone finally inside of the house, Millie sat at the table and took the glass of lemonade from Rachel. She took a drink and then set it down to briefly examine her ring. "I'm going to have to go shortly, Nancy hasn't been feeling well and I promised to fix her favorite pie."

"Dear, Millie," Rachel said as she sat down. "I do so appreciate your help." She sipped her drink and moved Clara's away from the edge as she came back with her pet and sat down.

"I love going," Millie answered. "It's just like old times. I haven't seen these statues in years."

"Clara, where did your Mama get these?"

Clara held the little possum up to her neck while she fixed his blanket. "I don't know, she always had them on the window sill with the plants."

Millie checked the two statues for cracks. One was a man and one was a woman. Scantily clad, one might add. They each held a bar of wood on their shoulders and at each end were cups to hold plants. They were solid green and would look very interesting among the green plants.

Rachel felt the little opossum. "Look at all the white hair he's getting in, Clara. He is really getting fuzzy."

Clara held the little fellow away from her so she could see him better. His tiny fat feet that looked like cherub's hands held her arm tightly. The prehensile tail wrapped around her arm for balance. He made a chuckling sound, so she laid him back in his blanket and gave him the cookie that Millie had gotten for him.

"I hear the men coming. I'll get out of their way," Millie said, rising and brushing crumbs from the front of her dress.

"You know, Clara dear," she said looking around. "I believe we have found everything of your Mama's."

John Rossi, just coming in the door, gave Millie a strange look. "I'm sure there is more to find," he said. "This can't be all."

Rachel and Millie both gave him an affirmative answer after seeing his strange discomfort.

"I'm sure we can never duplicate the house John," Rachel went on to say. "It will take us forever just to place all the nice things you found today. I'll get you something cold to drink after I help Millie home with her finds. Can you keep an eye on Clara?"

John went over to his wife. "Let's have something to eat at Jacoby's tonight, Clara. We haven't taken Simon there in such a long time."

Clara smiled her agreement and John put the little possum back in his basket so she could get ready.

Rachel saw Millie to her door and looked around for Charlie on her way back. He was still helping unload the truck. She would talk to him later.

Clara's room was already looking full, but cozy. The new picture was sitting by the wall it would soon occupy.

"It's going to be a warm summer," Rachel told Clara. "Which color lipstick shall we choose, the pink?"

Clara sat still while Rachel painted her lips. "That is pretty," she told her, putting the tube back on the dresser.

She heard Simon call her to the front door.

Michael! She had forgotten about her date with Michael! Simon was standing next to him in the doorway. Looking very intimidating, she thought.

"Michael, come in, it's good to see you."

Simon looked at her steadily while she introduced Michael to him.

The men shook hands while she went to tell John she had other arrangements for the evening and to make sure he didn't need her to help with Clara.

Michael was thrilled to know she was free for the entire evening and took her hand as they walked towards his car. Rachel didn't have to turn around to know that Simon was watching her from the door.

Night had settled over Stormont. Hundreds of fireflies lit Rachel's way up the driveway. The sound of her shoes on the cobblestones could hardly be heard above the sound of the cicadas and tiny tree frogs that called the old farm their home.

She passed the freshly seeded gardens and took off her shoes before she came up the steps. She didn't want to wake Clara.

"Could I talk to you for a minute please, Rachel?"

"Good lord, Simon," Rachel whispered. "Don't scare me like that!"

Simon stood and put out his hand for her to take.

Rachel took the assistance offered because she had trouble seeing in the dark. Letting go of his hand, she sat down beside him.

"What are you doing up so late?"

"I think the question is, what are you doing out so late?"

"I don't have to answer to you, Simon," Rachel said, looking at the floor of the darkened porch. She was very much aware of Simon being around her. She could feel his masculine presence in the house, and sitting next to her, he enveloped her in his aura. It was a strong, healthy, steady pull he had on her. Everything else became foreground noise when she was with Simon. Unfortunately, she couldn't tell if his reaction to her was the same as her reaction to him.

Simon leaned back and pulled at the edges of the quilt on the back of Clara's couch. He examined them in the half-light and then he looked at Rachel again.

"You know, Rachel, no one faults you for trying to have a life of your own."

Rachel's vision was getting use to the dim light. When she looked at Simon, she could see that he was looking steadily at her.

"Well, Simon, I already had a life of my own, and now, I have a life with the only two people who have ever loved me." Rachel's chin quivered slightly before she could turn away.

Simon didn't have to see it, he could hear it in her voice. He remembered the frightened young woman fresh out of the Business College that she had been sent to by the nuns. John had developed a soft spot for her from the very beginning and Simon had fallen in love with her before the interview was even over. He almost reached out to her, but it was such an imperceptible movement that she didn't know it. He cloaked his feelings and put his arms in his lap, leaning slightly forward. Another person could have sat between them, but he could still feel the warmth radiating from her perfumed body.

"What I thought we should discuss was the care of Clara and John."

Rachel turned to him in some alarm. "What's wrong, Simon?"

"Charlie's finding used deer blinds along Stormont's boundary lines. It means we have poachers in the area. He and Jake are also finding traps along the creeks and behind the old cemetery. They are both good Pinkerton men, but there are still only two of them. I'm going to hire four more that will stay out of sight of Stormont House, but will still be on the grounds.

If Clara sees them, they will tell her they are from the University and are looking for arrowheads. You know Clara, she won't care about that. The other thing I'm going to do is acquire about five horses and put them in the old barn. We'll enclose a pasture on the other side of the barn, so we don't interfere with the little graves. Charlie says he can take care of that many animals, and if he finds he can't, he can hire a local man to help. The vehicles make too much noise and the offenders are long gone before the men can get them in their sight and make an arrest. The horses are quieter, and faster than walking the grounds. I'm also going to see about some small plane air cover from time to time."

Simon put his arm back on the top of the couch and leaned back feeling a little more relaxed. Being in charge was his realm and he was comfortable with it.

"Simon, do you think we could have trouble here at Stormont," Rachel asked.

"I want to be ready for anything," he said to her. "Poachers mean guns and underhanded people are on the land. They don't belong on Stormont and we are going to run them off."

"Why has Charlie asked me to watch Mary?"

"Because Mary doesn't know who Clara and John really are. It's unfortunate she was hired to look after Stormont before Clara and John decided to live here. I would have had a Pinkerton agent in the house too."

Rachel felt a little sting with his last statement. "I think I can look after them as well as any agent you could find."

Simon realized the distance he had just put between them and the crease on his forehead deepened. He didn't know how to separate the employment end of their relationship from the intense love he wanted to share with her.

"I realize that you are loyal to them Rachel, but there is only one of you. I feel that putting a circle of men around the property will make up for fewer people in the house. That's all I was saying," he said, putting his hand on her shoulder.

Rachel softened at the touch. Simon didn't make judgment mistakes. She knew that he would study every aspect of the situation and then assign everyone his or her responsibilities.

Simon moved her closer to him until she was against his shoulder. "John has been making some very serious decisions lately. We will probably take another week to work out the details. While I'm here, I don't want to argue with you or have any conflict at all."

He turned in her direction and came unfortunately close. Her hair was soft and curly and he kissed her without thinking. It was a mistake, because once he had gone that far, he lost his armor. He became Simon the man, and Rachel responded to the affection the instant he gave it.

Rachel was completely giving to Simon. When he kissed her mouth, she felt as if she were one with him. His lips were firm, but softened as they kissed. She came closer to him and kissed the frown line that furrowed his forehead. Rachel loved Simon and continued to show him in her passionate kisses. She kissed his face and neck softly, her arms holding him tightly.

Simon closed his eyes and held Rachel around her waist. When she moved closer to him, he pulled her against his chest. She was everything to him, and in this special unplanned moment, he could let her feel his love for her. Unknown to the rest of the residents of Stormont, Rachel did not sleep in her own bed that night.

Rachel was in the kitchen early the next morning fixing coffee when she heard a strange noise on the porch. She went to see who was visiting this early. It was Charlie. He was changing the chains on the porch swing as quietly as he could. Rachel felt the weight of the one he had finished already.

"I'm glad you're doing this Charlie, I've been a little worried about them holding."

"Simon says," and he said now."

Rachel smiled, "How would you like some coffee?"

"Could use a cup," he replied with a nod of his head. He picked up his tools and the old chains and put them at the bottom of the steps. Then he joined her for coffee in the spacious old farm kitchen.

"When are the horses coming, Charlie?" Rachel asked him as she sipped her coffee.

"Tomorrow. The fence will go up today. I'll leave it to you to make it right with Clara."

"I think she will be receptive to the idea; after all, there were always horses on Stormont land in the past. I'll look for some old pictures and see if I can't approach the subject to her that way."

Simon came into the kitchen and joined the conversation. Charlie was facing the door so Rachel had time to compose herself. She watched Simon pour his coffee. She watched the way he moved and turned his head slightly when he was listening to people, Charlie in this case. When he turned around, she looked at Charlie also.

Charlie continued what he was saying, "I thought we would get some of those tan quarter horses because they would blend with the terrain. They are also heavy animals, so we don't have to worry so much about fragile legs on this rough land."

"Good choice," Simon said, sitting down next to him. "How about saddles, straw, hay, and oats?"

"Most of it will come from the farm. We still work some of the fields. Before we just sold it off, but now we have reason to keep it; so I'll have the boys just put it up in the barns at the far end of Stormont. We'll just bring it up here as we need it because this barn is so small. I'd better get started if the fence is going to get put up before the horses get here." He stood up and said, "Thanks for the coffee, Rachel," then left quietly so he didn't wake the rest of the house.

Simon looked at his coffee for a few minutes before he spoke. He looked at Rachel in the morning light and thought his heart would break with love for her.

"Rachel, I want to know something. I want to know if you are playing with my feelings." He looked at his hands briefly as he clasped them together. "I want to know if this is a game to you."

Rachel looked carefully at the man across from her, his dark blue eyes were clear and honest. The dark hair that curled slightly when it was damp was combed back straight and went with the suit pants and short sleeved white shirt he was wearing. His arms were already brown from the Midwest sun. Without hesitation, she answered his question.

"I don't play games, Simon. What I say is what I feel. The way I feel for you is the way it's always been and the way it always will be."

Simon brushed his hands slightly and then reached across the table to take her smaller ones. Looking down at them against the lace tablecloth, he was sure of his question. He looked at the woman he loved and said, "I would like for you to be my wife."

Rachel was stunned. She never expected to hear Simon say anything so remotely human, let alone say it to her.

"Simon, there isn't anything I want more, but what about Clara and John?"

Simon leaned back, letting go of her hands. The doves had come to coo from the wire by the back door and the sun was making a path across the floor through the screen door.

"I thought about that. I can't leave New York and you can't leave Stormont, and we can't leave John and Clara. I agree with you. I also believe that we can still be man and wife with the circumstances as they are."

Rachel looked at the half cup of coffee. "I won't be with you very much," she said as tears welled up in her eyes.

"We have never been married before," Simon said softly. He came around the table and sat down beside her. "We can arrange to be together at least once a month for now. What matters is that we know we have each other. And in the bargain, we have Clara and John." He paused to kiss her. "We have it all, Rachel. We're already a family! Please say yes."

Rachel held him tightly, "Oh yes, Simon. Many, many times yes."

Simon stood up, "I have a great deal of work to finish for John, but we will get the rings today and we will be married at St. Clara's before I leave. You will need to make arrangements with Father Kessler."

John Rossi walked into the kitchen just in time to hear the last part. He held them both. "This is a moment I have longed to see," he said to them.

Simple plans were made that day and Rachel went with Simon to get her ring. Millie was beside herself. The wedding would be simple, but she was to stand up with Rachel on Clara's behalf and they only had a week.

Two weeks later, the still new bride sat on the porch with Millie. John was working in his study and Clara was asleep on the couch. Stormont had been quiet since the new men and horses had arrived. Clara loved the horses and spent many hours down by the pasture gate feeding them special treats of apples and carrots. Simon had gone back to New York, but was making plans with Everett to connect Stormont with the main office and still keep the Rossi secret. John loved every minute of it. He had been out of the mainstream of his business too long and was anxious to be part of it again. He had perked up considerably when he realized he was needed again.

"Millie," Rachel began, " have you noticed that Clara hasn't been having any spells lately?"

"I was curious about that myself," Millie said, putting down her knitting. She looked at Clara. She was asleep, but instead of a kitten beside her, it was her little opossum. She had named him JoJo. The kittens were curled at her feet and Laddie was on the floor beside her. JoJo had his face covered, but his fat little fanny stuck out of the covers. The white down hairs on his tail gave it a bare look, but both Rachel and Millie knew it was soft when wrapped around your arm for balance.

"She sure does love that little fellow," Millie went on. "He looks big from here, but it's all that strange white hair he's growing in."

Rachel looked at the peaceful scene. Then she came up with an idea. "I can see into Clara's room from the other side of the porch. I think I'll peek in on her tonight and make sure she is all right. It's just so strange that she isn't getting up in the night. I want to be sure she isn't having any trouble breathing."

Millie lay her knitting aside. "I'll sit with you. Let me hurry home and get Nancy's dinner ready and finish the laundry for her, and then I'll be back as soon as it gets dark."

Rachel listened to the soft whistling and leaned back in her chair to have a small nap with Clara as Millie hurried home. The breeze was so heavenly on summer days and the book she was reading could wait.

She woke to JoJo pulling on her hands so she knew Clara was awake. "I guess you're looking for food," she said to the baby opossum. He got down and followed her into the house. Clara was already in the refrigerator looking for just a little something, as she put it, for her little pet. JoJo went over to help. He paced back and forth in a frenzy of anticipation that always made Clara hurry. They both disappeared into her room where a bigger basket had been placed at the foot of the bed for him to sleep in.

Rachel carried his water for her. "How does he like the little door Charlie put in the screen for him?"

"I think he likes it," Clara said with uncertainty. She brushed some crumbs from the corners of her own mouth as she spoke.

"Now remember, Clara, he can't have chocolate."

"No, I know," Clara said checking through his food once more before setting it down. She looked around but obviously couldn't remember where she had put her own cookie.

Rachel retrieved it from under the pillow where the chocolate chips had already melted slightly. "This one looks broken," she told Clara as she took her hand. "Let's go find another one to go with a nice tall glass of iced tea."

Clara, John, Mary, and Rachel enjoyed a light supper together. Rachel sat with Clara long after the others had gone about their business because she didn't mind waiting for Clara to finish. Clara ate the least and took the longest. She finally pushed the plate aside and pulled her cookie and iced tea closer to her.

"Did Mama make these today?"

Rachel looked at her carefully. These questions were difficult to answer. "They are her exact recipe, I know."

She leaned forward and pointed to the bits of chocolate. "Doesn't she always use the block chocolate and cut small bits for the cookies?"

Clara looked at the bottom of the cookie. Seeing the chunks were not uniform size, she went back to eating the cookie and drinking her tea. She seemed content, so Rachel went back to reading her book. Both of them were lost in their fantasy worlds when John came into the kitchen to see how they were doing.

"Shall I turn on some light?"

Rachel closed her book, "I didn't realize it was so late, John. Are you finished up for the night?"

"No," he said reaching for a handful of cookies. "Simon has set up my computer so we have a direct link with the New York office. I am enjoying being a part of the decision making again. Your husband is a clever man," he said, winking at her.

Rachel blushed slightly. Her marriage hadn't changed much of the routine at Stormont. If anything, it had improved it. John and Simon had drifted apart and John had felt useless. Now they were working as a team again. Rachel still slept close to Clara's room except when Simon was at Stormont, and then they had the entire upstairs to themselves.

"Clara, let's go get some petals for your bed," Rachel said, taking her small hand. "I'm going to give Clara a bubble bath tonight, John. I'll call you when she is ready for bed."

John nodded his O.K., it looked like more of a salute than a nod. He went back to his study with another handful of cookies and a cold drink.

"Clara," she said when they were outside, "last year's four o'clocks came up all by themselves on the other side of the house and have blooms already. Here is a bowl to put the petals in and a little tin to put the seeds in."

Clara took the little tin with great care and held it tightly.

"Shh, look Clara, at all the Sphinx moths hovering over them. They are as big as the humming birds we get later in the summer!"

Clara walked slowly over to the big moths, but they didn't fly away from her. Some even investigated the bright spots of color on the ladies' dresses before deciding there wasn't any nectar to be collected from cotton.

Clara picked the tiny black seeds out of the old blooms and put them in her tin. She bent at the waist and stretched her arm into the multi colored flowers. Many fell to the ground but it was impossible to see them in the last little bit of evening light. The sky was rosy in places, but the sun was gone. They would have to work steadily for the next few minutes.

Rachel pulled the fragrant petals from all the plants she could reach. She soon had a dish full and had left plenty for the moths. More would bloom tomorrow.

"Do you have enough, Clara?" Rachel asked, when she saw her trying to close the lid on the little tin box.

Clara handed it to her and Rachel shook the seeds until she could close the lid. She gave it back to Clara and they walked hand in hand back into the old house.

After a lengthy bubble bath, Rachel walked her powdered and perfumed charge into her room. She pulled back the covers and, in the soft light of the bedside lamp, she and Clara sprinkled petals all over the sheets. JoJo made little coughing sounds from his bed, so Clara sprinkled some in his basket and gave him a treat. Rachel was sure he probably ate both. She put the small tin of seeds on Clara's dresser and left Clara to do the last bit of arranging of her room before she got into bed.

Knocking lightly at the open study door, Rachel said, "She's ready John. I'm going to the kitchen to wait for Millie."

John laid his pipe aside and went to his wife's room where Rachel could hear him tuck in the opossum with a few kind words and then the creaking of the bed as he sat beside his wife and shared his thoughts with her.

Rachel sat for some time reading her book before she heard Millie at the back door.

"Am I too early?" she asked through the screen.

Rachel hurried to the door and opened it. "No, just in time I would say. The music box ran down about an hour ago and I haven't heard a sound out of her room."

"I brought some blankets in case we need to wrap up against the night air." Millie showed them to Rachel and looked at her wedding rings as long as she had her hand in the light.

It was catching. Rachel looked down at her own new rings also, and admired them in the light. Then, she thought about Simon for a moment.

"Shall I take some of these cookies along?" Millie said, eyeing the plate.

"We'll take them all," Rachel said, as she gathered up the plate and her book and they went out on the porch to the comfortable chairs Rachel had placed near Clara's window.

Millie and Rachel sat quietly until well after midnight. Rachel had given up trying to read in the dim light coming from Clara's room and all of the cookies were gone. In fact, so were the entire second batch Rachel had brought out and several cups of hot chocolate. Millie leaned forward slightly and gave Rachel a poke under the blankets that covered them. The air was cool and damp so they had turned to the blankets for warmth. Neither one of them spoke as JoJo got out of his basket and came around to the side of Clara's bed. He smelled Laddie's paw and it made the big dog jump slightly, but when Laddie saw it was the little opossum, he laid back down. He watched the baby opossum for a while and then drifted off to sleep again. The shy little creature put his front feet on the edge of the bed, then came over to his window door, and let himself out. He walked past Rachel and didn't even pay much attention to her when she reached out to pet him. Clara continued to sleep soundly.

"You know dear, I can hardly believe that little fellow can smell like fresh air and have such bad breath," Millie said.

Rachel looked at the comical baby opossum as he washed himself in the moonlight. "I know what you mean, Millie. It is quite distinctive. I thought he would smell up the house, but you really can't even tell he's around unless he starts giving those little coughs for Clara to pick him up."

The silvery little opossum shuffled off the porch and scuffed around in the foliage doing what Clara referred to as his job. Then he investigated the porch for a while causing a few kittens to bristle and hiss if he came too close. He chose a darkened section of porch rail and lay down with a sigh.

Rachel checked her watch. She felt warm and restless. Dawn was only a little over an hour away. It was that biological time when your metabolism picks up and prepares you to wake up.

A sudden movement from JoJo put both ladies on the alert. He stood up on the porch rail and growled slightly. With surprising speed he glided through his door and over to Clara's bedside. Millie leaned forward in alarm.

Rachel caught Millie's arm, put her finger to her lips, and shook her head no. However, both ladies were poised to take action.

"We won't know what's going on if we don't watch quietly," she whispered to Millie.

They put their blankets aside and knelt by the window.

Clara had started to toss and turn in her sleep. She was clearly dreaming. The little opossum went up to the sleeping woman and laid his head on her shoulder. She stopped turning and lay quietly.

The two women at the window leaned closer, they were hearing a strange melody. One they had never heard before.

JoJo had put his pointed nose as close to her ear as possible. His black eyes closed slightly and a little cherubic foot lay lightly on Clara's breast. By drawing air in and out of his nose in some secret fashion, he was able to create the most beautiful music anyone could ever be privileged to hear.

Clara's forehead relaxed and the lines disappeared. Her fragile body relaxed and her arm came around to rest on her pet.

Rachel and Millie sat at the window for a long time listening and watching a scene that had clearly been created in heaven. The morning light sparkled over Clara and JoJo's song was clear and sweet.

Rachel leaned back from the window, not wanting to disturb the two figures.

"Possums sing," she whispered to Millie, "possums sing."

Mid-July would have been uncomfortable during the day if John hadn't had the foresight to install air conditioning ducts above the ceiling fans when he restored Stormont. As it was, the ceiling fans carried cool and comfortable breezes through the entire house while leaving the house open. Rachel had to admit, it was great, the best of both worlds. She saw Charlie down at the barn and decided to go down and have a chat with him while Clara was asleep.

"Charlie, how does everything look with the extra men out there."

Charlie was leading out a very big horse, so Rachel stepped aside slightly.

"Looks good, Rachel, but how a thing looks isn't always how it is. We check every day for signs of trespassing. We aren't the only ones with problems. I talked to Mike Preiss the other day and he said his Mom is having problems with hunters on the fringes of her land too." He flipped the saddle onto the horse and went about adjusting the cinch.

"I feel sorry for these old people. They do the best they can to keep these guys at bay with signs and warnings, but hunters and poachers get a big kick out of getting away with what I call 'bordering'."

He put the stirrup down and the spirited animal stomped his foot to shoo some flies.

"I checked on a fire up at Russ Schull's farm and he had started the fire himself. It seems that they came home one night and found all their cats dead. Little Monica had a hard time—one was her kitten. Russ found out that some boys had had a party at that old barn on his land that's been falling over for years. It had been one of their games to throw the cats around until they just died. Russ called the sheriff, but you know the man's a coward. Hates animals himself and sponges off old ladies. He came out but didn't even report it. If he had, the States Attorney would have heard about it and he told Russ he hadn't. Russ took matters into his own hands. He burned the barn, threatened the boys, and bought two big Dobermans."

Rachel petted the horse while she listened to Charlie. "How safe are we from all this at Stormont, Charlie?"

"No one is safe, Rachel. All the money in the world isn't going to guarantee safety for anyone or anything. We don't even have the law behind us here. Remember when the Sheriff personally killed that old man's dogs and then threatened the jobs of anyone who told on him. I think it was Mary Lee that stood up to him on that one. He made a big mistake when he threatened her job. She and her friends waged a cold war on him that won't end until he either changes or dies."

He mounted up and reined his horse around. "I'm going to make rounds now. I'll check with you when I get back." He started to leave and then turned to her, "Remember, Rachel, what Father Kessler always says."

"What we don't see, all the animals of the forests do see. That's why he didn't give them speech. Man is too weak a creature to face what he does."

"God sees them, Rachel," he called back quietly to her.

Rachel walked into the barn and picked up some of the tack that the men had left on a straw bale. A familiar noise made her stiffen, but she didn't look around. The sound of laughter from somewhere in the distance made her cold and queasy. The pigeons became nervous and flew from the rafters to the windows. Their gentle cooing and preening stopped.

"Case in point," Rachel thought to herself as she left the barn to hurry back to the house.

Clara was asleep when Rachel returned, so she got John a cold drink in a regular glass and took it to him in his office.

"John, you never come outside," she said, sitting on the arm of his office sofa.

"Thank you, Rachel," he responded gratefully to the cold glass of tea. After taking a big drink, he leaned back away from his desk. The way he always sat straight made Rachel automatically emulate him. But, after a while the muscles in her back would cry for relief and she would find an excuse to lean slightly forward.

"Simon sent a fax for you," he indicated some white papers at the side of his desk.

Rachel nodded, she would get them in a minute. "We talked for two hours this morning," she said, "I can't believe he found more to say."

"He's making up for lost time," John said smiling at her. "I haven't heard him talk so much since I've known him. He turned to set his glass down before he continued. "We all face the world with a shield, his was just thicker than average. He was right to trust you, you won't let him down."

John looked out the window of his office. "Is it as hot as it looks?"

"I've been out, it's not bad; but I think I'll wait until the sun sets a little before I take Clara out."

They both turned as a rather large animal came in and made coughing noises.

"O.K. JoJo, I'm coming," Rachel laughed. She moved fast, but it wasn't fast enough. Clara was raiding the refrigerator and JoJo was circling the kitchen.

"Let me help you with that Clara," Rachel said, lifting a bowl set in the refrigerator just for JoJo. Since that memorable evening on the porch, Millie had made sure he had special treats ready at all times. She even baked persimmon cookies for him, holding the sugar and putting in other fruits and vegetables she thought he should be eating.

Clara sorted through, finding what she thought was a good assortment of things for him to eat and then put them in his dish by the kitchen sink. Mary was use to the strange pet even though she thought his appeal went the same way as his babyhood.

Millie's whistling was heard several minutes before she made it to the porch. She pulled open the screen door, letting herself in. "My dears don't go out, it's too hot for a dog!" She picked up a napkin and wiped her face before Mary could get a cool washcloth to her.

Clara picked up the cloth and washed JoJo's chin while he squirmed around trying to get back to his bed. When she put him down, he snorted and coughed all the way back to his basket.

Rachel turned away trying not to laugh at the look on Mary's face. She would probably throw both cloths away.

"Clara, are you hungry yet?" Mary asked.

We'll look at these pictures first, Mary," Millie said, taking Clara in tow. "Give us half an hour, dear."

Rachel and Mary finished setting the table for dinner. Rachel went ahead and baked a cake while they waited for the women to finish looking at the old pictures Millie had found last spring while she was cleaning her attic.

"At last, Clara!" John exclaimed tenderly when they came to the table. He got up and pulled the chairs out for them. "I am starving, you know!"

"Now, John," Millie said, as she passed a bowl, "you know we would have come if you had called us."

Clara spied the cake cooling on the rack and helped herself to a piece.

"Clara, it hasn't even been iced. Are you sure you want it like that?" Millie wanted to know.

"I just love warm cake," Clara said, and then pushed her dinner away to eat it.

Everyone looked at John. He shrugged his shoulders, pushed his plate away, and had a piece of warm cake with Clara; and so did everyone else.

"I have to go early, I'm afraid," Millie said to Clara. She held Clara's hand a few moments before she gathered up her purse and knitting bag. "Nancy is having the children over tomorrow and I really do have some baking to do. I'll be over for breakfast though."

She kissed Clara good-by and went out the door. Her whistling could be heard all the way to her house. A distant slam of a door was the last sound they heard from Millie.

"Clara, shall we go for a walk before the sun goes down?" Rachel asked.

Clara nodded, "I have to check on JoJo first."

She disappeared into her room for a moment. Rachel checked to make sure she hadn't taken him a piece of the chocolate cake. Clara was bending over his basket with one of Millie's cookies. Her little possum was sitting with his hand over his face, he couldn't eat another bite; so Clara covered him slightly and joined Rachel for her walk.

"Let's go over to the pond Clara, there are dozens of new catfish to feed. Wait, I'll get some bread." Soon they were on their way, with Laddie bringing up the rear.

The pier was new and was built in the shape of a T. Rachel and Clara went to the bench at the very end and sat waiting for the fish to surface. After a while Clara said, "I don't see any here, maybe they're along the edge."

"O.K.," Rachel said, "we can look around the edge as long as we don't get too near the water."

They walked around the pond scaring up dragonflies and causing bullfrogs to make giant squeaks and leaps into the water.

"There they are," Clara said, pointing to the water's edge.

"Your right," Rachel said, holding the trunk of a tree so she could lean over and get a better look. "They're right there in that big hole, it looks like a big school of them. We can get down to the edge on the other side of this tree." She worked her way around to a grassy patch and then helped Clara.

"Clara, did I give you the bread?"

Clara checked her sleeve, "No dear."

"I must have left it on the pier. If you wait right here, I'll go get it and be right back."

Clara sat on the grass-covered bank with Laddie and watched the wildlife around her. "I'll be right here."

Rachel walked around the pond to the pier and retrieved the little package of breadcrumbs. She looked up to make sure Clara hadn't moved from the spot where she had left her and noticed a small herd of deer had come into the pasture behind Clara. Clara had seen them also. She was standing by the tree, holding the bottom of her skirt so it didn't flap and frighten them away. They were grazing and taking little notice of Clara or her dog. Laddie sat quietly on the grass.

Rachel started back around the pond, and much to her horror, a shot rang out. It made her jump and she dropped the bread package. One of the deer had been hit and was falling slowly to the ground. It issued a dreadful call and tried to get up. Clara began to run towards it screaming,

"No!......Nooooo!"

Rachel ran. She ran faster than she ever had in her life.

"Clara!—Stop, Clara!—Clara, Please!"

Tears of fear ran down Rachel's face, she was too far and Clara was running steadily on, driven by the cries of the wounded deer. Laddie barked and barked and ran around to the other side of the pond heading towards the house.

Another shot rang out and Clara slowly fell to her knees.

Rachel's terror made breathing difficult. "Please God," she whimpered, "please let her have only tripped."

Blood began to show on the back of Clara's dress as she knelt there in the tall grass of the meadow. Rachel made it around the pond and put herself in a direct line between her beloved Clara and the direction of the shots. She ran with a purpose, she ran to save Clara's life.

Clara was poised for just moments with her hands slightly in the air, looking as if she were just kneeling over her flowerbeds and would stand up any moment. But the red spot grew quickly and she fell forward in the tall grass of her beloved Stormont.

"Charlie! ... Charlie!" ... Rachel began to scream "Please, Charlie Help Me!"

Rachel reached Clara's side and lay on top of her. She put her arm under her breast so she could hold her up to breathe. "Oh Clara, oh Clara," she sobbed. Another body fell beside her, it was Charlie. His face showed only hate and blind rage. He had a pistol in his hand and had already fired it twice to summon help. It was only minutes before four equestrians appeared at a dead run across the meadow. Two went past the tragic scene and two put themselves behind the two women. They jumped down and quickly ascertained what had happened. Charlie lifted Clara and turned her gently over. It was clear to everyone that she was dead.

Charlie let the pistol fall to the ground and threw himself over the fallen woman. He wept. Rachel began to shake uncontrollably and one of the other men took control of the situation. Charlie mounted one of the quieter horses and two of the men handed Clara's body up to him. He held her close and guided the horse back to the farmhouse. The dear lady's blood flowed down his leg and dripped thin, red droplets from the stirrup as he carried his precious burden home.

Rachel went into convulsions and the other horseman stopped and lay her in the grass. They tried to cover her and control her shaking until the ambulance could get to her.

John Rossi met the bloody horseman at the path near the house. He had been told what had happened to his wife. He took her gently from Charlie's arms and carried her over the threshold as he had done forty years before. He sat down at the table and refused to let go of his wife. He held her until the sun came up and the doves began to coo on the wire near the back door. And the only reason he let go of her then, was because his mind was gone.

Simon brought Rachel back to Stormont a week after Clara was killed. She had been unable to attend the funeral that took place in the old family cemetery on the other side of the meadow. All those days in the hospital she had thought she would never be able to return to Stormont, but John was still here and he needed her.

At the kitchen door she leaned against Simon and said to him, "I can't do this. I don't want to come back here."

"It's always this way, Rachel, when someone you love very much dies. Your life changes forever all at once. We have John to take care of now and I can't do it by myself."

Rachel went down the hall toward John's room but she had to pass Clara's first—it was too much for her. She went in, lay on Clara's bed, and cried. Simon came in and sat beside her much the same way John had sat beside Clara every night for forty years.

"Shh, Rachel," he said gently as he stroked her hair. She had lost weight during her stay at the hospital and her eyes were red from crying every day in spite of all the sedatives she had been given. Her fine bone structure and the aristocratic line of her nose were silhouetted against the long curly black hair. She hadn't bothered to pull it back from her face, as was her usual custom. She had just let it go. Millie had stayed with her night and day and cared for her like a child. Simon had handled all the affairs necessary on the home front.

"It was good that you got here so fast, Simon," she said holding his hand. "You are the only one left to depend on."

"Darling Rachel, we are together. I thank God I didn't lose both of you." He looked slowly around the room, letting himself grieve silently. The tiny tin of seeds was still on the marble top dresser. There were a few flower petals that had escaped into the corners and an empty basket at the foot of the bed.

"Where are Laddie and JoJo?" Rachel asked, suddenly remembering Clara's pets.

"Laddie is in the room with John, and JoJo . . .we don't know. He left and didn't come back. Charlie says he sees him from time to time back by the pond in the old persimmon tree, but he won't come to anyone."

"Have they found the person who did this, Si?"

Simon helped Rachel sit up and tried to brush her hair. He was very awkward at it, but Rachel let him continue to try. She was just too weak and tired to care.

"Not a trace, Rachel, whoever it was only left behind two shell casings and that is all. Pinkerton men have been crawling all over this town. Charlie pushed them on for three days and nights straight, but they didn't find anything. All he found out was that nearly everyone in this town has a gun and a license to kill."

"Did he check Gib?"

"He checked him first, in fact he stood outside his house and yelled that he knew he did it for hours. Jake had to take over the investigation until Charlie could deal with his grief." Simon held Rachel for a long time before he spoke again.

"It's strange about Charlie, he looks like he could bite nails in half, but he sure had a soft spot for Clara. I think he would have killed McNiff if he'd seen him, but he didn't. What aggravated him even more was the fact that Gib's gun was clean and he had an alibi."

Rachel sat up and looked around the room. It was hard to bear but she tried to think of Clara without falling apart. The tears still flowed, but she had to see John, so she got up from Clara's bed and walked out closing the door. For now, she thought, for now I will shut out the pain.

John's room had been altered. It resembled a hospital room, which in fact was exactly what it had become. The big oak bed had bottles hanging beside it and an oxygen tank stood directly behind it. On the bedside table were bottles of medicine and plastic water jugs.

Another table at the end of the bed held intercom systems and computerized equipment that was directly linked to the hospital. A nurse sitting near his bed relinquished her seat when Simon came into the room and went to get John's charts. She hadn't any idea exactly who Simon was, but she knew he paid her wages and they were handsome wages at that.

Simon took the chart from her and dismissed her for the moment with a curt, "thank you."

Rachel went to John's bedside and kissed him. He looked at her but he didn't speak and he didn't appear to know who she was, and then he turned away. Tears ran down his face from time to time but that was the only reaction they could detect to indicate he was still a thinking being.

Rachel sat beside him and held his hand, while Simon went about the house seeing to everything that needed to be done for John.

Laddie lay on a rug by John's bed. He didn't get up but he raised his head and wagged his tail a bit. Rachel took pity on the dog and called him over to her.

"Come Laddie, come to see me."

His ears perked up a little at the sound of her voice, and he came over and sat down beside her. She rubbed his ears and scratched his chin while she talked to him. Her thoughts kept coming back to him. Something, what was it? Something she wanted to remember about the dog.

The nurse came back in the room. It's time for Mr. Rossi to have something to eat, Mrs. Garrett, do you wish to stay?"

"Yes, I wish to stay, in fact, I wish to help you with his care." She turned to the nurse and continued, her strength and her will returning in spades, "I would like you to instruct me on everything I can possibly do to care for him."

She smiled and took Rachel's hand, "Very well then, we'll start with dinner and then I'll show you everything we need to make his evening a comfortable one."

"Thank you," Rachel replied gratefully.

It was late before Rachel emerged from John's room. A night nurse had replaced the day nurse and John had been given a sedative to help him sleep. She went to John's office to find her husband. Simon was hard at work over the computer and was referring to some of John's notes. He looked up at her when she entered.

"John was up to something here," he told her. "I can't figure it out. It doesn't seem to have anything to do with the business either. There are codes all over the place that I didn't set up for him."

Rachel sat down, "Do you think you will be able to ask him?"

"Time will tell Rachel, the doctor said he should come out of this. It was just a shock and his brain needs time to accept it. He say's there isn't anything physically wrong with him and he has a good chance to enjoy many happy years." He kissed her. " We just have to give him time." Simon pushed the papers away he had been looking through and turned off the computer. "Let's walk over to Jacoby's and get something to eat."

"Jacoby's? Why Jacoby's? Where is Mary?"

Simon stood up and leaned toward her, "We'll talk about it on the way."

Rachel felt a little better about being in the house. Some things were still familiar. Simon was still here, and John and Laddie, and Clara had lived here. They walked down the big hall into the kitchen after checking on John. Rachel could see Clara every place she looked—she couldn't help it. The tears started to flow again. Laddie followed them out onto the porch and she bent down to pet him and remind him to stay.

What was there about the dog she was trying to remember? "Simon, let me sit here on the steps with Laddie for a minute. There is something I'm trying to remember and I get the feeling every time I pet him."

Simon did not say anything, he did not want to break the spell. They had all hoped Rachel could remember something about that day that would lead them to Clara's killer. He watched the sun setting and listened to the frogs start their chorus down by the pond.

"Simon! It was Laddie, he didn't run after Clara with me. I know he didn't, he ran the other way, in fact!"

Simon was alert to everything she was saying. "Wait here, Rachel, I'm going to get Jake and Charlie. Keep the dog with you," he added.

Charlie and Simon were back at the house in record time. A couple of minutes later, Jake arrived riding one horse and leading three other hastily saddled mounts. The sun had set but there was still enough light to see.

Rachel didn't wait to change her clothes. She let Simon help her up, trying to keep her dress at a modest length while still being able to sit in the saddle.

"Come on, Laddie," Simon called.

"Show us exactly what happened," Charlie said, his face grim.

Rachel noticed that both men wore side arms. There were also rifles in the scabbards on all four horses. These were bad times if men had to bear arms on Stormont Land.

Rachel tapped the sides of her horse with her summer sandals. Her bare brown legs lightly gripped the horse as he moved down the path.

"We came down this path. We followed the brick all the way to the pond." She paused at the pier, "It was here where we waited first for the catfish. We sat on the bench at the end of the pier for a while. Then we decided they must be along the bank because it had been so hot that day; so we came back here to the end of the pier and moved along the left side of the pond." She moved the horse on, stopping from time to time and showing them where they had paused to check for the fish, "And then we got to this tree, and we saw a whole school of them in that hole right there underneath this big old tree. I had forgotten the bread crumbs we had for them and so I had Clara wait here while I went back to the pier."

Rachel started to cry, "I shouldn't have left her, I know I shouldn't have left her," she leaned sobbing into the horse's mane. "She was so cute, looking for the bread crumbs in her sleeve where Millie always puts her little handkerchief. Simon," she turned to her husband, "its all my fault. I should have been with her."

Simon dismounted and gave the reins of his horse to Jake. He got up behind Rachel and put his arms around her.

"Listen, Rachel, listen to me. No one is responsible for another person being where they are when something like this happens. The fault lies with the person who shot her. You were doing the right thing, my love. She wanted to be here with you feeding those silly fish and watching them jumping for the breadcrumbs. She wouldn't have traded those moments with you and you wouldn't have traded them with her. She had all the money in the world, Rachel, but it wouldn't have bought anyone who loved her as much as you did. The pain is deep right now. I know it's hard to relive it so soon, but you can help us. Keep in mind the dog, put everything else out of your mind and concentrate on where he was and what he did."

Rachel sat in the saddle looking at the spot beside the tree. Simon took the reins but kept his arms around her.

"I left him here with Clara. He was sitting beside her the way he always did. I was over there at the pier. I had gotten the bread crumbs we had left on the bench and was just stepping off the pier and started this way." She paused trying to get her thoughts together.

"Take me back to the pier, Simon."

The group made their way quickly back to the place Rachel indicated. The light was nearly gone.

"O.K., I was here when I heard the first shot and the deer we had seen fell. Clara started to run and I started to run. I was running this way . . .to the left of the pond, Clara ran into the meadow behind the pond, and Laddie . . .ran . . .he ran away! That's it, that's what was so odd. After the first shot, he ran along the right side of the pond toward the house. He didn't go to Clara. He went the opposite direction, and he was barking like crazy."

Rachel took the reins and moved the horse midway between the pier and the tree where she had left Clara. In the dark, she told the men. " This was the last I remember seeing him. He was straight across the pond from me and running as fast as he could in the other direction."

Everyone sat fairly still on their horses assimilating the scene Rachel had just recounted for them. Laddie lay down in the grass, he didn't seem to want to be very far from the people.

Charlie spoke up first. "This is the best lead we have, Rachel. I'm sorry we had to put you through this but the trail to Clara's killer is a mighty cold one."

To Jake and Simon he said, "The dog will have left prints, if we can follow them, it will lead us to the exact site the killer was standing. We have a computer image of where the killer might have been, but it was too broad and we didn't find anything. It hasn't rained so we still have a good chance to follow the path Laddie took."

Jake cleared his throat. He didn't like to talk very much and when he did it always seemed like a big effort. "The beaver might have left prints all over the place. They have spent most of the summer closing off the far corner of the pond. They have probably walked all over the ones Laddie left. Those wet tails would have swabbed the ground like an old mop."

They all looked toward the area where the beaver dam was. They couldn't see it, but they could hear the noises that came from that special place. Water trickling off the branches from the higher areas of the structure. Small waves lapping against bark and the green smell of freshly stripped branches left lying on the damp earth. The heavy sound of a beaver coming out of the water. The small sounds of the young and answering mutters of the parents. Peaceful, untroubled, uncomplicated lives.

Rachel was leaning against Simon and she felt him sigh. The swishing of the horses tails and the occasional stamp on the ground were just patient ways horses had of waiting for people to make up their minds. Rachel leaned forward and played with the mane of her horse and then she said the strangest thing, as strange as her meeting with him.

"I know an Indian."

"Rachel," Simon said laughing lightly in her ear, "honey, just because a man is an Indian doesn't mean he can track dogs."

"I know that Simon, and don't laugh at me. I just met him and I think that he could probably track a dog. He just looked like he could do things like that."

"Who was he, Rachel?" Charlie asked.

"I don't know. I met him at the auction and he sat beside me for a time. All I know about him was that he raised horses."

Simon moved his horse in the direction of the house. "We're going to Jacoby's for dinner. Why don't you two join us and we'll ask Robert and Di what they know."

"I'm for it," Charlie said. "How about you Jake?"

"I'll stay and put the horses up and tell the other men what we know. We'll all meet you at the tree tomorrow morning at dawn unless you let us know otherwise."

"O.K., and check in with my wife would you. Fill her in as much as you can and tell her not to wait up," Charlie said to him.

Charlie brought up the rear of the group. When they approached the house, Rachel looked over Simon's shoulder to make sure he was still behind them. His gaze was fixed on the riderless horse that Jake was leading. The symbolism seemed to be a moment for Clara. She turned back and leaned against Simon's chest.

"We were going to walk over to Jacoby's. Charlie, does that idea suit you?" Simon said as he helped Rachel dismount.

"Sounds good to me."

Jake took the horses on to the barn while Simon and Rachel tried to smooth their hopelessly wrinkled clothes.

"Put the dog in for the night please, Rachel," Charlie said. "Try to stay with him if he has to go out tonight. I haven't seen him down by the pond this week, but now that we know what we're looking for, I want to keep track of where he goes."

Rachel put him in, "I'll keep a watch over him, Charlie."

The threesome walked to the restaurant in silence. It was a nice evening and kids were playing and riding bicycles. Dogs were barking in every neighborhood, and mothers were shouting out the doors trying to keep track of their broods. They passed an open door where the smell of fresh popcorn drifted out to them.

"I'm definitely hungry," Simon said, taking Rachel's hand and hurrying towards the restaurant.

They sat down at a corner table and a friendly waitress took their order. There were only a couple of people lingering over coffee, so Robert and Di joined them. Di had a dishtowel in her hand and dried the table a bit before she sat down. Her husband stood next to her.

"We are so sorry about what happened. We just want you guys to know that," Di said. She adjusted the stained glass rocking horse. It was one of the centerpieces she had made for this table. It caught the light and everyone took a moment to reflect. Robert stood next to her and shook his head in agreement as he added, "Everyone in town is in shock. We all loved Clara."

She turned and spoke softly to Charlie. "We've been keeping our ears open and we haven't heard a thing. Robert's even been going over to the tavern every so often to listen in on conversations over there, but they just aren't talking."

Robert agreed with what his wife said, and then added, "I don't think anyone knows who did it. To be honest, I think if even the lowest skunk at the tavern knew, he would tell it. Most men are pretty upset. They all have families and it could have happened to anyone. There are new No Hunting signs going up all over the county."

Charlie entered the conversation. "Stormont had wall to wall signs and more, and it didn't stop a tragedy from occurring."

Rachel noticed that when he said, "and more," his jaw muscles clinched tightly. The 'more' was, of course, himself. If his shoulders were weak they would have sagged when he thought of his failure to save Clara.

Their dinner came so the conversation changed.

"Robert," Simon said, "do you happen to know any Indians around here who raise horses?"

Robert looked at his wife and they conferred slightly a bit on who married whom and what strangers had moved into town in the last hundred years and then, finally agreed to whom Simon must be referring.

Di got her thoughts together and then leaned slightly forward, absentmindedly folding her dishtowel as she spoke. "It has to be the man who bought the Shelly estate. You know the place, Simon, it's where John bought that old marble top dresser for Clara."

She looked at her husband. "He was in here a while back, remember, and you talked to him for a while. Remember, he sat over there at the counter?"

"Oh yes, I know who you're talking about. He had a strange name. It was Nicholas something, what was that now? Lightening . . .no . . .Longtree. That was his name, Nicholas Longtree!"

Charlie pushed his half-eaten food away, put a ten-dollar bill on the table, and left without saying a word. Even Simon was surprised, as that was more his style of doing things than Charlie's.

They stayed at the restaurant until it closed and then walked back to Stormont. That was the nice thing about summer in a small Midwest town. It was close to midnight but lights were still on in houses and bigger kids played quietly in the cool, late evening. Screen doors were left unlatched and windows were open above the beds of children. In spite of the recent tragedy, the town was still safe. It was only the woods, the fields, and the lonely roads that people feared at night. The places where their neighbors did unspeakable things when they felt no one was watching them. The fear was in happening on someone and then knowing, knowing when you looked at them in the daylight, they were capable of killing.

Simon walked around a bike left on the sidewalk and knew it would still be there in the morning when some little child ran out trying to remember where he had left it. The dark side of human nature was only among a few, it was time to weed them out.

"Simon," Rachel said taking his hand," you were going to tell me about Mary?"

"Oh yes," he said without smiling. "Mary. One of the nasty things Pinkerton agents uncovered was the fact that Mary was letting her nephew trap beaver at the pond behind the house. They checked everyone who was dealing in any kind of fur trade and one of the new undercover agents happen to overhear a conversation a boy was having with his Aunt Mary concerning how much money he had made on beaver pelts. Knowing we had poaching going on, coupled with Charlie's earlier suspicions, we were able to go right to her door."

He stopped a minute to kiss Rachel under the street lamp before he went on. "Her father came to the station when she was interviewed and it was very interesting to note that he had a jagged scar on his right cheek." He put his arm around her and pulled her closer to him. "He probably still has some of your hair under his nail, if I had to guess."

"Simon." Rachel was aghast, "Mary knew all along what had happened at the picnic and she didn't let on at all."

"That's right, but let's don't worry about her anymore. Outside law has stepped in and the Sheriff, Mary, her dad, and a lot of other people have a lot to answer for.

The next morning Simon was up before dawn and went out to meet Charlie. Rachel went into John's room to help the nurse with his bath and breakfast.

"Shall we get him up?" she asked the nurse.

The nurse looked a little concerned. "I haven't been able to get him to sit up at all. And he hasn't been eating well. Dr. Brown took the IV's out, but he might have to put them back in if he doesn't eat."

"John?" Rachel tried to get a response. "John, do you want to sit up for me?"

Again, no response.

Rachel turned to the nurse for answers. "What can I do? He can't continue like this. What are we doing wrong? Dr. Brown said he should be himself again any day now."

The nurse poured some water into a dishpan. "Sometimes it takes longer for a person to adjust to their loss. Meanwhile, we can still do what we can."

She smiled gently at Rachel. "You can help me turn him for his bath and here is some lotion. Be sure to put it on his elbows, heels and hipbones."

Rachel helped the nurse as well as she could. She felt a little awkward, but she could see some things that didn't seem right. After doing all they could for him, he fell into a peaceful slumber. Rachel pointed to the intercom and then to the kitchen, indicating to the nurse she wanted a quiet moment to speak to her.

They sat at the table near the speaker so they could hear the amplified sound of John's even breathing.

"Why are his heels so red and soft?" she asked the nurse.

"We have a little friction and pressure problem. It will go away as soon as he is up and around. We just need to keep him turned every couple of hours and make sure we massage those red areas with some lotion."

"Do you have a schedule for this?" Rachel asked.

"Every even hour we shift him. But I think we should increase that to every hour. His skin is breaking down fast. It occurs quickly in some people and other people don't seem to have a problem with it no matter how long they are bed ridden."

The nurse returned to John's room and Rachel went outside with Laddie. While she waited on the porch for him, she looked out over the pond. The area was crawling with men, all following several feet behind one single individual. She knew it was her Indian friend in the lead. She recognized the figure of her husband and Charlie and thought she knew which one was Jake. They were pretty far away. It was nearly eleven and they were just coming around the beaver pond. It looked like there were at least ten men in the group. Laddie went to the edge of the little brick sidewalk and looked their way.

"Laddie, come here," Rachel called to him.

He came in the house with her and she closed and locked the screen door. "I have to remember what I'm doing," she said to herself. Looking around the empty kitchen, she realized that there also wasn't any food in the house for all those men. Rachel consulted her watch and started the water for iced tea. She looked hopelessly around the kitchen trying to think about how she should start to organize things.

She heard a faint but familiar whistling and she ran to unlatch the screen door. She went out on the porch remembering to push the door shut tightly and ran down the path to meet Millie.

"Oh Millie, it's so good to see you!" She hugged the little woman and took her knitting bag to carry. "Millie, I just don't know where to start. I'm not sure which jobs to do first and I'm not sure which ones I should take over. And to top it all off, I think that all those men out there," she said, pointing to the pond, "are going to be here for lunch in about an hour."

"Not to worry dear, first things first," Millie said as she let herself in the kitchen door and put her things on the table. She sat down and accepted the glass of tea Rachel brought her. "You have always run the household. You just must be tired from your ordeal." She stopped to squeeze Rachel's hand and take a second to look at her ring. Rachel took a moment to admire hers for a moment also. Millie's habits were so easy to catch, probably because they were things that made you feel good; like her whistling, calling you dear, giving you hugs, or admiring gifts she had been given.

"I know how to do things. It's just that John always checked over my lists and put his O.K. on everything. It's their money and I feel uncomfortable just taking over as if it were mine."

"I see, dear," Millie said sympathetically. She glanced around the kitchen and spied the cookie jar. "Do we happen to have any cookies?"

"Sure, Millie, let me get them."

"First of all Rachel, just let me tell you," she said as she munched the cookies, "Charlie talked to me early this morning about the plans they had for today. Simon is going to be busy trying to catch Clara's killer and taking care of John's financial affairs. You have to take over the house until John gets his health back. It's the only thing to do. What will happen if you don't? The lights won't get paid; the water won't get paid; there won't be food on the table. Which brings us to the point of lunch today. Call Jacoby's right now and order lunch sent over for fifteen people. Then run down to the pier and shout across to Simon that you have lunch and I'll check in on John and see what the nurse thinks we should get for him from town. That will take care of all the immediate problems." She bent over and kissed Rachel's head.

Rachel walked down to the pier feeling a lot more like her old self, and things were under control for the moment. She called to Simon that lunch would be at the house for everyone in about forty-five minutes. Simon took a minute to acknowledge her, but there was more to Simon than just a wave. He was a different person with her. She was the trusted keeper of his inner most thoughts and secrets. With her he could be the person he was meant to be.

She watched them working their way through the grass, mostly on hands and knees. However, it didn't look as if they were finding much. She would know more when they came to lunch. She turned to go back to the house; but when she got to the fork that went to the barn, she turned that way instead. She walked into the pasture and over to the little white crosses. The old crumbling wood had recently been painted and the vases had been filled with white roses. Rachel stood and looked at the little graves for a long time.

Robert! This is great!" Simon said, as he sat down with the rest of the men.

"No problem," Robert said, smiling at the compliment. He was unwrapping hot packages of food and handing them to Rachel to distribute. Millie had taken two dinners to John's room.

The big kitchen was full of men, all discussing the mornings events. The man who was the new addition to the team looked pleased to be an important part of the mission.

"Nick here, managed to track the dog all the way around the beaver pond," one of the men told Rachel.

"I have every step that dog took on film," another added.

"We should be at the spot the shots were fired from by mid-afternoon," Charlie said. "Then, we'll cordon off a fifty foot by fifty foot square and go over every inch of it."

Nick ate quietly, but it was easy to tell he was enjoying the notoriety his skills were bringing him among his peers.

"How do you know how to do this?" Rachel asked him.

Nick smiled at the question. "You can believe one of two things; that I learned to track animals from my ancestors, or that I learned to track animals because, in addition to raising horses, I am a free-lance wildlife photographer."

Rachel sat down with her plate and began to butter a piece of Di's homemade bread.

"Well, I believe it's because of your sweet an-ces-te-rys," she told him.

Nick countered her answer with another idea. “Then, it appears to me that a lot of us had the same ancestors.”

The men nodded their agreement. All of them were thinking about Clara and people like Clara.

“Robert, I can’t thank you enough for helping us out. Can we make this a regular arrangement for the time being?” Simon said.

“Sure, we’re glad to help out; just let us know how many for each meal and we’ll have some of our special dinners fixed for all of you. Di can watch the restaurant while I run it over so that’s not a problem.”

“Can everyone be here for dinner about five?” Simon asked, as the men got up and headed for the door.

The vote was unanimous. They followed Robert out with worthy suggestions for the evening’s dessert.

Simon lingered, to be alone with Rachel for a few minutes. “It’s hard to know what we’ll find at the end of the tracks. Maybe if we can find out who did this, John will come around for us.”

Rachel put her arms around him and kissed him. The sleeve of her dress fluttered up in a feminine way against his cheek, and when he turned to go, he took that memory with him.

Rachel cleaned up the kitchen and joined Millie and the day nurse. John had eaten very little, and lay with the biscuit he was given to try still clutched in his listless hand.

“John, did you have a nice lunch?” Rachel asked. She bent to kiss his cheek, and wiped away some Jell-O that had escaped to the corner of his mouth.

John did not answer her. He wasn’t answering anyone; if in fact, he did hear them.

“Well, ladies”, Rachel said to the nurse and Millie, “let’s try to sit him up for a few minutes so his lunch can digest a little better.”

“Will that be O.K. with you, John?” she asked, doing it anyway.

It took all of them to get the big man to the edge of the bed, and it was very difficult to keep him there.

“This is no good,” Rachel told them as they lay him back down with a great deal of struggle.

"John, you're like a big rag doll. You need to help us a little next time. Will you do that for us? Can we get you anything? Millie and I are going to walk to town and bring back a few things we need, just tell us what you would like to have."

Rachel went on talking while she put salve on his heels and helped the nurse redress them. They also worked on his shoulders where the skin was becoming a little soft. Then, she and Millie got their things together to go downtown.

It really was a pretty afternoon, and if they hurried, they would get back in time for supper. They had noticed that the men were getting nearer and nearer to LaDue, the street Stormont House faced. All of them were fanned out and crawling on their hands and knees. If there was evidence there, they were determined to find it. Some of the people in the town had turned out to watch the proceedings. Some had even brought lawn chairs to sit in. All of them stayed a respectful distance from the yellow tape and all of them hoped they would find the evidence they needed to catch Clara's killer. A table that held iced drinks and cookies had been set up along the far tape. It had been set up by the senior citizens, and one of the members was being allowed to bring them refreshments, as long as she stayed behind the working men. She was obviously very happy to be given the opportunity to be on the working side of the tape. She wore her apron like a flag, proud to be *helping the boys*.

"Well, I must say," Millie told her as they walked the block or two toward the store, "if the killer is seeing this, he should be in a high state of worry. We're going to get him if it's the last thing we do." And with that, she shook her little fist in the air. And then, checked her ring in the sunlight.

Rachel automatically checked hers too, and thought about Simon working back there with the men.

"Girls!" Mary Lee said upon seeing Millie and Rachel come into her shop. She came around the corner to give them a perfunctory hug.

"What's happening at Stormont? I hear all kinds of rumors. Have they found out who did it? I can't believe it you know, I just can't believe it. To be shot in your own back yard is just too much."

She stood by the open window and lit a cigarette. Millie half closed her eyes and went to the other side of the shop to look at the doilies, but Rachel went over to talk to Mary Lee.

Mary Lee blew a little smoke out the window and leaned toward Rachel and whispered, "It was that little weasel, McNiff, you know. I'd stake my life on it."

Rachel looked at some lingerie Mary Lee had on display and confided to her, "I have to agree that he is the most likely suspect. Unfortunately, his gun checked out and he had an alibi."

Mary Lee laughed at that, "An alibi? Which one of his relatives gave it to him? The thing that gets me is that the killer had to be standing on the street side. Surely someone saw him."

"Take the lace honey, it suits you," Mary Lee interrupted herself.

Rachel held onto the lace slip while she browsed the shop a little more. After Mary Lee snubbed out her cigarette, she followed Rachel and rained more wisdom down on her head.

"I would say it's just a matter of time before he gives himself away, Rachel. We just have to be patient. Actually, I think that's why the town is taking this all rather calmly. It's not as if a stranger came into town and started killing all the women and children. It's old Gib, and everyone knows him. The question is, why? I never understood Clara myself and I don't even have a cat, let alone the zoo she had. It's the hair. I hate the hair. And who has to feed them all . . .the person who brought them home to begin with. So you feed them, so they can grow more hair. It's not for me, Rachel, I like my apartment just the way it is. I really like coming home and being the only one in there. Nothing creeping and crawling around."

She paused to comment on another item Rachel had picked up. "The print is perfect, light and airy, perfect for summer," she told Rachel.

The door opened and Grace came in with a couple of her friends. Rachel went back to browsing and Mary Lee didn't move from where she had been folding a few blouses.

Grace immediately began with an unpleasant insinuation. "Who do you think will be the next Mrs. Rossi?" she giggled to her friend.

"I don't know," her friend said a trifle loudly, "maybe he will just keep things the way they are."

Mary Lee stepped in. "Can I help you?"

"Just looking," Grace said over her shoulder. They left laughing.

"It is really hard to believe she is a grown woman," Mary Lee said after they left. "And sores, has anyone ever seen the woman without a band aide on her face, or some other medical problem? And what is that smell?"

Millie joined them, and listened half-heartedly to Mary Lee's tirade against Grace. Nothing was new, she and Grace had been at war since grade school, and Grace had been insulting everyone since high school.

"We still have to stop at the pharmacy," Millie reminded her.

"I'm ready," Rachel said to her. "I just want to get something a little new."

Mary Lee and Millie exchanged glances. Of course, Rachel was still a new bride, and in the wake of the tragic happenings, everyone had lost sight of that. They both set everything aside and looked at the dresses with Rachel until a smile came back to her face, and she even laughed with them a little. She picked a pretty, yellow print dress, and even bought matching undergarments and shoes.

"Simon will love it, mark my words," was Mary Lee's parting comment.

They had to hurry to the pharmacy and then home, but they didn't mind. They had some new ointments and bandages for John, and Rachel had her new dress. There would hopefully be news at dinner, as to what they had found. Rachel put her arm around Millie and gave her a hug.

"I love you, Millie," she said.

Dinner was on the table when they arrived. Millie checked on John but the nurse had already gotten their plates, so she and Rachel sat at the table with the men.

"We are at the exact spot the killer was standing," Simon informed them.

"There was a lot of ground torn up, we should be able to get all the evidence we need. The forensic team will be here tomorrow. Meanwhile, we are going to take four-hour shifts, two men each, to make sure no one touches the area. Charlie's out there right now, his wife brought him blankets and dinner. He say's he's going to stay there until we have done everything we possibly can.

Nick spoke up, "The dog had a go around with someone, that's for sure. We found blood on some leaves and the trunk of the tree and bits of clothing."

Another man spoke, "Lots of dog hair though, not only is he shedding, but he lost some in the tussle. The man probably pulled on his hair to get him off."

"The computer printout they gave us, had the gun fired close to the house. The guy was actually farther over towards the woods," Simon commented. "We've got him, and that makes me very happy."

Millie stayed pretty quiet throughout the conversation, but Rachel was curious.

"Do you think we can tell John what we know, or should we wait?"

"Let's wait until we know for sure, and then we'll tell him. I don't want to get his hopes up. We'll tell him what we know tomorrow, and then he will have all day to get used to the idea. If I tell him tonight, I'm afraid he won't be able to sleep." Simon told them.

After dinner, everyone drifted out. Rachel and Millie helped Robert carry the empty containers out to his car, and then Millie went home. They promised Rachel they would be there at breakfast the next morning.

The house was quiet when Rachel went in. She thought about putting on her new dress, it lay between sheets of gauzy white paper in a box of delicate pink. It still had the light scent of perfume from Mary Lee's little shop. Rachel sat down to think about her life for a few minutes. The new dress seemed somehow inappropriate with John lying there and not being able to enjoy life. She put her new things away and went to find Simon in John's study. She had something important to discuss with Simon.

Rachel went up and put her arms around Simon while he continued to fuss with the computer. He reached behind when she kissed the back of his head and unclipped her barrette. Her hair fell forward and he kept one hand in it, playing with the curls.

"You know, Rachel," he said, pushing the chair back and pulling her onto his lap, "I am really confused about what John was working on. I just keep wondering if I was suppose to be doing something for him and wasn't getting his messages."

Rachel leaned back against his shoulder and looked at the computer.

"He was in here a lot, but he didn't say anything about what he was doing. He just said you had set this up so that he could be in direct contact with the New York office and so that you could be here at Stormont more."

She turned towards her husband. It was very pleasant to be alone with him, but there was more to share with him.

"This morning, we got John up because his skin is breaking down, but he's too heavy for us to manage. What should we do?"

"We are doing everything we can for him. He would get the same care in the hospital as he is getting here. We could get more doctors and more nurses, but they would just be in each other's way. This is something John has to come to grips with himself; we can't bore it into him, or give him a pill. He has to overcome it himself."

"There is just something about him that reminds me of some of Clara's orphans," Rachel told him. "Remember the rabbit that just gave up and died?" She turned to look at him before going on, his steel blue eyes very close to hers.

"And there were others, it seems that they would just be a little sick, and the next minute they would be dead. Another thing about them was that they always wanted to be held those last hours, every one of them. But they had made up in their own mind that life wasn't worth living. I always had the feeling that wild things didn't have as much trouble with the transition from life to death that we have. Maybe they know something that we don't know."

Simon put his arms around her and smiled as he kissed her hair. "Rachel, they know a lot more than we know. And they sure act better than we do."

"Did you know Mary Lee doesn't like animals?"

Simon laughed at that. "So she says, I happen to know that she spends a fortune trying to preserve everything from the rainforest to the elephants."

"How do you know that?" Rachel wanted to know.

"Because Mary Lee Denehea is on the side of every cat, dog, and kid in this town. I know that as a lawyer, because lawyers talk to each other about their cases. Everyone likes to represent Mary Lee, because she either wants to win or make the other side so poor they don't have time to bother little kids and small animals." He kissed her pouting mouth and then added, "I think you two would be great friends."

He checked his watch, "Let's go help with John before we go to bed."

Simon gave instructions to Rachel and the nurse after checking John's charts.

"What we will do is, let him sit up; and then after a few minutes, we will help him stand up. I will lean him against me and hold him, while you two massage his body. If this doesn't work, we will get more people."

Simon got John to his feet with little effort. Simon was slightly taller than John was, but John was the heavier of the two. He held him while the women massaged his skin until it looked pink and the circulation was improved.

Rachel left to get more towels, and when she came back, she saw a different Simon. John's head lay on his shoulder, and he had both arms around the ailing man. He held him carefully, but tightly. John Rossi had been a rich and powerful man, and now he had in his own fashion, stepped down to let the younger man take the reins. Simon was clearly the head of the family now. Both women worked steadily until Simon told them he was going to let him rest again.

He laid the white-haired man gently against his pillow and leaned down to kiss him good night, as naturally as a small boy kisses his father. His vital signs were stable, so the young couple bid the nurse goodnight. She would call them if they were needed before it was time to turn him again.

The next morning went as planned. Robert showed up with breakfast and the men in charge of forensics came in for their instructions. Nicholas Longtree stayed with the group now, as one of them. He seemed happy to help. Millie came over, as she had promised, and took a plate in to see if she could encourage John to eat. She thought that with all the activity in the house, he might be more alert.

Everyone ate quickly, and most took their coffee with them. They were all anxious to see what the day might bring. Millie came in to sit with Rachel after everyone had left, and showed her the full tray.

"I can't get him to eat a bite. The nurse tried too, but he just wouldn't eat."

"I know the feeling," Rachel told her. " I tried to get him to eat a little toast and drink a little coffee this morning, but he wouldn't even try. John's different to work with than Clara was, I just don't feel like I should tell him what to do."

"John's always been the strong one, he seemed invincible. He always looked as if he were handling things just fine. Now that he is sick, there doesn't seem to be any common ground with him. I never really knew him, only Clara did."

A light knock at the door surprised them.

"Father Kessler, come in," Rachel said, getting up and opening the door. "John will be so glad to see you. Have some coffee with us before you go in. There are some donuts left from breakfast, if you would like one."

"Yes, I would like some coffee," he said, sitting down beside Millie. "I must tell you, this nasty business has me completely upset. I have tried for years to get people to stop and think before they commit such wicked acts upon the innocent. Now look what it has brought us. Clara's gone, John's ill . . ."

Rachel felt truly sorry for the man as she handed him a cup of coffee. His hands dwarfed it as he held it waiting for it to cool a bit.

"I'm so tired of this," he went on. He sighed, and looked tired. "What are we coming to? How is our John?" he asked, turning to Millie.

Millie patted his hand and told him their fears about John's health and about the job the men were doing outside.

Father put a fist to his chin as he listened, and gazed at both Rachel and Millie in turn. He nibbled nervously at the food placed in front of him.

Father Kessler put down his empty cup, and with the two women, he went to visit John. After the prayer for recovery and for strength and confidence, Father stayed with him the rest of the afternoon.

"I must go, dear," Millie said, after a substantial wait for Father to emerge from the room. "Nancy will be coming home soon, and I haven't begun to put the house in order."

"Stay for dinner here," Rachel implored. "We have more than enough for everyone. You know how Robert and Di are, always putting out plenty for extra people."

"Oh, I know I'm welcome," Millie went on, "it's just that I have so many things I need to see to. You can count on me for breakfast though," she said smiling. "I will want to know all the details from Simon about today's work."

"Good-bye then, see you tomorrow," Rachel said, waving to her dearest friend.

At dinner, Rachel asked Simon about the results of the afternoon. Most of the men had left the grounds to work on other cases.

"We have bags of evidence, but there is one little snag to it leading us to Gib McNiff. Gib has disappeared, and no one seems to know where he is. And if they do, they won't say."

Everyone was quiet at the table.

"He has to show up sometime," Charlie said. "We'll just wait."

"It's true," Nick said in full agreement. "He'll make a mistake somewhere, he has to eat. He'll probably need to buy ammunition, because people like him don't give up hunting for anything. He's just going to lay low for a while. I'll keep my ears and eyes open. I'm in the woods all the time sitting quietly, and I'm hard to see. I know a lot that goes on in the woods. If he comes by, he will leave a print, and it will give us the direction he is coming from, and going. If he's around here, which we think he is, he will surface eventually."

Charlie and Nick had become fast friends. Probably because they were so alike, Rachel thought.

As the evening wore into night, Rachel and Simon took their turns helping the nurses with John. They managed to keep his skin healthy, but as the weeks went by, he became thinner and weaker. Doctors were brought in as well as more medical equipment. But in the end, John Rossi won the battle to join his wife without ever speaking another word to anyone. The funeral, as expected, was small and simple. Rachel sat between Simon and Millie in the row designated for family. They were his only family. The one thing Rachel was to always remember at his funeral were the last words in the hymn Father Kessler had picked for him.

Justice to the orphan and oppressed, so that mere mortals may strike terror no more.

She had closed her eyes, and before her came an image of Clara and John trying to help those two baby raccoons over the fence and taking them to the other side.

The following week at Stormont was hectic for Simon and Rachel. Visitors came by to offer their condolences and to bring food and all the affairs of the farm had to be seen to. Millie came as often as she could, but her grandchildren were visiting and she was needed at home.

A knock at the front door brought Rachel out of the kitchen looking puzzled. Everyone visited everyone else in the big old farm kitchens common to the Midwest houses. Front doors usually meant strangers.

"I am looking for Mr. and Mrs. Garrett."

"That would be my husband and myself," Rachel told him. "Please come in."

"Thank you," he said, taking the offered chair. "My name is Cole, Mr. James Cole. I have come at the request of the late John Rossi. I am the lawyer he chose to represent the estate of he and his late wife."

Rachel was startled," I hadn't even thought about a will," she said. "Mr. Rossi and his wife have already been generous to a fault to my husband and myself. Years ago, he established trust funds for the charities he and his wife had chosen to leave their money to."

The little man in the black suit smiled and took out a monogrammed handkerchief to wipe his brow. He looked around at the modest furnishings and then turned back to Rachel.

"He changed his will several weeks before his wife died so tragically. It is all very legal and straightforward. It also concerns you and your husband."

"Simon is in the study, I'll call him to join us. Would you like something to drink?"

"Yes, please," he said. Then he took off his glasses and proceeded to polish the surface of the lenses and wait patiently for his hostess to return.

"Simon," Rachel said at the study door. "There is a Mr. Cole here that says he is representing John Rossi's estate. He wants to talk to us in the living room. I'll get some cold drinks and meet you in there. And please turn the fan on."

Simon was puzzled, he put down the paper work he was doing and went into the living room. Rachel joined them with the drinks and then sat down beside her husband.

Mr. Cole opened his brief case and laid out a few papers. " I have here the last will made by John Rossi. There is a copy for each of you. As you see, the bulk of his estate has been bequeathed to the two of you to manage. He has left you both a handsome share of his wealth also, but this is aside from the money you will handle for the charity he has established."

He paused to take out a folder for each of them.

"In essence, and the exact details are inside, you are going to form a charity that is going to radically change the course of history. That is my opinion of course, but I don't think I'm too far off the mark." He smiled as he picked up his briefcase and zipped it shut with a loud tearing sound.

"My fees have already been paid, so this is the only contact you will have with me, unless of course you have any questions. My sole purpose was to deliver these papers to you upon his death. And I can assure you, he did not intend it to be so soon, nor did I. He was still working out the details of his plan when his wife was killed. I'm afraid none of us know exactly what it was he had in his mind because he wasn't able to finish his work and commit it to paper. From what I have seen, he had a grandiose idea. I wish you all the best in carrying it out."

He rose and shook hands with both of them, and then he was gone.

"Simon, did he ever talk to you about any of this?" Rachel asked, when they were alone.

"Rachel, I don't have any idea what all this is about. I think we are about to see why, too. I would have been completely set against it. He would often talk about doing things for us and I would always remind him of how much he already had done."

"I was the same, I have more than enough. They have been so generous to me that I wouldn't ever need more. I am curious as to what John had in mind for us to do for him. NOW THAT, I am interested in."

"So am I," Simon said to her. "What ever it is and what ever it takes, we'll do it."

"Here, Simon, you read these papers over and I'll run to Robert and Di's for our dinner. You can tell me about it while we eat. And pick out a bottle of wine to chill, honey," she called on the way out the door.

When Rachel returned, it was to a very shocked husband.

"It can't be done Rachel, we can't possibly do what he asked us to do. I haven't even gone into the computer yet. He left all the codes so I could find the detailed instructions he had intended to leave. But I can see that this is too big for just two people to organize."

He dropped into a kitchen chair and stared at the table.

"Simon, it can't be that bad. We have all this money to work with and a small request to follow up on. We can do it."

"Rachel, it *is* that bad. Not everything is possible."

"Look, let's set the papers aside, have a nice dinner, and get a fresh start in the morning. It's late, and we can't possibly figure this all out when we are so tired."

But Rachel had been wrong. The days wore on as the two people tried to figure out how to meet John's last wishes. It wasn't going to be easy at all.

Rachel had moved all of their things to the upstairs she and Simon shared. She sat cross-legged in blue jeans on her bed. Simon sat quietly in front of the computer. He looked at the blank screen and folded and unfolded his hands.

"O.K. Simon, lets look at what we have figured out. With the annual income from the estate, we have to basically do just a few things throughout the United States. We have to establish free veterinary services exclusively for children and their pets. We must provide counseling for children who have traumatic incidents with the loss of their pets and subsidies for rehabilitation of wild animals. Most places have humane societies established. We just have to help finance the ones who do not practice euthanasia. This all looks reasonable to me, Si."

Simon looked at the papers around him, "When you put it that way, it does sound easy. Maybe we can pull it off. There is just something here that I am sure he wanted to let us know, but he didn't have time to write it down. I worked for John a long time and I got to where I just had a feel for these things. These are rough, rough drafts, of a plan he had hoped to put into place himself."

He smiled at Rachel and came over to hug her and sit beside her on the bed.

"You know, John was an interesting man, a very interesting man. He knew a lot about human nature, all those things that make people tick. I'm telling you the truth when I tell you that John would have left us a back door. He never came up with any business venture that didn't have one."

"What can go wrong Simon, it just looks so easy. There is only so much money to be given out monthly. We just have to work out a budget and stick to it. And make sure, from time to time, that everything is going as it was planned to."

Rachel started to pick up her papers and put them away. Laddie came upstairs and whined to go out, so she said to Simon, "I'll take him this time, I want to stretch my legs."

" They are pretty ones at that," Simon told her as she went down the stairs.

Laddie whined louder trying to hurry Rachel up.

"I'm coming, I'm coming," Rachel told him. It had gotten dark and there weren't any lights on downstairs, so Rachel felt her way along the wall to the switches. It was a cool evening and was raining off and on. All the dust had washed off the roof and had made some of the windows a little muddy. There was still a threat of a big storm coming. When Rachel stood on the back porch, she could fẹel that the wind had picked up.

Laddie walked a little way toward the barn and growled low. The hair stood up on his neck and he lowered his head. A light laugh, carried in on the wind, chilled Rachel to the bone.

"Oh my God! He's right here at Stormont," Rachel said to herself.

Laddie went crazy at the sound of the laughter and tore down to the barn, barking as he went. Rachel ran into the house just as fast.

"Simon!" she yelled, running down the hall. "He's here! Gib's here at Stormont! I think he's down at the barn!"

Simon passed her in the hall carrying a rifle and a pistol. "Call Charlie," was all he said.

Rachel dialed his number and his wife answered.

"Laura," Rachel said. "Gib's at Stormont."

"Charlie knows, Rachel. He heard the dog and he went out the back way. Are you all right?"

"Yes, I'm fine. I just thought he would be miles from here. I never expected him to be so close."

Charlie's wife was young, pretty, and blonde, just the opposite of her husband. She never worried about him, either. She always felt he would come out on top. She would have the coffee on when he got home and they would talk about the case, but she never questioned his judgment.

"Charlie doesn't think he's going to go very far, he knows the land here and he knows the people. Charlie says, if he goes anyplace else, he'll get caught because he just won't fit in. Not too many people will miss an old man who's playing at being Daniel Boone."

"So you think that Gib's just going to stay here and tease us till he dies?" Rachel speculated.

"I think that's exactly what he is going to do, Rachel. Did you know Charlie quit Pinkerton?"

Rachel sat down by the phone, "No, I didn't know that."

"This is a personal thing he's got with Gib now. He shouldn't have killed Clara. Charlie won't let go now, and that means Gib has to die."

Rachel couldn't believe what she was hearing, but knew it to be true. In fact, the whole town knew it. Charlie was after Gib McNiff and everyone was waiting to see who was going to win.

"Isn't there someone we can call in to help out with this?" Rachel asked a little worried. After all, her husband was out there right now, too.

"They did everything they know how to do, or can do. They have to go on to other cases, and all they can do is keep the file open and hope Gib shows up someplace. Old ladies get killed every day and someone loved each and every one of them. It's up to us to corner Gib."

"I know you're right, Laura, it just all seems so primitive."

Laura laughed, "Rachel girl, we are a true cross-section of humanity. There are still headhunters among us." She paused for a minute and then said, "I hear Charlie coming in, so I better go. Simon should be coming any minute, too. It doesn't sound like they caught him. I'll see you tomorrow, Rachel."

"I know the guy was around here," Simon said, when he came in the door. Laddie came in with him. Both of them were still bristling from the audacity of the man.

"Simon," Rachel said, "you're going to have to start wearing heavier pants and different shoes. Maybe some jeans?" she suggested.

Simon looked up at her as he took off his muddy shoes. The shine was definitely gone. His white shirt was covered with dirt and straw and there were holes in his suit pants. He padded through the house to lock up his guns while she made coffee for them. When he came back, he was nice and clean and had on some casual slacks and a light pull over.

"He was here wasn't he old boy?" He petted Laddie's head and gave him a cookie.

"Simon," Rachel said, "he'll get cavities."

Red flashing lights shown in the kitchen window. "Would that be the local police?" Rachel asked.

"Yes, it would," Simon told her, sipping his coffee. "I don't intend to play games with that crazy bastard all night. In fact, that old man is going to be chased all night by bloodhounds while I'm in bed enjoying the company of my wife."

Rachel blushed and did not comment.

Simon came around and picked her up out of her chair. "Do you know I'm crazy about you?"

Rachel put her arms around him and whispered in his ear. "And I'm very much in love with you, Si."

Stormont was quiet over the next couple of days. News of Gib's visit to Stormont was all over town. The local people speculated that he might be after Rachel next, or even Clara's dog. This didn't stop Rachel and Simon from going about their business on the farm. Clara's gardens needed weeded and the house had a certain amount of upkeep. John had intended it to be the headquarters of his new charity and had left the farm to the couple he had loved so dearly in life.

Rachel brought some flowers into the new study Simon had fixed up in the room connected to their bedroom. It had been a sunroom, of sorts, at one time. It was really a very pleasant room. They had decided that being downstairs brought too much sadness to them right now, so they had closed John and Clara's rooms and just left things as they were for the time being.

"The south flowerbed by the porch," Simon tried to guess.

"Right," Rachel said. "Tell me what you have accomplished so far."

"This seems easier than I expected. I phoned the agency responsible for each state and they will contact at least one vet per 200-mile radius. Each one that agrees to it will establish a free service for the kids. They will be put on a set salary. Then, I contacted the humane society and they will establish a shelter for each area, all animals neutered free. Last, but not least, I contacted each state's conservation department and they will set up rehab programs and keep records as to who has wild animals in their care and who gets paid. We'll have our own staff who handles specifically, loss of pet trauma. All of the information will be kept on a computer and all we have to do is direct the funds.

Everett will run the New York office from now on. I set this system up for John and myself and we had all the bugs ironed out a week after it was in place. Everett and I will use the same system. That means we go to New York when we want to, and we stay here when we want to. At least, until we decide what we want to do with our lives and where we want to live."

"What about Stormont, Si?"

"I've thought about that, Rachel, what will happen to it when we're gone. I just don't know. We don't have to decide right now at any rate. So, what do you think of my progress?"

"You have done very well, Si. We don't seem to have any worries, let's hope it stays that way. Let's celebrate. Let's go out to a really nice place and have dinner and dance a little."

"I'm for that, get your new dress on and let's go. I'm going to take Laddie out one more time and then leave him at Charlie's. I know he will be safe there. I'll be back in a minute to get you."

Simon was anxious to please his new bride, so he made time for her in his busy schedule. Like tonight, he thought, she looked beautiful in her new dress. If only he could shake the strange feeling he had about John's set up. He could tell from the notes that John had made that he expected trouble of some kind to develop. Simon had gone over the whole thing so many times that his head hurt. He couldn't see anything that could be a problem.

He opened the door of the car for Rachel and waited for her to get in. She moved over so she could be closer to him. He got in and put his arm around her.

"Rachel, can you see any problems that might develop from this plan of John's?"

Rachel thought about it as she watched the lights from passing cars flash by. "Nothing, I can't see where there would be any problems at all. In fact, it should do exactly what John and Clara would have wanted; make people more caring and teach the children early about compassion and caring for the natural balance of the earth. The only reason wild animals are treated as badly as they are, is because this is a money world and they don't have any. They are exploited by people to make money from their fur or save money by eating their flesh. Either way, the problem is greed. Giving wild things money just evens it out a little. At least people can learn more about them and the people who advocate animal rights will finally get a chance to enlighten the people about the natural role animals play in our lives."

"We could just live on concrete you know," Simon told her smiling.

"Some people would be happy doing just that! But even they have to breathe, which brings us to trees which brings us to how everything is interconnected."

"I hope you're hungry, my little wife, because we are almost there."

Rachel was very happy. This was the first time in her life she hadn't any responsibilities heavy on her shoulders. She was in her new yellow print dress and with the man she loved. The restaurant was charming and a world away from the life at Stormont. After dinner, she danced every slow dance with Simon, savoring the closeness of him and the way he held her as they moved lightly with the rhythm of the music. The dance floor was softy lit, rosy almost from the table candles and the hidden ceiling lights. The music was sweet and unhurried. The stone tiled area set aside for the band and the dance floor was cool under her feet. The footsteps of the dancers, the rustle of dresses and the wonderful scents of colognes were light years away from life at Stormont.

"Simon, my love, do you know what I will miss about this earth the most, when I die?"

"Me?"

"Of course, you," she whispered in his ear. Then she put her head on his shoulder and half closed her eyes. "And the other thing I will miss is the music. We have so much beautiful music on this earth."

The music ended and he led her back to their table. The candlelight flickered softly. He ordered a drink and then leaned toward her with a little twinkle in his eye.

"I think I have a name for John's charity that is just perfect," he said.

"That's right," she said. "He didn't have a name for it, did he? He was still trying to come up with just the right name, as I remember from his notes. Well, Simon, tell me what you think is so perfect."

He leaned back to enjoy the drink he had ordered and to admire the glass, taking his time to answer. "Anticipation is half the fun," he teased her.

She didn't answer, just folded her arms, and prepared to out wait him.

He leaned forward, still smiling and said, "Arakun."

"Arakun?"

"Yes, Arakun, I got the name from Nick. When I told him about the little graves, he told me the Indian name for raccoon. It's Arakun. It means, he who feels the earth with his hands."

Rachel was entranced with the idea. "It's perfect, Simon, it's perfect. They would both have thought it was perfect. Arakun, it is."

Good morning, Rachel," Simon said, sitting on the bed with two cups of coffee. What are your plans for today?"

A sleepy Rachel turned to look out the window before answering his question. "If it rains, I'll work on scrap books; if it doesn't rain, I want to be outside as much as I can." She looked at her arm, "I think my tan is fading."

Simon laughed at her. He had a gift of looking tan all year around even if he was outside very little during the day. "Here, have some coffee and don't worry, you look very brown."

Rachel sipped her coffee slowly. "That breeze is heavenly, I hope it stays this way all day."

They both watched the lace curtains flutter around the wooden sills for a while. It was very relaxing.

"Well," Rachel said lazily," I suppose I need to see what is being set up around town for Arakun, if anything is yet."

"I would give it another month to get off the ground, although there should be rumblings about what's going on. I think we should watch this town very closely because it will be very indicative of what is happening all over America. Everything in every town will be identical, so we will see first hand how the operation is progressing. Everett is going to handle the business while I'm here, and I'll handle Arakun exclusively, with a check from time to time on the New York office."

"Right now," he said, putting his coffee down, "I'm going to get back to the computer and phone and see how John's little charity is developing. Another thing, Rachel, that I may have forgotten to tell you. The John and Clara who were hired as impersonators are still alive and well. As far as the world knows, they are the ones who are behind the charity, not our John and Clara."

"I had forgotten about them," Rachel said. "What provision did John leave for them?"

"It was simple. If they out-lived John and Clara, they would continue as if nothing had happened. John foresaw that if they were suddenly disposed of, then what he and Clara had tried so hard to build up and hide would be headline news. People would want pieces of every bit of their private lives here at Stormont. So, they have their lifestyle until they die. Their will has already been made up with the help of John Rossi and is with the attorney John hired to represent them. I told you, John always left back doors. That's what I don't like about this set up. He didn't have a chance to write down what could go wrong and what we should do about it."

Rachel got her clothes together and went over to kiss the frown line on his forehead that had deepened as he spoke.

"Simon, has it ever occurred to you that you might be able to figure out how to solve these problems as well as John would have?"

The couple looked out the windows of the peaceful Stormont, hazy trees waved in the distance. Some Canadian geese were flying in low and heading for the pond. And faintly in the distance was Millie whistling.

Two weeks later Rachel and Simon were up at dawn to answer a ringing telephone.

Simon picked up the phone, but before he said hello, he put his hand over the mouth piece and asked Rachel, "Have we or have we not had a honeymoon?" He went back to the call.

Rachel laughed but put a pillow over her head so she didn't have to listen to the conversation.

He finally hung up. "There are snags everywhere. I'm going to go to Robert and Di's and get our breakfast. I am not going to try to even put cereal into bowls. I have to at least get the office to fax messages rather than call. The phone is driving me nuts." He was trying to get his shirt buttoned. "How in the hell is it that you give people a fortune in free services and all they can give you in return is grief? Honey," his voice changed as he snuggled her under her pillow, "can we talk about this over breakfast?"

Rachel moved the pillow. "Breakfast sounds good. I'll shower while you're gone and meet you downstairs." She kissed him and ruffled his hair. "We'll get control of this situation, it's just new that's all. It's the novelty of the whole thing; all of the sudden animals have money. Think about it, Simon, it's not just a rich pet owner or someone who really wants to save just one species; this has actually been set up so that every animal out there has a money value other than for its flesh or fur, or sport. They have a money value on life, their life, and their right to life. It was actually a clever idea John had."

She kicked back the covers so she could get up. "Hurry back, or I'll be first one finished."

The kitchen was sunny and open compared to the rest of the downstairs. Rachel went into Clara's room for a minute while she waited for Simon to get back. The room still smelled fresh and sweet like Clara. Rachel went around the room just touching her things, the things that had grown even more important since Clara died, because there weren't going to be any more memories. She stopped at JoJo's basket. She hoped that wherever he was, that if times got tough, he remembered his clean bed and the little white-haired lady who loved him so dearly.

"I'm back," Simon called from the kitchen.

Rachel hurried out to the kitchen to help him.

"It's a little warm, so be careful."

"So, tell me about the phone call," Rachel said.

"It would seem that adults have already figured out a way to get in on the free clinics for kids."

"Yes, we expected that problem to crop up."

"Well, the problem, dear wife, is that already very few legitimate kids are getting the service. Instead of the little kid down the street that doesn't have any money and has a puppy with a snotty nose getting the service, it's the middle class mamas getting their kids to take the overstuffed dog in so she can save a few pennies"

"Middle class mamas is not very charitable, Simon," Rachel smiled.

"It's not what I want to say either, Rachel, but I'm trying to keep my language on a gentleman's level," Simon smiled back.

"Well, what are we going to do?"

"We could try to have all the kids register their pets. It might work to go to the local schools and take names and pet names. It's still summer vacation right now, so the idea will have to wait until fall. It's for all kids, so we can't go by need either. People have their pride and they don't want their kids labeled poor. Any ideas at your end?"

"I think that after a certain period of time, the vets that run the clinics will get to know their new clients. Maybe they could have a Meet the Vet Day or something at the summer camps. Everything takes so much time to establish, that's my gripe."

"It isn't the only problem, Rachel," he said, taking her plate to the sink and kissing the top of her head. "Since we stipulated that our shelters not practice euthanasia, we have to enlarge them until the animal population is under control."

"Can we do that, I mean can we afford the expense?"

"I'm going to run up some figures this morning, then I can better answer your question; but we have to remember that many shelters already exist that do not believe in euthanasia and they are surviving. It's hard to accommodate them all, but they manage."

"Do we have any more problems I should know about?" Rachel asked.

"Plenty. The people that have started up the clinics are already being questioned as if they were pedophiles with a new avenue to the young. And last, but not least, we come to the rehab situation. City people, who wouldn't know a wild animal if one came up and bit their behinds, are robbing the zoos. They don't understand that a lot of the zoo animals are not indigenous to the United States. And since they already have a home, they don't count."

"Well, Simon, one very good thing about this is that no one knows we started this mess. And hopefully, they won't find out until we have it running smoothly."

"If we do get it running smoothly," Simon said, as he leaned against the sink. "I found one more little item in fine print on the documents our dear friend Mr. Cole left us. Should we be unable to fulfill this last request, it is to become a corporate venture. A large ranch in Texas comes to mind, it's not run by the heirs anymore, just a lot of business men. That's what will happen here, if we die, or decide to willingly give it up."

"If we don't make this work, and we knew what Clara and John wanted; then, how can someone run it who hasn't a clue as to what they had in mind?"

"I've seen that before, too, Rachel. Another good example is the Tully case, an old women died and left her estate to the Humane Society for local use. Within a year, all of the assets had been used up and the kennels closed, and it was very far removed from what the dear lady wanted."

"I remember that case, Si. There isn't even a humane society in that town in her name. Well, we have to make it work, no matter what," she came over to hug him, "and we will. I have to go pretty soon," she continued, "I am going to attend one of the meetings here for the kids. Evidently, they are having quite a turnout and I promised to help with refreshments. It gives me a chance to spy on our progress too."

"O.K., that will work out for me, too; because I have a lot of papers to go through and I want to work out some hopeful solutions to our problems. I'll take care of Laddie, so you won't have to worry about him."

"Simon," Rachel said, as she went out the door, "I'll bring something to fix for dinner tonight."

Simon rushed to the door and teasingly said, "Dinner for two, with wine?"

"Yes, now let me go or I'll be late."

Rachel walked to the town hall since it wasn't far from Stormont. All the streets were tree-lined, so it was cool and breezy. Everything was old, the sidewalk, the houses, and the brick streets. It was also something more, and it was that something more that always brought her home to the Midwest. It was the stability in the old things, the history. On the side of the newspaper office, there were still the faint remnants of a sign painted on its wall. It had been a veteran's hospital during the war. Many of the homes had been in families for generations, and the old people weren't just old people. They had been someone at one time; they had done something that the town remembered them for. Even if that something was a simple paper route or poetry contest.

Rachel had been so carried away by her own thoughts, that she was surprised to find herself at the town hall steps. She entered quietly because she was a little late. There were seven or eight children sitting around a little table in the basement. One was talking when she arrived.

"My Mother always drown the new kittens at the farm because she said there were too many."

"Why did that bother you?" a young woman asked who was obviously the counselor.

"Because they use to splash in the bucket until they were dead and then she would just throw them in the garbage. We knew we couldn't get attached to them because we couldn't have them. Sometimes we would sneak one to save, but she would always find out and drown it anyway, and then it was harder. Then we would cry, and Dad would say if we didn't shut up, he would give us something to cry about. I was always afraid of that because I used to hear them say there were too many mouths to feed, and I was afraid they would drown me in the bucket too."

"You're older now," the women said. "How do you feel now?"

"I just feel sad when I think about it. I just wanted my Mom to be a nice Mom. I didn't want to think of her as someone who would kill something so small."

"What about the rest of you, what do you think of Helen's story?"

Another girl spoke up, "My Dad was the same, he kept hunting dogs and he use to shoot the puppies. The Mother dog would cry and try to save the puppies. She would drag them back by their necks and Dad would kick her, and then, kick the puppy to the other side of the pen, and then, either kick it to death or shoot it. They would cry and cry, and then they would be dead. And I just hate my Dad for what he does. I can't ever tell him that. When he tells me he has to do it, I tell him I understand because that's what he wants to hear. But in my secret heart, I hate him; and as soon as I find a boyfriend, I'm going to move away from him."

"How about you, Josh?"

"I just hate the blood. I have bad dreams at night because there is so much blood in my dreams, and if you bleed a lot, you die. So I'm always dreaming that I'm bleeding to death."

Rachel looked around the room at the tragic faces of the young people. She felt terrible about having a happy walk over here when these kids were on the way over with such a burden on their hearts. She got up and went to the kitchen to fix some Kool-Aid and cookies. Some of the teenagers were sobbing and many of the boys looked as if they had been. It was unusual to have both sexes together, she thought. Usually boys wouldn't be caught dead telling their feelings in front of girls. Rachel pondered this as she set up the tray on which she included Kleenex. There was a boy about sixteen years old standing against the door jam, but he wasn't coming in, so Rachel left the group on the pretext of getting some air. She sat on the steps some minutes before the young man came over to her. She kept looking down, waiting for him to speak. She noticed he was wearing large, heavy boots, a very hot choice for summer. They looked about two sizes too big and she noticed a hole on one edge.

"Is your name Rachel?"

"Yes, yes it is, how did you know?"

"I know Clara from some time ago. I only live two mile from you. I liked Clara, she was nice. I want to ask you if you know something."

"Sure, I'll try to help."

"I want to know why my dog has a hole this big in his hip?" and the boy showed her his fist.

"Well, I don't know, I would have to look at it."

And so, the young man took her hand and they walked down the street in silence. They went down a narrow alleyway next to a tavern that stunk of something Rachel wasn't sure of.

"Isn't this building back here, where the kennels are for the humane society?"

"There is no such thing," the little boy assured her in a matter of fact voice. He led her past two empty cages and walkėd down a dirty, oily path through some weeds. He stopped near some small trees in a slightly wooded lot. The smell was worse here than in the alley, and soon Rachel could see why. They were standing above a big pit, and in it, was a dead deer and something that had decomposed beyond recognition; and then, there was the boy's dog. It had been there for awhile and was slightly swollen with decay, but the boy didn't seem to be concerned with that. He pointed to the dog's hip, and sure enough, it had a big hole in it.

"Well, what happened to him?" Rachel asked.

"My folks had him put down cause he was old, and the shot made that big hole."

The boy was still holding Rachel's hand. She looked at the ground and could see that there was a bare spot worn by the boy's visits to his dog.

"We need to bury him, don't you think?" she asked the boy.

He just nodded his head, yes, so she couldn't tell how close to tears he was.

She kept holding his hand, and started walking away from the awful sight. "I know a perfect place for him, if you don't mind my suggesting it."

Again, he shook his head without answering.

"Do we need to ask your folks if you can go with me?"

"They work," was all he said.

They walked back to Stormont and Rachel changed into jeans and got several garbage bags and the big farm truck. She sent the boy down to the barn for a couple of shovels. Before she left, she stopped at the door to Simon's study.

"Simon," she said, "I'm not bringing anything to cook tonight, and I will be a little late and I'll need a very long bath."

He came over to the door. "Do you need my help?"

"No, not this time, I've got help. Kiss me now, you might not want to later."

"I trust you will tell me what happened at dinner."

"Probably before dinner," she said. She re-joined the young man and they drove back to the pit."

"What is this place?" Rachel asked, as the boy climbed down to get his dog.

"It's the death pit, they throw dead animals here."

"Remember to walk only on the plastic bags," Rachel told him, gagging slightly. "There have to be all kinds of germs in this place."

"No, miss," he said, as he rolled his dog into one of the bags. "My dog didn't have no germs."

"I see, of course. I was just thinking there might be germs here from another time."

The boy shook his head that he had understood her error. He was having trouble with the smell himself, but he wouldn't let go of a dog that had obviously been his best friend.

Rachel leaned over the pit to take the dog from him. It had been a very big dog and she had to drag it up the side. The boy pushed from the bottom. She had put plastic bags every place, but while cleaner, it was also slicker. Between the two of them, they managed and finally got him onto the bed of the truck.

"O.K., that's it. We're ready to take him to Stormont. Can you tell me his name?"

"His name was Pal."

"Pal, that's a perfect name," Rachel said.

"I'll ride back here with my dog," the young man told her. He proceeded to get in the back and pull the dog up close to him.

Rachel didn't say anything; she didn't even try to get his name out of him. He needed her to help him do what he couldn't do alone, and that was all she needed to know. She drove down to the pine forest east of Stormont

"This is a perfect place for your dog," she told him. "The wind in the evening makes a rushing sound and it's always peaceful here. Up there in the trees are some big hoot owls, but that's about all that you can ever see. The pine needles are so thick that nothing can grow, so you don't have weeds or bugs. I'm sure this is the perfect place."

The young boy looked up at the tall trees. He was holding the very big, very dead dog in his arms. He finally looked around for a place to lay him. He chose an open spot between two trees.

"Pal always liked to lay in the sun," he explained.

It didn't take much time to bury the dog, and finally, the only smell in the air was from the pines. Rachel got down on her knees and helped spread needles over the fresh earth.

"You know," she said, "all animals go to heaven. I had a dog once that I loved very much and she died; but, every once in a while, I can see her happy and running towards me. There is an invisible barrier between us but she tries to run and get through."

The young man's eyes shown with understanding, "That's the same way with Pal. He keeps wanting to play with me, but he can't no more."

Rachel leaned against one tree and the little boy leaned against the one across from her. "When you see, Pal is he happy?"

The little boy thought about her question. "Yes he is. He's running and almost laughing it seems."

"That's what I think, too," Rachel said. She picked up one of the shovels and put it in the truck. The little boy picked up the other one and got in the cab beside Rachel. "You come back anytime you want to," she told him.

Rachel drove the youngster back to the barn at Stormont. That's where he wanted let out and she respected his decision. He disappeared down the block with a lighter step and she knew he wouldn't be spending his days by the edge of that old death hole watching his dog decay. She went in and fed the horses some hay and said to herself, "At least something is working out right."

Rachel walked up to the house, having left the farm truck at the barn. It was getting dark and she could see a light on in the upstairs at Stormont. Since there weren't any on downstairs, Rachel surmised that Simon hadn't taken much time away from his work while she was gone. She came up on the porch and saw Laddie inside the screen door. Simon might not have heard her approach, but the collie had.

She opened the door and let him out for a few minutes. "Hello boy, what have you been up to today?" she said, petting his fluffy neck.

He wagged his tail and then went down the steps. He smelled the air and stood alert until he was satisfied that all was well around him. Rachel sat on the step and waited for him, watching the growing kittens play in the grass. Laddie's tail was fanlike, and the long hair blowing in the prairie breeze attracted at least one of the kittens every time he went outside. Rachel let them play while she fed them all and then called Laddie in with her.

"Simon, are you still working?" she said, when she saw he was still at his computer.

Simon turned toward her and stretched, then he looked at his watch. "Where has the time gone?"

"It goes fast when you're having fun," she called back from across the hall. She filled the tub with hot water and bubble bath.

Simon came to the door. "I'm hungry, is it going to be Jacoby's tonight?"

"That is a good idea," Rachel smiled, as she got into the tub.

"What have you been up to today?"

"If you take my clothes down and put them in the washer for me, I'll tell you all about it."

Simon picked up her clothes and squished up his nose. "Did Laddie roll in something?"

"No, I did," she said, sinking below the bubbles so she could get her hair wet enough to wash.

Simon returned from his task and then scrubbed his hands in the sink.

Rachel couldn't help but smile; Simon would not have touched the clothes if he had been informed about her afternoon first. Of that, she was sure.

Simon came over to wash her back. "How did the counseling session go?"

"Si, it's the best thing I have ever seen to help kids. I was amazed at how many teenagers were there. I was sure no one would show up, but when I got there, eight children were already there and talking to the counselor."

"That's a hopeful sign," he said.

"What I found difficult to believe, was the fact that there were both sexes there. I would have expected all girls."

"I have the figures and apparent reasons for kids of all ages for the rest of the country compiled by the authorities on the subject. I'll get the papers while you wash your hair."

Simon returned and sat on the floor with his printouts while Rachel soaked in the tub.

"It works out to about a fifty-fifty ratio when we add up the number of kids that have come to the counseling sessions so far. After talking to the kids individually, they have come up with the reason for the interest."

Simon pulled out some more notes and spread them on the floor in front of him. "It would seem that the study of DNA, biochemistry, genetics, and the general advanced education they are getting is making the children a more informed group of people. They realize that life is a tremendous accomplishment and they have more respect for life than their parents do. They are simply more enlightened. The media tells them the state the planet is in and the fight going on to save the environment for their generation. They want it back in balance and they resent what their parents are doing, even if it is out of ignorance. It is even a state mandate now to teach compassion and preservation of life in the classrooms. These kids are having a rough go. When they go home, their parents tell them this is the way it's always been and ever more shall be. They go to school and learn that the road is getting narrow; things have to change or they will loose their natural resources in their lifetime. It's there in black and white for them, but the parents are so out of touch that the kids can't reach them."

Rachel got out and dried off. "We'll have to hold on until these kids grow up then."

Simon picked up his papers. "Well, I feel sorry for them, most of the counselors are finding the same thing to be true. They live at home, hate the cruelty in their parents, and want only to get away from them. They have to reach out to strangers because they are the only ones that are on the same educational level they are."

"Then, what you are saying is, the kids are actually grouping together because they want to pull away from what they see going on around them, that is considered the norm," Rachel said. "I can't comprehend it myself," she went on sadly. "People that I have thought well of, turn out to be just sickening and ruthless when it comes to animals. Its no wonder small children are shocked by their parents behavior, so am I."

"Let me help you with the buttons," Simon said, coming up behind her.

She reached behind her and ran her fingers in his hair leaning back on his chest. He held her tightly for long moments. "I just thank God there are people in the world like you, Simon."

Rachel pulled her wet hair back in a braid, and taking Simon's hand, they walked over to the restaurant. It was a nice evening and many people were out, some even had the same idea for a late supper.

"Hey, you two," Mary Lee shouted, just coming out of her house. She lived between the grocery store and the pharmacy. Her house was pink and narrow, about half the width of an ordinary house.

It looked more like a doll's house with its white shutters and fancy wood trim. "I'll bet you're going to Jacoby's, mind if I tag along?"

"No, join us," Rachel told her happily.

Simon turned into the aloof stranger he was with other people, but Rachel was getting used to it. They would talk at home. Meanwhile she would enjoy her friend's company.

They walked into Jacoby's and found a large booth for themselves. It was pretty crowded and Simon and Rachel were in hopes of picking up some feedback on Arakun.

Grace and a few of her friends were in a booth nearby, but the heat was off Rachel and Simon and was directed towards the new charity.

"I personally don't think the world needs another charity," Grace was telling her friends.

Mary Lee spoke up, "Grace, you don't have to give to a charity you know."

Grace ignored her remark and Mary Lee flounced her red curls back so she could light a cigarette and order something to eat. Her lips left a brilliant orange streak on the white filter. She was also keeping one ear open to the conversation in the next booth.

Nick came over and joined the conversation. "I think it's about time someone put a stop to the cruelty that is going on. It makes me sick to see what these kids are doing. They come from good homes too, but their parents don't have any idea what they are capable of and wouldn't believe you if you told them."

"No kidding, sweetie," Mary Lee added. "They killed some kid's dog last week and drug it all around town behind their car and no one did anything to stop it. It finally came down to a fight between the kids. These are the same kids that are going to wind up doing time somewhere."

"Like you know anything about raising kids, "Grace piped up.

Mary Lee looked up through half lids and blew smoke in her direction, "Wasn't that your kid that was throwing kittens out of barn windows last summer, Grace? And where is the little angel now?"

Grace ignored her. Rachel looked at Simon sipping his coffee. He wasn't going to comment, just take it all in. It would show up on some report in the future, of that she was sure.

One of Grace's friends spoke up, "The place will be overrun with deer and rabbits if my man don't get out there and control the populations, they will be up to our back doors!"

Rachel felt Simon tense up and clench his teeth, but he was determined to stay out of the conversations. His job was to make Arakun work, not fight with the likes of Grace and her friends.

Several people started talking at once, but Robert's voice was louder than the others were, so everyone had to listen. "It would be nice to see nature get back into balance. We may have a few population problems, but since we made the problem, we can certainly live with finding a solution."

"Hunting is the only recreation we have," one woman complained.

"How nice," Mary Lee chided.

"You don't have a bunch of kids to feed!" The woman was shouting at Mary Lee this time.

Mary Lee lit another cigarette, turned to the angry woman, and quietly said, "That's because I keep my legs together."

The woman became incensed and glared at everyone who might have been snickering at Mary Lee's remark.

Di came over to join the group and, oblivious to what had just transpired, she asked, "Have you heard about the new charity being started by that rich couple?"

Rachel spoke up, "What do you think of it, Di?"

"I think it's great. I'm so tired of the things people do to those poor animals they don't want, I think it's got to be some kind of help. I'm not sure about the rehab though. Did you hear about the black market on wild animals that started up?"

Simon perked up on, "Haven't heard, what's the news on that front?"

Evidently, no one else had any of this news, so the restaurant became fairly quiet.

"People are live trapping anything they can get, except skunks, and selling them to folks for ten bucks apiece. That one animal assures them of an income for about a year."

"I can't see how that will work," Simon said to them. Aren't there regulations that the animal has to be known to have an injury or to be an orphan?"

"Injuries can be arranged, Simon; but so far, no one is checking on that part. They are just checking to make sure there is an animal and that it has good care. I'll be back, I've got a customer."

"I saw some boys with a fox tied in their back yard," a woman said who had been quiet up until now.

No one commented.

"I will be grateful for the free vet care. My kids always have pets and there are always vet bills to pay and too many kittens to take care of. We just can't find them all homes so we wind up keeping most of them."

Rachel looked at the woman. She seemed like a nice lady, and she was the kind of person they intended to help. She gave Simon a nudge.

"If you ask me," Mary Lee spoke up again," none of us should have to have a handout. We should all be taking care of our own, and making sure our kids and husbands set a better example then they have been."

As Rachel expected, Grace and her friends had nasty comments for Mary Lee. It never really seemed to bother either one of them that they always totally disagreed on everything.

"We need harsher laws," Robert spoke up. Start throwing some people in jail and giving out a few well deserved fines."

An old woman spoke from the back of the restaurant; "I'd like to know how it can be a sport to teach our children to kill things. They should be playing basketball or going to dances instead of learning this bloody business."

Father Kessler had joined the woman at her table. "I have to agree with Ida," he said. "We pay with a human death every time an animal is cruelly killed. It's God's way of punishing us for what we are doing down here."

Everyone kept a respectful silence while he spoke, and then went back to discussing the subject quietly at their own tables. Robert and Di drifted off to visit other customers.

"I must go," Mary Lee told Rachel. I want to get to the shop early tomorrow because I have a new shipment coming in. And Rachel, we have some more dresses that would look delicious on you."

"I'll stop by to see them," Rachel told her. "Good-bye," she called after her as Mary Lee breezed out.

Simon was miserable. He hated being stuck in situations like this one. Rachel knew that she was lucky he hadn't insulted everyone, one at a time.

"Are you ready to go?" she asked him.

Simon didn't answer; he just left a tip and went over to pay Robert while Rachel said good-bye to Father Kessler and Ida.

On the walk home, Rachel told Simon about the little boy and the events of the afternoon.

"Who was he?" Simon wanted to know.

"I don't know," Rachel said, taking his hand, "but I'll bet from time to time you can find him up there in the pine forest. When you or Charlie are out riding, maybe you will run into him."

"I didn't like what I was hearing about the black market or the injuries that could be made to happen," Simon said to her.

"That bothered me too. I suggest we don't stipulate that the animal has to have an injury."

"I'll get that information out before we go to bed," Simon told her. "You know, just talking about this stuff is depressing, it's no wonder John was so preoccupied and kept to himself all the time. Poor Clara, she realized all of this when she was a child and had to deal with it for over sixty years. If it's this depressing to hear about it, how must it be to people who live it? No wonder they are unhappy people."

Rachel leaned on his arm. "We learned a few things that might help us," Rachel told him. "By the way, what was that Father Kessler said?"

"I didn't catch it," Simon said, leaning down to pick some chicory.

"You know," he said to her, "this is one of the prettiest flowers I have ever seen."

Rachel took it to hold while he picked some more, "This is only chicory, Si. It grows along all the roads and in vacant lots like this one. I think there is some in the pasture up there where the raccoons are buried too. What do you like about it?"

Simon turned the bunch he had in his hand to get the best view. "I like the color, it's the same color as the sky. It's like looking down and seeing heaven. It has a perfect shape for a flower."

Rachel took the flowers from him. "I like the wheat. I think that has to be one of my favorite colors in the summer. It's the same color as the sun."

They walked hand in hand for some distance before Rachel asked him what he was thinking about.

"Oh, I miss New York. I miss the theaters and the lights and it just seems a million miles away from all the problems here."

"You have the same problems there, in a way," Rachel told him. "Here we have innocent animals being killed and there you have innocent people being killed. Just the prey is different. The people doing it are the ones that are the same."

When they arrived at Stormont, the house was in complete darkness.

"I thought you left the light on," Simon said to Rachel.

"I thought I did to, the back porch light is the one I always leave on."

Simon smiled at her. "*Always leave on* are the key words here, it must have burned out. If you can manage to go in and turn on the kitchen light, I'll get Laddie from Charlie's. When I get home, I'll change the bulb."

"I'm not afraid of the dark Simon, I just can't see very well in the dark. I know my way around in the kitchen. I will have a light on when you get home and the new bulb for you to put in the coach lamp."

Simon stopped to kiss her under the giant maples. "I'll leave you here so you can hear the bricks under your feet." He kissed her again. "I don't want you to get lost."

Rachel watched him walk down Spring Street in the soft glow of streetlights toward Millie and Charlie's. He had a long stride and would be there in no time. She would have to hurry if she were going to get all the things done that she had promised before he got there. She hurried along the bricks in the opposite direction towards the house. She could smell Clara's flowers all around her, but she couldn't see them. She reached the back porch and opened the screen door. She went in and walked over to the wall where the light switches were.

"What is on this floor"? she thought to herself. Something felt gritty under her feet. She kept feeling the wall for the switches and finally found the one that illuminated the table area. When the light went on, she looked at what it was she was stepping on. Pine needles. Rachel froze where she was. There was a trail of pine needles leading from the back door down the hall. From where she was, she could see that Clara's door was open. Rachel backed into the corner of the kitchen and sat on her knees on the floor. She kept her hand over her mouth to keep from screaming. There wasn't any noise at all. The frogs weren't singing in the pond, the pigeons weren't cooing on the wire by the back door, and the wind wasn't even blowing the curtains. Nothing was moving.

The first noise Rachel heard was Laddie. He was mostly collie, but he lacked the high pitched bark of a collie. When he barked, it was the German Shepherd you could hear in him, low and full; and he was on his way to the back door. He broke through the screen door and his nose went straight to the pine trail. He tore around the house barking and growling. Rachel leaned back against the sink and put her hand down from her mouth. She could hear the sound of his nails as he raced around the house and jumped on furniture and windowsills. Then he was back in the kitchen and out the screen door. His fanatic barking faded into the dark as he ran.

Simon came in the back door with Charlie right behind him. They both saw the pine needles on the floor at the same time. Charlie pulled out a gun from a shoulder harness that he had grabbed on his way out of the door and hadn't had time to put on.

Simon went to Rachel and helped her up. "Are you all right? Did you see him?"

Rachel shook her head. "I'm O.K., and no, I didn't see him." She nodded her head toward Clara's room.

Simon pointed it out to Charlie. "We keep it closed," he whispered.

Charlie didn't give it much of a glance. "He's been here, but he's not here now." "I'm going to go get Nick to track Laddie. We've got a fresh trail now, I hope nothing happens to that dog."

"I'm going to check the house with Rachel, and then I'll join you two. Horses again?" Simon asked him.

"I don't know," Charlie said. "I'll have to see what Nick says. We may be on foot, so you might want to change."

Simon looked down at his slacks and shoes after Charlie left. "I don't have anything to wear into the underbrush in the middle of the night. I'll have to put jeans and boots on my priority list if this man is going to continue to play games with me." He looked at Rachel. "Does he have any idea who he is playing with?"

"I think he does," Rachel said to him. "He found a game animal to challenge him."

"We'll see who wins," Simon said to her, "we'll see."

They followed the trail into Clara's room. Rachel turned on the light.

"Do you see anything missing?" he asked Rachel.

Rachel looked around the room carefully and then she said, "Oh, no, he took her music box."

They continued to follow the trail upstairs. Simon had laid the notes for Arakun on the bed, and the rest of the things they had been working on were all around the room. Nothing was disturbed, but there was something very chilling in the middle of the floor. Out lined with pine needles was the word, Arakun.

"He must have been in the pine forest when we buried the boys dog. Do you think he dug it up?"

Simon unlocked the closet and was arming himself. "If he had dug it up, I'm positive it would be in the middle of our bed right now. No, I'm pretty sure he left it in the ground. I'll check to make sure there aren't any empty holes around the pines anyway, for the kids sake."

Simon went around so that he could read Arakun better and looked at it thoughtfully. The frown line in his forehead deepened. He looked up at Rachel. "There is more at stake here than one or two lives, Rachel. What's at stake here is a way of life. Gib's way or Clara's way."

Simon paused on his way out of the kitchen door. He cupped Rachel's face between his hands and looked her full in the face. "I want you to lock up after me, and don't come to the door for anyone but us." Hearing a car, he looked toward the barn and Charlie's headlights glared in his eyes for a second before they were turned off. Simon turned back to Rachel. "If he had wanted you dead, he would have killed you in the pine forest. He wants us to leave so that he can have the old ways back again. He knows who we are, Rachel. He knows we're behind Arakun and he's going to try to stop us by frightening us into leaving. We have to be very, very strong. Don't call the police yet. We don't want them walking or driving all over Laddie's tracks."

Rachel nodded through her tears and put her arms around her husband for a quick embrace. Then Simon left her and went down the path to join the other two men.

Rachel locked the door and made coffee. She sat at the table for some time trying to think things through, and then got up and went to the kitchen door and unlocked it. She went out onto the porch, changed the bulb in the coach lamp, and then walked down the path to Millie's house that was illuminated slightly by the security light over the barn door.

Her precious friend opened the door after the first knock. "Come in, my dear," she said, when she saw it was Rachel.

Rachel stepped into the cool living room and looked around. Millie's house was constantly being changed. Millie would move a chair here for a while, and then move it there for a while. She had decorations for every season and even changed her drapes to go with the changes in the weather.

"I see you are into the lace season," Rachel told her. "It's beautiful."

Millie moved some handiwork out of the way so Rachel could sit down. "Well you know, I owe it all to John and Clara." She sat across from Rachel in an overstuffed chair. "Clara and I had been close friends all of our lives and I even used to travel with them from time to time." She leaned back in the chair and adjusted the doily on the arm that wasn't lying as neatly as she wanted it to. "They put a trust fund in my name many years ago, in fact when Nancy was born." She smiled at the memory, "Clara was like Nancy's Fairy Godmother. The trust was put in my name and its purpose was so that I would be able to stay home and be with my child. I have had a very good life because of Clara and John. But the best part was knowing Clara."

Neither one of them spoke for several minutes. Rachel leaned back and enjoyed the comfort of the fairy tale house with its lace curtains and overstuffed furniture. Unlike Clara, Millie had only a few objects that reflected the past. Most of her house was up to date with the current fashions.

Rachel broke into their silence first. "We had a visitor at Stormont tonight."

Millie sat straight up in her chair. "We'll go over to your house and discuss this, Nancy is due home with a gentleman friend any moment. We need to talk about serious matters in private."

They strolled along the brick walkway, looking down from time to time to avoid those bricks that had shifted and had a corner sticking up. Rachel told her all the developments that had occurred up until that moment.

"My dear girl," Millie said, "you must have been frightened out of your mind to think that murderer was actually with you in the house!"

"I was at first," Rachel confessed. "I tried not to scream because I wanted to be able to hear him if he was in the house."

"You did the right thing," Millie said, holding her arm as they went up the steps.

Rachel poured them both some coffee. It was going to be a long night waiting for the men to get back. While she looked for cookies, Millie examined the pine needles on the floor and went over Clara's room carefully. She came back out to the kitchen and sat down with a sigh.

"I think all he took was her music box, too. I can't see anything else missing. It's all so eerie to know he has been watching everything we do so closely."

She picked over the cookies until she found the one with the most chocolate chips. They had been frozen, so Rachel had warmed them in the oven. Millie took the first bite and had bits of warm chocolate on her lips and fingers. She licked one finger, and then adjusted her ring before she spoke again.

"I agree with you Rachel," Millie said. "I don't see any point in locking your doors against Gib. He's like the bat Clara once had that had a broken wing. When he got well and wanted to be on his way, he just got out of his cage through a crack no bigger than the side of piece of paper. Not only did he get away, but also we never saw him or heard him. Gib's like that too; he just comes and goes with no one the wiser. I think Simon's right, if he wanted us dead, we would be dead."

Rachel had a cookie. She was beginning to feel as if it were old times with everyone there in the kitchen at Stormont; Clara's mother's fresh cookies, Clara and Millie, and Clara's music box singing softly to itself while John sat on the edge of the bed smoking his pipe. And Simon, the two of them would start a new life at Stormont and they would someday be part of its history.

Millie got up and started to tidy up the kitchen.

"Now, Millie," Rachel said. "I didn't have you over to clean up."

"I know, I know my dear, I want to have something to do while I wait for the men to come home. You know it's rather nice having Charlie living right next door. All I would have to do would be to open my window and shout and he would be right over. He is usually in the back yard weeding the garden and watching the children. Those twin girls of his look just like Laura. When I wash dishes, I look out the window and see them collecting dandelions in the fields and taking them to their Dad. They are as fair as Clara was when she was a child. That man dotes on those girls."

She was sweeping the pine needles into piles in the hall when she called to Rachel, "You can tell a man did this, a woman would never deliberately put these on a carpet because she knows they are the devil to get up!"

Rachel laughed, "I don't think Gib ever had a Christmas tree, Millie, or a wife."

Rachel was on her knees pulling the last bits out of the carpet in her room when they heard a scratch at the screen door. Millie was sitting on the bed, broom in hand. She jumped to her feet, but said to Rachel, "You hurry along, I'll catch up, you can get there much faster than I can."

Rachel ran down the steps as fast as she could, and there at the broken screen door, was Laddie. He was filthy and had burrs stuck all over his fur. His tail was one big glob of them, and he was covered in mud. Rachel held the door open and hugged the dog. What a relief to have him back.

Millie came into the kitchen slightly out of breath. "Oh, I was so afraid he would shoot him."

"I know that feeling," Rachel said. "I'll try flickering the porch light to tell them he's safe."

"He needs a bath before he goes past this kitchen," Millie pointed out.

Rachel took him into the laundry room and set him in the old wash tub. "I'm not going to worry about the burrs, we'll have to work on those for a week. I'll just get the mud."

Sounds in the distance told them the men were calling it a night. They came into the kitchen looking only slightly better than the dog. Millie passed out coffee and made scrambled eggs and toast. It was close to dawn, and all of them were feeling the come down from the recent excitement.

Simon was talking to the other two men. "Where can that son-of-a-bitch be hiding?"

Charlie added some milk to his coffee. "Nick and I have been all over this property so many times, we can't even count them any more. We can't find anything but old camp fires. All that tells us is that he spends a great deal of time on Stormont, but basically stays on the move."

Rachel came in with Laddie, he shook, but she had dried most of the water out of his fur with towels. "Who's next?" she asked.

The tired men laughed. Gib was gone for now. Simon had called the police and reported the break-in before he sat down, so once again the lights and the dogs assured the neighborhood of several nights free of worry.

"Were you able to follow his tracks?" she asked Nick.

"We were," Nick said. "The dew made it just damp enough that he left perfect paw prints. He didn't catch up with Gib, either. We're lucky he didn't," he said, scratching the wet dog's ears. "I would like to take him back to my place, if you don't mind. He will be safe there. No one will know where he is and we won't have to worry about him making another crazy move like he did tonight."

Simon and Rachel looked at the screen door with the screen hanging down one side.

Simon spoke for the two of them. "It is the best thing for him, neither one of us would forgive ourselves if anything happened. I think we've counted on him too much to tell us if Gib is around. We're going to have to find a different way to deal with the man."

The group broke up just as dawn was peeking over the rolling hills of Stormont. Millie went home, but was too tired to whistle. She had a funny little whistle anyway. They were not tunes anyone ever recognized and could hum to. They were just tunes of her own making. They were always the same kind, lilting, music that made you happy to be around her.

Laddie went with Nick willingly, he always had been rather fond of the man. It seemed the natural thing to get in the truck beside him. He was a tired dog and Nick had promised some special salve for his paws when they got home. Charlie was the only one who didn't seem tired. He went off to the barn to feed the horses. Simon again had ruined his shoes and ripped up his slacks. He threw them away and showered. He had welts on his legs where they had been scratched in the underbrush, but he didn't say anything. He only noticed them when the soap ran over them and made them sting. The sting didn't make him think of his legs, it made him think of how much he hated Gib and the wreck the man was trying to make of their lives.

He dressed and sat at the computer for a few minutes. "Wasn't that stipulation we were talking about, something about not having to check if animals were injured before they get their monthly money?"

"Something like that," Rachel yawned getting into bed. The fax machine ran for a while and then, she didn't hear it anymore. She was asleep.

She woke about noon hearing Simon swearing to himself. He hadn't been to bed yet.

"What's wrong, Si?"

"We have parents trying to close down the counseling service because they don't want anyone telling their kids they have a problem. Those aren't the exact words, but that sums it up. They feel that the kids are just coming to the meetings for the free food and drinks and that the counselors are putting words and ideas in their heads. Most of the kids are forbidden to come to meetings, if their parents find out they are attending. The parents say that's the way they have to live, so the children might as well get used to it."

Rachel rolled over and looked out the window. She remembered the kids at the meeting. "That's not the way it looked to me, Si. The kids really did look like they hated what was going on in their homes. They were very honest and emotional about it. There may be one or two that aren't being totally honest, or are just there for the sympathy; but, overall, I think the kids just want to be heard."

"I agree, that's what all the counselors are saying. But here is another problem, we have vets out there that are taking Arakun money and still charging the kids for taking care of their pets. On top of that, people are dumping their domestic pets at humane societies and keeping wild animals instead, because wild animals bring income that domestic pets don't."

"Did they find Gib last night, Si?"

Simon rubbed his weary eyes. "They not only don't find him, I'm not even sure they keep him away from the house. Look at all the animals there are in the woods, and yet, if you take a walk, how many of them do you bump into? Gib's like that, which is one of the mysteries about the man. He is more like an animal than a human, yet he kills them on a regular basis and eats them. He has even taken to killing humans, just as some of the larger animals have. He's sort of a rogue human. And I intend to hunt him down as such."

"He's a very old man. Where does he get his energy?"

"There again," Simon turned his chair around to face the bed, "another very good point, Rachel! All of the transcendental beliefs tell us that if we wish to have a serene long life, we must take time to enjoy nature, to be one with the earth, to feel the earth with our hands, so to speak." Simon stood up to better make his point. "We have a man who is doing just that, on the one hand, and exploiting it with the other."

Rachel rolled over and looked at the ceiling, contemplating Simon's thoughts. "Do you think his behavior is innate or learned?"

"No question in his case, Rachel, it's innate. You can have the worst upbringing in the world, but after the age of twenty, everyone has seen enough of the world to make choices that express their own genetic make-up. He's rather like Barabas, he just doesn't get it."

"Are you tired, Si?" Rachel asked.

He looked at her with affection. "A little, but there is a lot to do," he said, indicating the flashing light on the telephone. The ringers had been disconnected and all the lines had been fitted with lights instead. It looked as if they were all on.

"This whole project has me intrigued. I didn't know my feelings ran so deep," he confided in her.

"Let's go have some breakfast and walk around town to see what is going on," Rachel said, getting up. "You need coffee, boots, jeans and a new screen door, in that order."

Rachel and Simon were ready to face the rest of the day in no time and were soon crossing La Due on their way into town. Father Kessler waved to them from the churchyard. He was mowing, trimming, and talking to himself. It was unusual for him not to rush over and say hello. Terry Griffin, the altar boy who had grabbed her arm at the pens, was putting up the letters on the church sign. When he saw Rachel, he quit what he was doing and went inside.

Rachel saw a little girl she recognized. "Hello, Bonnie. Goodness, what did you do to your cheek, honey?"

The girl felt her face with her hand, "Daddy got a new pet and put him in the back yard, but he forgot to get my doll."

Simon knelt down beside the little girl. "Can I sneak a look at your new pet, Bonnie?"

Bonnie put a finger to her lip and looked shyly to the ground. She shook her head yes and pointed to the back fence. She pointed with a wet finger. "There is a hole right there to look at him."

Simon walked across the yard and up to the fence. He had to bend down to see in the hole, and after he did, he came back to the girls.

"Bonnie," he said, "don't go near that doggy again, O.K.?"

Bonnie shook her head yes. The swollen face with the new stitches reinforced his belief that she would stay away from the back yard.

Rachel bent down and asked, "Did you get your dolly?"

Bonnie shook her head no. "He ate my doll."

"I see, well, is that a new one you have there?" Simon asked her.

She shook her head yes, went back up the walk to her porch, and began to play.

When they were a good distance away, Rachel asked, "Well, what's behind the fence?"

"It's a big old coydog, healthy as a horse and terrified out of its mind. They don't have any business having it penned that close to a girl that small."

They entered the restaurant, and inside, a heated discussion was going on between two people they didn't know.

"I'm telling you those coons are driving my dogs nuts and that's why they bark. You've got too many in that pen and they fight all night. You could try feeding them once in a while!" a big, red-faced man yelled.

"Mind your own business! Keep those dogs on your side of the fence, if you want them to live!"

Robert broke it up, and the two men left, still screaming at each other. Rachel and Simon sat down in a corner booth. Robert came over to take their order, still slightly shaken. "Sorry about that, you two," he said, as he passed out menus. "Shall I bring coffee?"

"Please," Simon agreed.

Rachel sat in dead silence, taking in the conversations and contemplating the events they had encountered just getting to the restaurant. "Things aren't going well," she whispered to Simon.

Simon turned to Rachel. "Do you think we need a house keeper? Everyone knows that John left us his estate, so we don't have to worry about showing a little money. We are going to have our hands full with this mess. It seems to be taking a nasty turn for the worse."

Robert brought their coffee and left.

"Who do we trust, Si?" Rachel asked.

"Good question, we can just look for someone, I suppose. For now, we can manage, but just know that I hate doing dishes."

He brushed his hands and put one arm around her briefly. They finished breakfast in silence.

As the afternoon wore on, Simon and Rachel outfitted themselves with hiking boots, heavy socks, and country clothes. They stopped at the hardware store to order a new back door, one a little sturdier. Frankie Wakeland waited on them.

"Have you heard about the them opening up the old Deaconess Hospital to handle all the animal bites that are getting reported I hear they may have to send experts in to have the dead animals tested for rabies right on the spot and they have to quarantine all the live ones for at least two weeks I just want to know who's going to pay for it all some of the women have moved all the children to a big house in the country and are turning their homes into animal shelters did you folks need something?"

He paused to look at them in his earnest way and put a roughed index finger up to the corner of his mouth to brush away a small drop of spittle. Rachel was used to Frankie's speech patterns, but Simon wasn't, so he missed his chance to answer and Frankie went on.

"Of course you can look around all you want to and when you decide what you want just let me know so what kind of animals are you folks keeping I kind of like the Canadian Geese myself they aren't for everyone some people like the smaller birds but I find they die too easily and so I like the bigger birds they tame down real well too and then it's fun to feed them now I have a friend who likes the ducks and that's O.K. for the people with little ones because they sure are harmless when they pick up corn in those flat old beaks another friend likes the deer now for sheer beauty you have to go for the deer the guy has them so tame they come up and eat right out of your hand a great learning experience for the medium size child would you like me to show you the other side of the store?"

Simon was ready this time.

"Screen doors," he said.

Frankie looked at him as if he was waiting for more, realizing that Simon was a man of few words he went on about the virtues of each kind of door they had to offer.

Simon's jaw was set in a harsh line when he left the store, but Frankie was smiling delightedly with the order.

"Are we finished with everything we had to do?" he asked. Rachel checked her list.

"We are finished," she announced.

"Good, then let's go to Gib McNiff's."

"What!"

"He lives just down the street down by the old tracks. It's not far from here, so let's go."

The closer they got to Gib's house, the more they stood out, and the more nervous Rachel was.

"Simon, what if he's home?" she said, shifting the packages in her hands. She looked up and down the streets and between the houses. There weren't any children out playing and the people they passed were thin and sullen. They didn't look at Simon and Rachel, just their packages.

"I hope the police have the sense to check every so often to see, if indeed, he is home," Simon told her, and he took some of the heavy packages from her hands.

They stopped in front of the house they knew to be Gib's. It wasn't painted, in fact, probably never had been painted. It looked as if it had been made out of driftwood planks and old pieces of tin. They walked up what was left of a sidewalk. Grass had grown in it's cracks and where chips had broken out the weeds had taken over and grown so high they had to push them aside. Simon knocked on the door that someone had boarded up. They both felt a little odd standing there for a second, listening, as if there was a chance anyone would come to answer a boarded up door on the porch of a fugitive.

Simon walked around the porch looking in windows and watching for loose boards. "Come on, let's walk around back," he said.

"Simon, is this the brightest thing you have ever done?" Rachel asked, plowing through the weeds in her summer dress. She had to stop and pull the hem away from a nasty looking scrub tree.

"Let's go in," he said, ignoring her question.

"Go in, Simon! Go in Gib McNiff's house and do what!"

Simon looked at Rachel amused, the hair around her face was damp and she had weeds up to her waist. The heavy packages weren't making her life any easier and she refused to set them down for fear of them being stolen.

"Let's ask ourselves," he said to her, "did he or did he not ask if he could come into our house?"

"Of course he didn't ask, Si, he's a murderer and an ass."

Simon proceeded to kick the back door in, which really wasn't any great feat. They walked into what had been a kitchen. There were dishes still piled and smelly in the sink. Roaches scurried off the counters and into open cracks in the wall. A cheap aluminum table sat in one corner. Two chairs with gaudy torn seats were at each end. Simon opened all the cabinets and looked in all the containers he could see.

"What are we looking for, Simon?" Rachel asked him. She held her packages closer and looked down at the floor, making sure nothing was crawling on her shoes.

"Clues," he told her. "What did he expect to find at Stormont? He didn't know. But now he has a lot of information about us. And all he did was walk in and have a look around." Simon smiled at her and put out his hands like a song and dance man.

Simon's mood changed and he went through the man's house as if he were expecting to find gold. He pulled an old box out of the closet. "Look at this, Rachel, pictures. Do you know any of these people?" Rachel sat on the dusty floor beside her husband.

"No, I don't, but Millie might."

"We'll take them with us, put them in the bag."

Simon looked under some loose boards and pulled an old cot out from the wall of a bedroom so small, it could have been a closet. He pulled the thin mattress to the floor and it made a strange, heavy thunk. Simon knelt down and pulled the old army blanket off it. One edge of the mattress had big safety pins in it holding it together. When he pulled it apart, most of the pins flipped to the floor. Leaning over Si pulled out an old-fashioned scrapbook. The pages were stuck together so he gave up trying to open it.

"We'll look at this at home," he said, putting it in one of his bags.

They went back out to the kitchen and he pried open what looked like a closet door. It gave, and swung open over an old dirt basement. There weren't any steps and Simon had to catch the door jam to keep from falling.

"Si, don't you think we've had enough fun for one day?" Rachel said, when she saw the gaping hole.

"I'll take a look to make sure we haven't missed anything, and then we will leave."

He dropped down to the dirt floor and disappeared under the boards that supported the floor Rachel was standing on. She could hear him shuffling around down there, but it didn't help her anxiety. Gib could be down there, too. It was just his kind of place. Rachel felt cold and afraid.

Simon came back into the light, "Not much down here, except this," he said, showing her something in his hand.

"What is it?" she asked, bending closer. It looked like a glob of dirt.

"Go outside to the cellar steps, I'll come out that way."

Rachel picked up all of their packages and went back outside into the weeds by the side of the house. That whole portion of the house was caved in and open.

“You could have saved yourself the trouble of kicking in the door,” she smiled.

“It would appear so,” he said, looking around. “It would appear so.” He handed her the soiled article he had in his hand and took the packages from her.

She wiped away the dirt and looked at him in surprise, “Clara’s music box!”

He shifted his burdens and turned the music box upside down showing her the bottom. “Not Clara’s music box, but one just like it. Clara’s is an original piece, this is an imitation. See, this one doesn’t have the date and signature on it. Claus made only one that he signed, and he made it for Clara. This one looks like it fell through the floor with a lot of other trash. Let’s go home and see what we have here.”

It didn't take the couple long to get back to Stormont. No one had noticed them going through Gib's house and no one really cared if they went through it. They put Gib's things on newspapers on the kitchen table.

"I'm going to shower and change," Rachel told Si. "I feel like I have bugs clinging to me."

"So do I, I'll shower down here and then go over and get Charlie and Millie. I think they should be in on this. By the way," he called to Rachel as she walked toward the stairs, "this is one more reason I miss my apartment. All the filth in the whole building doesn't amount to what I saw on just one of Gib's plates."

Rachel came back into the room.

"We're trying to catch a murderer here, Simon, and bring about an enormous change of thinking. No one said it would be easy. Besides, you never really get dirty; you have too much class. You just get dusty." She gave him a light kiss and then went upstairs to shower.

Simon immersed himself in water, soap, shampoo, and aftershave, then called Robert to have dinner brought over for all of them. Feeling cleaner, he went about collecting their friends. Charlie telephoned Nick to join the group.

Robert brought a wonderful dinner as usual, but couldn't stay. The restaurant was filled with people and he had to get back to help his wife.

After dessert, Rachel and Simon cleared away plates and brought out the things they had found at Gib's.

Millie picked up the scrapbook, looking more than a little amazed. "This is Clara's scrap book," she told them. "I'd recognize it anyplace, we worked on it together. There was a dime store in town that used to sell things reasonably cheap, and we bought many of these to keep our memories in."

She tried to open the pages, but realized, as had Simon and Rachel, that the pages were stuck together. "That was the problem with them. If you didn't put wax paper between the pages, the pictures would stick together."

Millie got up and fixed a small pan of soapy water, and then she and Charlie went to work.

Rachel tried to get the music box in working order while Simon and Nick cleaned and laid out the pictures in the old shoebox.

"Charlie," Rachel said, "why didn't the police take this stuff?"

Charlie kept working on the pictures but looked at her with some amusement. "This is old-fashioned detective work," he said. "We looked for anything that could be tested for DNA, and the murder weapon. The rest is not as important as it used to be. The crime boys obviously looked at the box because I can see it was dusted for prints. They missed the mattress and the stuff that fell through the floor. Or if they did see it, they just left it."

Rachel got the last bit of dirt off the music box and oiled the hinges, and then she wound it up and lifted the lid. The music was the same that had echoed through the house for many years. The original musical apparatus commissioned by Claus had been sold with his original music box design. Every one stopped talking to listen to it. Rachel picked up some items that were in the box and began to clean them. When everything was clean and lying on the towel in front of her, she stood up and got herself a cup of coffee. She leaned thoughtfully against the sink and said quietly, "Gib McNiff didn't kill Clara."

They all looked at Rachel, waiting to hear the rest of her musing.

"Gib was in love with Clara." She reached over, picked up a faded gold locket, and opened it up. She handed it to Simon and everyone had a good look at it.

"Millie, wouldn't you say that is a high school picture of Clara on one side and a high school picture of Gib on the other?"

Millie looked at it closely and then put it down on the table. "That is exactly who the pictures are of," she said.

Charlie stood up and paced the kitchen, "If I had killed him, the real murderer would have gotten off scot-free. I can't believe this, everything points to Gib." He paused and ran a thumb over the locket. "He might have been in love with her a long time ago. A forgotten love or a love turned to hate when she married John. The locket and scrap book were compiled when they were children."

Rachel sat back down, "I think we overlooked the most obvious clue."

They were all looking at her now.

"The deer, we looked at everything but the deer. Gib was there, and he was right by the tree, right where Laddie attacked him. But what if he was watching Clara. Clara was beautiful to watch. She was graceful and fair. Gib probably stood close to the tree. His leathery skin and tattered clothes probably blended perfectly with the bark.

Then off to his right, a shot was fired. Probably in the exact spot the computer said the bullets were fired from. The deer cried out, remember, he kept screaming and Clara started running. Whoever fired the first shot realized the deer was only wounded and he fired another shot. Only this time Clara was in the way. And the second shot hit Clara. How do I know Gib didn't fire the first shot? Because Gib never missed. He was known for always making a kill shot. How, do we know he didn't kill Clara? Because the bullets came from the same rifle."

Rachel went on, "how must he have felt when Clara was hit. His angel falling slowly to the ground. The only person in the world he loved."

Charlie and Nick looked at each other. "It's true, the deer bled to death. The only reason he didn't run was because he was overcome with fear and so he just lay there and screamed." Charlie said.

Nicholas nodded his head in agreement.

"Who did do it?" Millie spoke up.

"It's probably someone Gib knows," Charlie said. "He might be letting us believe he did it because he is protecting someone."

Simon leaned forward and indicating the pictures they were cleaning, he said, "These are probably his relatives or close friends. It could be one of them. Millie, can you go over these pictures and put names to these faces?"

Millie came around to his side of the table. "Of course, dear, I'll start right now."

Rachel was still perplexed, "So why is he bothering us? If he didn't kill Clara, then why go through our things and hang around Stormont?"

"That goes back to what I was talking about yesterday, Rachel, it all ties in!" Simon was getting excited. He got some coffee and then turned to the group. "Gib isn't afraid of death. I'm not even all that sure he cares about anyone enough to take the rap for them. But he knows one thing. If we find him, the law will bother him. Gib doesn't fear these things and he doesn't fear death. He lives too close to it. What he fears is the thing all animals fear, loss of habitat. And that, dear wife, is where we come in. He doesn't see that we are trying to preserve the earth's natural balance, so he's trying to stop us." Simon set down his cup and then went on, more to himself than to the others. "Actually, if natural order is restored, there would be a place for our Daniel Boone. We are both fighting cruelty and sport hunting. It's upsetting the natural predator prey relationship.

Charlie was thoughtful for a second, and then he said, "We still can't rule out Gib as a suspect. I admit it is beginning to look as if he didn't fire the first shot, but he knows who did. What matters is who fired the second shot. Anyway we cut it, Gib McNiff knows who killed Clara. If we catch him, there is a very good chance he won't want to go to jail, and there is also a very good chance he might talk."

"How do we know Gib isn't looking for the killer also?" Nick asked the group. "If he was in love with Clara all these years, he might not be too happy about the fact that she was gunned down right in front of his face. And why didn't he shoot the guy when he had a chance? Was it because Laddie came up and kept him busy?"

"Maybe it was one of the youngsters in his family and he couldn't bring himself to kill him. Even Gib might fall short of being able to shoot a child." Millie said.

"How are you coming with those pictures?" Simon asked.

"Well, I can make out some of them," Millie said. She was writing names down on the backs of the pictures. "But if it was a child, it wouldn't be in one of these pictures, the pictures are too old. The children in these pictures would be the parents of whoever you are looking for. And it could also be that it isn't any one of these people, maybe it was someone from town not even related to Gib."

Everyone sat back in their chairs at that revelation.

"What about the scrap book, Millie?" Simon asked her.

"It will take me some time to get all the pages unstuck . . .it looks like it's been closed a long time. I don't think he has added anything to it. But it may tie together someone they both knew. We'll just have to be patient."

Charlie leaned back in his chair, "How about we go out tomorrow and look at that other area indicated by the computer, Nick?"

"Early start?" he said.

"Sounds good," Charlie said standing up. "We'll say good night, then, and thanks for dinner."

After they left, Millie got another cup of coffee. "I'll stay here a while longer if you don't mind. These things are very interesting and I'm not in the least bit tired."

"Go ahead and work on them," Rachel told her, giving her a kiss on the top of her head. "But sleep in Clara's room tonight so we don't have to worry about you walking home."

"O.K. dear. Good night, I'll see you in the morning."

When Simon and Rachel reached the top of the stairs, they could hear the fax machine running. Simon turned on the light in his office; he couldn't believe the sight! There were so many messages they had run off on the floor.

"The thing must have been running steadily all day," he told Rachel.

The telephone was lit up as usual, but neither one of them bothered to answer it.

"Most of these are from Everett," he said picking them up off the floor. "Oh, no!"

"What is it, Si?"

"Everett has been in a minor car accident and needs me to take over for a couple of weeks. This is one more thing we didn't think of, who takes over if something happens to Everett. And look at the rest of these. They are from all over the country." He sighed heavily. "The only thing we can do here is to group them by problems."

They sat on the floor and worked long into the night putting everything into four main concern groups. The fax machine continued to run and the lights still flickered on the telephone lines.

"Si, what are you going to do about the phone?"

"Don't answer it," he said. "When I get to New York, I'll get an answering service to take these calls. I'll leave the fax set up as it is so you have a copy of what is going on. Remember, the same information is running on both computers, the one here at Stormont and the one in New York. You won't have to worry about the funds for Arakun. The money from John's businesses will be channeled automatically once a month to a manager for each state. From there, it filters down to individuals."

"Yes, I saw one of the checks already," Rachel said. "They have a collage of white animals on a light blue background. The signature, Arakun, is scrawled at the bottom."

Simon looked up and smiled at her after she described the checks. Rachel blushed and went back to sorting the fax messages.

"Simon," she said, holding stacks of papers in her hands. It seems we have a new batch of problems cropping up. They aren't very big, but there are many different ones. Like this one, who pays for the flea sprays in the humane society facilities."

"We'll pay, as long as we can, on the money John and Clara's estate provides. The money goes into the main concerns first, and the rest will be divided among the little problems. Let's get some sleep right now. We have a big day tomorrow. Are you sure you can handle anything that comes up here?"

"I can't think of anything that I would have to deal with," Rachel said, getting up and giving her stacks to Simon. "It looks as if everything is being handled as smoothly as possible. The only worry I have is Gib, and he's more of an annoyance at this point than a worry."

"Do you want a security system put in before I leave?"

Rachel looked around the room. "Well Si, I don't really think there is anything to steal. If anyone wanted any of these things, they could have out-bid John at the auctions. Most of my things are in storage, and I haven't decided where to put them yet. That just leaves the only thing that needs guarding as me." She fluffed her pillow and pulled the sheets down before she looked at him and said," But we have to remember Millie stays by herself nearly all the time, and Laura is by herself every time Charlie goes out in the middle of the night. I should be all right," she finished up, right before she fell asleep.

After he turned the lights off, Simon sat on the edge of the bed and looked at her for a long time in the moonlight. The worry line on his forehead softened as he watched her sleeping on the flowered sheets. How strange this all is, he thought to himself, looking at the colorful pastel sheets and his sleeping wife. He could understand the business matters of Arakun much better than the lace and flowers he lay on next to the mysterious creature that he had won as his wife.

The smell of coffee woke them both up in the morning. It took them a moment to remember that Millie had stayed the night. Simon got up and reluctantly began to pack while Rachel went downstairs to see Millie's progress on the pictures.

"Oh, I hope I didn't wake you, dear," Millie said, when she saw Rachel.

"Not at all," Rachel said, giving her a kiss on the way by.

"It is the smell of your luscious coffee that was too much to bear. Simon and I have been spending so much time on what has been happening at Stormont that we forget it's mealtime until it seems too late to fix anything."

Rachel sat down at the table with her coffee and looked at the array of pictures set in order in front of her. She didn't touch anything. Millie was making scrambled eggs and toast and she knew that Millie stuck to her one thing at a time rule. When it seemed near breakfast, Rachel got the plates out of the cupboard and put the silver and napkins on the table. Simon came in with his suitcase just before the women were ready to call him. They all sat around the pictures and had breakfast. They were careful not to disturb the obvious pattern Millie had made with them.

Millie sat down to her breakfast after she added a cookie to her plate. "Simon, are you going someplace?"

"Everett Martin, the man who handles the office when I'm not there, was in a traffic accident."

"Oh, dear!" Millie said, putting her hand to her mouth. Her eyes seemed very large as she looked at him through her slightly thick glasses.

"He's all right," Simon assured her, patting her arm. "It was just a fender bender, but he did manage to get pretty banged up and broke his knee cap on the steering column. I think he also broke his nose, but I assured my friend that it could only be an improvement," Simon laughed.

"Si," Rachel said, "that wasn't nice. Everett has a nice nose for a man."

Simon looked at Rachel, amused.

"He is far from having the perfect nose you have, my love."

Rachel looked at Millie and sighed, but her friend wasn't any help. She could tell by the twinkle in her eyes that Millie was enjoying the lighthearted conversation the young people were having. She went on with her breakfast in silence, but Rachel noticed that when Millie put her coffee cup down, she looked at her ring a lot longer. She adjusted the diamond with her little finger until the morning sunlight made it sparkle. Perhaps remembering those long ago light hearted moments in her own life.

"I shouldn't be gone much more than a week, and I'll keep in touch. I can be reached at a moment's notice in case something happens here before I get back."

Millie waved her hand over the pictures, "All I've done here is lay out who married who and who is family and who isn't. Some of these people I don't know so I just put them aside. As for the scrapbook, I'm still working on it. Nancy is gone on a cruise and won't be back until next week, so if Rachel doesn't mind, I'll just bring over a few things and stay in Clara's room until I finish it."

"That will be perfect," Rachel told her. "I'll do what I can to help, and then we'll show it to Charlie and Nick. It could be that we have a picture of Clara's killer right here on this table."

Simon stood up and put his dishes in the sink. "I must go if I plan to get to the airport in time."

"I'll walk you to the car," Rachel said.

After Simon had put his luggage in the trunk, he turned and said good-bye to Rachel. He was still stiff about hugging her, although he wanted to, but it was something they would work out as time went on. Rachel didn't have any such qualms and she put her arms around him and kissed his neck in her guileless way.

"I will miss you, Simon," she said, leaning against his shoulder.

His suit had already made him a stranger to Stormont and for some reason, it made her afraid. She moved her bare toes to stand on the ends of his shoes so she could better fit into the tall man's arms. The tie at the back of her dress fluttered against his hands. He held her tighter.

"I will miss you, Rachel, more than you will ever know," he said, and then he kissed her tenderly before lifting her off his shoes and setting her carefully on the already warmed cobblestones of the driveway.

She waved until he was out of sight and then walked slowly back to the house. The four-o'clock bed that she and Clara had gathered seeds from was fragrant in the morning air although the flowers were closed. She paused to gather a few of the black seeds, and then joined her friend.

"There are plenty of seeds this year," she told Millie, when she went back in. "I think I'll try to get as many as I can before summer is over."

"Mine are flowering nicely, too," Millie commented, drying the last plate and putting it away.

"I'll do dishes tonight," Rachel told her. "I'll fix us something nice for dinner, also."

"That will be just perfect dear, I'm so tired of my own cooking. Now, let's take a long look at these pictures." Millie fussed with them a little more until they were laid out much like a game of solitaire.

"I put our generation in this row," she explained, pointing to the pictures near the top. "Anything above it are possible pictures of their parents and I don't know them. But this row is the McNiff boys. It was Gib, Clyde, and Nelson. Their dad was a skinny old man, worked hard, but never made much money. Their mom disappeared after the youngest was born. That would be this man here, Nelson. Gib was the oldest, so he helped his dad take care of the younger ones as best he could. You were pretty much on the mark when you said Gib probably never had a wife because of the way he threw the needles on the rug. As far as anyone knows, he never took a wife. But, no one really ever paid much attention to Gib, unless their pets were missing. That part about Gib is true, he does kill other people's pets." Millie leaned back at this point and tried to remember something. "Conan, that was it. Some little girl found her golden retriever dead in a ditch right in front of her house, and the dog's name was Conan."

"Who would want a husband who did things like that?" Rachel remarked.

"Very true my dear, very true," Millie commented. "But there are men around here who have big families and do a great many thoughtless deeds more or less along those same lines. They even shoot the poor woodpeckers that drum on their drainpipes."

"Drum on their drainpipes?" Rachel asked smiling.

Millie laughed and got another cup of coffee, "Woodpeckers make noise during the mating season by drumming on hollow logs, but if they discover the wonderful, loud noise a pipe makes, they use that instead."

"Millie, it seems to me we don't know nearly enough about nature to have ever, ever interfered with it."

"You're certainly right about that," she looked down at the pictures again. "Now here, old Clyde McNiff, the one who grabbed your hair at the picnic. His daughter is Mary, as we found out later. She married a man named Sam Kendall. When he took off, she kept his name because the McNiff reputation kept her from getting jobs around here."

"Did Mary have any children?"

"I never heard her speak of any, or even indicate that she might have had any," Millie said. "The way she was around JoJo after the initial thrill of finding him sort of seemed like she never had kids. She didn't seem to have any developed mothering instincts."

"Clara mothered everything. Can you imagine how she would have been if she had had children too?" Rachel said.

"Clara was one of those women who was born knowing how to care for young things. That's rare, it usually develops with the pregnancy." Millie looked towards Clara's room for a moment.

"Mary's father didn't seem that old to me, he seemed strong as an ox," Rachel said, her hand going to the back of her head.

"They were all strong men. You were lucky he was old, or he would have had you over that fence with one hand and would have choked you with the other. All they do is roam these hills and woods all day. They have twice the strength and endurance the rest of us have. Nelson, in particular, since he is the youngest. He spent most of his young life trying to keep up with his brothers. Rumor has it, he's been in jail more than once. His son is the father of Ben McNiff, and Ben was the one that was caught trapping beaver on Stormont land."

"Which one of the people that we know about here do you think might have killed Clara, if Gib didn't do it?" Rachel asked her.

"Let's see," Millie said, putting the pictures back in her original order. "Gib is, of course, a prime suspect. Clyde isn't too happy with you, but I don't think he would carry the grudge to Clara. Nelson is seldom seen around here, but his kids still live in the area. His grandson Ben is a teenager now, and he is the one who put out the traps in the pond. But when the police questioned him, he said he didn't own a gun. He just trapped."

"Can't they check and see who has a hunting license and who doesn't?" Rachel asked.

"Some of the guns in the families in this town have been handed down for generations. If they poach, then it really doesn't matter if they have a license because no one sees them anyway. I don't know most of the younger kids. There could have been someone else trapping with Ben."

Millie picked up the pictures and put them in the shoebox. "They sure don't have many pictures of each other."

"Shall I help you with the scrapbook?" Rachel asked.

"I'm going to go home and check the mail and tidy up. I'll get some things and come over later this afternoon. Then we can look at the scrapbook." Millie decided.

"I'll go over and show these to Charlie, and then I think I'll walk downtown and see what is going on." Rachel said, picking up the shoebox.

"You mean see how Arakun is progressing, don't you?" Millie asked, winking at her.

"Millie," Rachel said with a smile, "I swear, you are a friend to beat all friends. You know all this stuff about Clara and John and never let on to anyone."

"My dear," Millie said, as she went out the door, "that's why our friendship lasted sixty years."

Rachel sat at the table and listened to Millie's cheerful whistling all the way to her house. Even after she heard the closing of a door, she could hear the faint whistling through her open windows. It mingled with the sound of children playing, the occasional car passing in front of Stormont, and dogs barking. It was too bad about the leash law. All that the kids and their pets could do now was to stare at each other through fences. The concept of a boy and his dog was somehow being lost because someone found manicured lawns more appealing.

The day was growing warm, so Rachel went about the errands she had told Millie about. She stopped at the store and then hurried back to Stormont to fix dinner for herself and Millie. She had formulated an idea that she didn't want to share with anyone just yet. Rachel would enjoy the evening with her friend and then put her plans into actions.

"Millie," Rachel said, as they lingered over their after dinner coffee. "The grocery store seemed a lot smaller to me today when I was in it. Are they redecorating?"

"No," Millie said, "the woman has blocked off some of the store so she can keep rats."

"Rats?"

"For the money," Millie went on to say.

"But not to raise them, is that what she is doing?"

"It would appear so, but you shouldn't worry your pretty head about it. Let Simon work it out at his end. It could just be an isolated case. At least, she stopped putting out poison for them. That's what always bothered me. The occasional animal would stagger out into the middle of the floor gasping for air, and there was plenty of it around. They couldn't get it into their systems, and then off they would go to die someplace. I told the woman I would take my business someplace else, if she didn't put a stop to it."

Rachel got up and washed the few dishes she had left, and then sat down beside Millie and helped her with the scrapbook.

"This is where I have gotten to," she said, thumbing to about the middle of the book. Turning back to the beginning, she showed Rachel some of the pictures she had salvaged. "This all happened a long time ago. Look at the snowsuits we had to wear! This is a picture of Clara and I on our bikes. It didn't snow that Christmas, as you can see." She looked at the picture a little closer. "I remember this bike, when the chain wasn't falling off, it was catching my pants legs. Clara and I always asked for the same things for Christmas. Most of the time our parents went along with it, but not always. Our coloring was different, so sometimes our Mothers would insist our clothes had to be different." Millie patted her short, curly gray hair and then went on to explain. "Clara had the blonde hair and blue eyes, and I had the brown hair and freckles." Thinking herself a little vain, she blushed a lovely rose color.

Rachel looked closely at the woman bending over the scrapbook. She could see the faint freckles through the heavy, pancake make-up; and looking behind the awkward glasses, she could see the perfect soft doll eyes that still hadn't lost their shine. Rachel could see Millie the young girl, the young wife. Her husband had lived only two years after they were married and Millie had never chosen another. She had been a war bride. Those years had been fast paced and ended tragically. Maybe it had been enough for a lifetime.

Millie spent the rest of the evening going over each picture and giving Rachel a full account of who was in each of the pictures and what event was taking place. While it was all very interesting and a lot of fun, they hadn't figured out one clue that would tell them why Gib had stolen it. At last, they closed the book, and Rachel got up to get them some coffee and a cookie or two. While she waited for the coffee to perk, she absent-mindedly wound up the music box and let it play.

"Do you think those pictures were taken about the time Clara found the raccoons?" Rachel asked Millie.

Millie had another quick look through the pictures, and then stopped at one of the pages. "It was exactly at that time. This dress is the same one Clara was wearing when she went over to Gib's that first day to yell at him."

Rachel took Millie her snack and looked over her shoulder at the picture. There in a white dress with sailor trimmings was a very young and beautiful Clara standing beside what must have been her father's car. She was holding something up and pointing to it while her long blonde hair was blowing in the prairie wind she loved so dearly.

"Wasn't that when she won the spelling bee?"

Millie nodded.

Rachel put her hands lightly on Millie's shoulders, and then said, "It seems that Clara left more of an impression on him than anyone could have possibly guessed."

Millie patted one of Rachel's hands. "Clara stood for what was true and important in this world, and she never backed down from anyone. I remember her walking down Railroad Street to have it out with young Gib." She laughed a little at the memory. "She was shaking like a river aspen in a strong breeze, but she never thought once about giving it up or having someone else handle it for her. When I think back, she must have left quite an impression on everyone within hearing distance.

She was just a little bit of a thing in her pretty dress standing outside Gib's house and calling him every name she had ever heard in her life. She was crying and choking and her fists were clinched up into tight little balls. I went with her down Spring Street as far as the tracks, and then I had to stop. We had been told so many times not to go beyond the tracks that I thought the devil himself lived there. But I could see her and hear every word she said from where I was; and I didn't know where the most trouble was going to come from, Gib coming out and getting her, or her daddy hearing the racket she was making and coming to get her."

Rachel smiled at the picture Millie had painted of their girlhood. "I can just imagine it, believe me," she said. "I was with Clara at a dinner party, once, and a woman arrived in a fur coat. Clara wasn't nasty, she never was mean to people. But the next day, she anonymously sent the woman tickets for one of those expensive health and beauty spas. The woman used the tickets; and when she got back, Clara sent her the most beautiful dresses I have ever seen. Along with them was an elegant cloth coat, and she attached a sealed note to it saying, '*Only women who think they are ugly have to wear the beautiful fur of an animal, and you're not ugly!*'."

"Do you think the woman ever knew it was Clara?" Millie asked.

Rachel laughed and began to tidy up the table. "I'm sure she knew it was Clara, but neither one of them ever let on. The woman looked astonishingly changed when she came back from the spa anyway. They had shown her how to expose so much of her natural attractiveness that she didn't need to rely on the beauty of a dead animal skin. Giving up fur coats was all the thanks Clara wanted, and she got it. So everyone was happy."

Millie closed the scrapbook and lay it aside. "We haven't watched television in such a long time, I think that would make a perfect evening."

"I was having the same thought," Rachel told her. "Let's make some popcorn." She glanced at the clock. "We have about fifteen minutes before the eight o'clock movie comes on."

Millie made some iced tea while Rachel made the popcorn. Then she rummaged in the pantry for some cookies.

"We're getting low," she said, bringing out a package of another one of her favorites and looking sadly back towards the shelves.

Rachel smiled at her while she shook the popcorn pan. Her cheeks were turning rosy with the heat. She was making quite a racket with the popping noise and grating the pan over the burner, but it was a happy combination. Rachel shouted to her friend, "I'll not only get more at the store, but I'll have Simon send us some special ones to try from New York."

Many hours after their special evening, Rachel tiptoed downstairs. The light snores from Clara's room meant that Millie was asleep. Rachel was dressed in blue jeans, hiking boots, and a light flannel shirt. She didn't take a flashlight out of the drawer, but she did take the telephone off the hook. She let herself out of the new screen door as quietly as she could and stood on the porch, letting her eyes adjust to the dim light. Then, she tied back her hair with a scarf, so it wouldn't blow in the wind, and followed the brick path to the little graveyard.

Coming near her destination, Rachel stepped to the side of the bricks and moved slowly, stopping every so often to listen. In spite of the bright moon, she still had trouble finding her way, but what she couldn't see, she could remember. Rachel walked until she had put the small graves between herself and Stormont hoping she was downwind. The breeze in her face told her that very possibly she was. Rachel lay down in the grass and pulled Simon's pistol out of her back pocket. She flipped the safety off and put the pistol in the grass in front of her. She waited, the frogs in the pond started their chorus again, and the night birds called to one another. And still she waited. One of the frogs in the pond made a high pitched squeak, and then she heard a splash. It was followed by several more squeaks and splashes in rapid succession. Rachel looked toward the pond but couldn't see anything. She was about to raise her head above the grass, when someone nearby lit a cigarette.

Rachel flattened herself to the ground, but she really didn't feel close enough. Her heart was the only sound she could hear, and she pressed herself tightly to the grass. She put her fingers on the gun, but she didn't lift it. It was Gib McNiff; she knew it had to be him. She could see his outline against the light on the porch. He crouched down in front of the little crosses and took something out of his pocket. Soon the air was filled with the crystal clear sounds of Clara's music box. After the music died down, he seemed to wait and listen. Rachel heard it too. Off in the trees was a low melodic whispering sound, like wind blowing through a sacred tree. It was JoJo. Gib listened for some time, and then picked up the music box and left. Rachel didn't see him or hear him, but she knew when he passed the water because the frogs gave their warning squeaks and jumped into the pond.

Rachel got up and followed him. She couldn't see him, but she knew where he was going. She went around the pond the other way and came up behind Stormont's family cemetery. It was the place where Clara and John had been laid to rest. She was feeling a little disoriented when she heard some crashes in the brush. She dropped to the ground and pushed her way under some brambles. A man ran closely by her, and another man soon after. Rachel couldn't see either one of them and could only guess that one of them was Gib. The sounds of running faded and soon there were only sounds of the night creatures fading into sounds of the day creatures.

She waited for first light and crawled out from under the bushes. She put the safety back on her gun and went over to check the graves of Clara and John. It was the first time she had been there since she lost them both. They were both untouched by vandals. She bent down before them because she was sure that the prairie wind had picked up their voices as they whispered happily, Arakun, Arakun.

The walk home was shorter in the light. She came up on the porch and smelled coffee. That meant that Millie was already up. She opened the screen door and went into the kitchen.

Millie came out of the pantry with the flour canister and gave Rachel a casual glance before she asked, "Did you find out anything?"

Rachel sat down at the table and checked herself for ticks, especially her socks. "Nothing that I didn't already guess." She told Millie about her midnight adventures.

Millie poured pancake batter into the pan. "What you are doing is dangerous, Rachel honey. Gib is not a man to play with." She shook the spatula in Rachel's direction and said," And I don't want to be around if Simon finds out."

Rachel smiled and took off her boots. "I don't either." She ran into the shower room just off the kitchen. "I'll be out before they come off the griddle, Millie!" she shouted.

"I'll be going home today, Rachel, if you don't need me to stay," Millie said during breakfast.

"Oh, Millie, you have done so much to help us. I hate to see you go, but I can get along by myself," Rachel said. She was wrapped in her robe and had put a towel around her hair. "So, who else do you think was out there in the woods last night, besides Gib and myself?"

"I have a guess," Millie said. She adjusted her ring and then had a sip of her coffee. "I could be wrong, but it sounds as if Gib is chasing someone or someone is chasing Gib. I'm surprised they missed you thrashing around in the woods the way you were. No, they were only interested in each other. Gib must be feeling challenged, someone out there is as clever in the woods as he is. At first, I thought it was Charlie, but I could hear him working down at the barn before daybreak. All the lights were on inside the building and his radio was playing." She set her cup down and pursed her lips, as if the coffee had been bitter. "No, I think that the other person who is out there is the person who actually killed Clara."

Rachel gave a small shudder. "I wish I could have seen who it was. I could only hear them moving through the grass and brush. I couldn't even see boots or shoes or anything like that. What I guess I could do is figure out if someone is missing in town."

Millie got up and put her dishes in the sink. "I'll listen to the local gossip and see if I pick up anything. The knitting shop is a great place to start." There were big overstuffed chairs in the store for customers who wanted to linger. Rachel could envision Millie sitting with big needles and balls of yarn on her lap and on the floor.

"Leave the dishes, Millie, it's my turn to do them. Besides, I have the cats to feed. Shall I tell Charlie about last night?"

Millie came out of Clara's room with her things. "I'll tell him if you like, I'm going that way. I want to drop in and see Laura and the girls."

"That would be nice, thanks, Millie."

After her friend left, Rachel sat for some time deciding what to do next. She put the telephone back on the hook and called Simon.

After the initial intimate conversation shared by a husband and a wife, Simon confided in her. "Rachel, I fear this whole idea is going to blow up in our faces. I think we should let it go. There are some mysterious deaths happening out there that could be related to Arakun."

Rachel was shocked, "Mysterious deaths! Simon, what do you mean?"

"I'm not sure I know exactly what I mean, myself. I just have the feeling something is going horribly wrong. I've already had to limit the number of animals people have in the rehab program. It was going way over the predicted budget. There are people claiming hundreds of animals in one dwelling. The money just isn't there for those kinds of numbers. We were thinking along the lines of one or two animals per several hundred households."

Rachel related the possibility that some people were raising wild animals, such as the incident at the store.

"What else have you noticed there, Rachel?"

"I haven't been out that much. I'll go all around town today and see what I pick up. I'll call you tonight."

After Rachel hung up, she knew exactly what she needed to do. She fed the pets, dressed and left the house. She followed the path

Clara must have followed nearly fifty years before. She followed Spring Street to Railroad and stood on the tracks, much as Millie must have done when she witnessed Clara's wrath. She followed the tracks that ran between Division and Railroad Street. She had dressed in an old pair of jeans and shirt.

Her hair was tied back in a simple braid and she walked slowly between the rails, stepping on the ties whenever she could. The smells of the odd vegetation that grew along the tracks mingled with the heavy smell of creosote. Now and then, she could smell a homey cooking smell and see smoke rising from a wood cook stove. It wasn't as hot as it had been earlier in the summer. There was a hint of fall chill in the morning air. She walked along until she was directly across from Gib's house. She sat down on the rail. "Who was with you last night, Gib?" she asked aloud.

Acting on a hunch, Rachel crossed the street and went up to a neighboring house. The grass had never been cut and the screen door was off its hinges. There were children playing with a ball in the side yard, so she felt it must be occupied.

A large woman in a housedress answered her knock. "Yes?"

The woman was fairly attractive and about Rachel's age, so Rachel was slightly shocked to see that she didn't have any teeth.

"I was looking for a Ben McNiff."

The woman stepped out onto the porch, "I ain't seen Ben for some time." She looked around and then said quietly, "I hear there's bad blood between him and his Uncle Gib." She nodded her head towards Gib's.

A man wearing dirty trousers and a T-shirt came out and stood beside her. The large women stepped aside a little and plucked at a tear in her dress. The man hiked his pants up but his belly kept them from staying in place. He put his hands on his hips and Rachel couldn't help but notice how beefy and dirty his hands were. He didn't smile, or shave much either. His wrist was wrapped in, what looked to Rachel like, black electrical tape. "We don't know where the boy is and we don't know where Gib is. Ben don't live around here anyways. His folks live down the road apiece." He jerked his thumb in the direction of the hospital. He looked Rachel up and down and then bullied his wife into the house.

“Thank you,” Rachel called, as she descended the steps.

She stood on the sidewalk until she was sure the couple had gone back to their loud television and then went over to Gib’s house. She went in through the door Simon had broken and looked for evidence that someone had been in the place since they had. The dust on the floor didn’t have any prints in it, so she presumed she was alone. She went over to the closet and put his pictures back and then went into the bedroom and put the mattress back on the bed. She put the scrapbook on top and covered it with the old army blanket. It wasn’t his, but she had a feeling it would mean more to him than to anyone else who had it. She kept the music box. Rachel walked around the rooms. It was odd. For being as dirty as the house was, it didn’t have the feeling of sadness she expected. She sat on the edge of the bed and tried to imagine what it was like to be Gib McNiff, an old man on the run with not a lot to show for a lifetime of living.

Late in the afternoon Rachel crossed the tracks and continued on Magnolia Street to Jacoby’s. She was getting used to the cages that were going up in front yards. She was hopeful that having Si put a limit on animals would put an end to some of this. The smell of animal waste was almost overwhelming.

“Hi Robert, Hi Di,” she said, when she walked in. “Could I have a glass of tea?” she asked, when Robert came over.

“Sure, Rachel,” Robert said. “I haven’t seen you in a while. Did you finally get a dinner schedule worked out?” he said laughing.

“There isn’t a schedule,” Rachel told him. “Simon and I just stopped being such big babies and started fixing our own meals.”

“I see,” he said.

“Where is everyone?” Rachel asked Di.

“We were just trying to figure that out ourselves,” Diane said. “There hasn’t been a soul in here all afternoon. I haven’t even seen anyone to ask what’s going on. If things don’t pick up, I’ll send Robert over to the tavern to see what’s up.”

Robert smiled. “I have to do all the hard work,” he said, winking at his wife.

"Well, I'm on my way to Mary Lee's. She said she had some new dresses in, so I think I'll have a look."

Rachel crossed the street and went into the Boutique. "Hi, Mary Lee," she said, spying her in the back part of the shop.

Mary Lee ran out, her face white. "Rachel, have you heard what happened!"

"No, what?" Rachel said, putting a dress back on the rack and giving Mary Lee her undivided attention.

"Those people killed their little girl!"

"What! What people!" Rachel said.

"Down the block. Oh, it's so horrible."

Rachel went over to try to calm her friend. "What have you heard?"

"They said they killed her because they needed her room and she wasn't bringing in money, but the coyote would."

"I can't believe this," Rachel said, sitting down. She felt weak with emotion. "No one would do such a thing."

"It's true, Rachel. What's more, they are talking about organizing a hunt for people that are just plain useless because they are just eating up the world's supply of food and apparently aren't worth anything. They say there are too many people just sitting around taking up space and pretty soon there will be so many lazy humans they will be up to our backdoors. They say we'll be overpopulated with them and they will just starve or turn to crime if they don't shoot them." Mary Lee started to cry.

Rachel tried to console her friend, but secretly, she thought that she had lost her mind. "Do you want to come home with me?" she asked her.

Mary Lee shook her head no, "I want to stay here so they can see I'm worth something."

Rachel suddenly had some bad feelings. If it came to that, what were her qualifications for being important?

"I'm going to go out and see what on earth is going on. Maybe Father Kessler knows what's going on, or Frankie Wakeland."

Mary Lee picked up on the last name. "Frankie has disappeared."

"He's not at the hardware store?"

"No, his son has taken it over. When I asked him where his dad was, he just said, 'Well, you know, he was getting old.' What did he mean by that, Rachel?" Mary Lee was sobbing quietly by this time.

"I'm going to see about these things one at a time Mary Lee. There has to be some explanation. Will you be all right?"

Her friend shook her head, yes.

As Rachel was leaving, she called back to her. "Come to my house if you need me."

Again her friend shook her head yes, but didn't look up.

Rachel ran all the way to the church. When she went in, she saw Father Kessler kneeling at the altar. She sat and waited for him to finish so she could have a word with him, but became impatient and went back outside. Terry, the altar boy she had seen at the picnic, was working in the flowerbeds. Rachel went over to him. This time he didn't run.

"Terry, when do you think Father will be coming out of church?"

He looked up at Rachel and shook his head. "He's been like that all day. I can't get him to come away from the altar and he hasn't eaten any of his meals."

"Thanks, Terry," Rachel said. She went back into the church, and after making her obeisance to Jesus, she went up to Father Kessler. He had a hold on the altar, and she could see his knuckles were white from gripping it so hard.

"Father," she whispered. "Please come away, I must speak to you about matters of great importance."

He didn't pay any attention to her, he just kept praying and gripping the wood.

Rachel pried his fingers up while talking to him the whole time. His curly lashes were wet with tears, and he was shaking uncontrollably. She wasn't getting anyplace, he was just gripping all the harder. Rachel ran outside and got Terry.

"Terry, we have to get Father out of the church because I have to talk to him about some urgent matters. I can't make him let go of the altar, and we have to get him out here, even if we have to carry him."

Between the two of them, they managed to get the man out on the church lawn, even though he had clutched the altar cross and would not let go, so they had to bring it out with him. Both Terry and Rachel were winded from their efforts.

"Father, tell me about the little girl. What happened?"

He continued to pray unceasingly.

"Terry, do you know where the altar wine is kept?"

He nodded that he did.

"Please, go get me some for Father Kessler."

Terry brought back the wine and an empty glass. Rachel forced some on the overwrought man, then had some herself.

"Father," she tried again, "do you know anything about a little girl's death?"

"Rachel," he finally said, "Rachel, you believe it don't you?"

"Tell me about it again, Father, tell me about our belief."

He held the cross against his breast and spoke so quietly that Rachel had to get down on her knees to hear him. "This is all part of our Master's plan, Rachel, that every act of cruelty against a lower form of life is repaid by us acting out a form of cruelty on our own."

Rachel sat back on her heels but still kept her arm around Father Kessler. Terry was openly sobbing on the grass, so Rachel moved to hold his hand. "Father, you have a very good point, but look carefully at the situation. These people aren't harming animals, anymore. In fact, they are going out of their way to give them a fair chance. There hasn't been an act of cruelty in over a month, and the children have learned more about the spirit of life in the past week than they would have learned in a lifetime."

"It's come too late, Rachel, we have too much to answer for."

"Father, can you tell me about the little girl, please?" she asked again.

Father Kessler let his large hands run over the cross. He caught a tear with his tongue that had run next to the corner of his mouth. Rachel tried to brush some of his hair back from his eyes and then put her arm around him, and waited.

"Do you remember how bleak it gets in February? How miserable every one is?"

"Yes, Father." Rachel was having trouble being patient with the poor man but realized that he was leading up to his point painfully slowly. A point she was having trouble getting.

"That's because of the harvest," he laughed strangely. "Can you imagine calling killed animals a harvest! A basket of apples is a harvest! A field of corn is a harvest! A life is not a harvest!" He turned and clung to her arm. "Then, they blame God. They say that His bible condones their behavior. But it doesn't, Rachel, it says they are created to serve man, such as the donkey served to carry Mary to Bethlehem. Such as the birds serve us with their songs. The Bible doesn't say to mutilate them for our pleasure."

He went back to staring at the cross. "Think of all the hearts that stopped beating, and think of what all of the animals of the forest have witnessed us doing. That's why it's so still, Rachel. Everything is so still and so sad. All animals sing when they are at peace, and it is part of our world and part of our happiness and inner peace. When they stop singing, we suffer sadness, feeling of abandonment, and melancholy."

Rachel was trying to take in what he was saying. It was very profound and she had to take a minute to assimilate it in her mind. "But Father, that was months ago, and it happens every year."

"That's right, Rachel, and He's sick of it and so are so many of his children. Now, little Bonnie is dead."

"Father, how do you know she is dead?"

"They brought her to me for last rites, and then they put her in a plastic bag and buried her."

Rachel couldn't believe her ears. Arakun, a name she had grown to love, a symbol of her devotion to Clara's last wishes, was taking on new meaning.

Rachel sat down on the front lawn of the church with a broken man and a child. She held the bottle of altar wine to her lips and took a very long drink. From across the street and deep down on Stormont land, she heard laughter. She stared silently into the distance at where Gib had to be standing. She deliberately took another drink of wine and then set the bottle aside. She reached down and brought the priest to his feet. She fixed his coat and wiped away his tears. "You will be needed, Father Kessler. There is a lot happening here, man-made problems' developing from greed. Whether it's punishment for evil deeds or not we are not all guilty and there must be a sanctuary for the innocent. You must open the church and be sure to do what you can for the people who seek your help."

"Terry," she asked the boy getting to his feet, "what do you know about the hunt for useless humanity?"

"Old man Clyde McNiff started it. He says there ain't enough money to go around to everybody, so it has to go to them that can take it. He says it will be like the old days."

"Terry honey, the old days are gone. Let's try to fix whatever it is that has gone wrong. Can you stay with Father for a while and get the church doors open? And Terry, can you fire a rifle?"

Terry looked at the ground. "Yes."

"Then, please get it and barricade the people who need your protection in the church. " Father, can you handle this?"

The frail man was looking around the parish and listening more to what Rachel was saying. "It's true, we aren't all guilty, there are good people out there." His face took on an enlightened glow. "I'll stay here and do what I can," he said. "Will you try to find Ida and bring her here?"

"Who is Ida, Father?" Rachel was standing with one hand on her forehead and the other on her hip. How could there be so many people she didn't know very well in such a small town.

"Do you remember the lady with me in the restaurant, the one that wears the little hats?"

"I remember her, yes, I will try to find her. Now listen, Terry has gone for his rifle. You must be in charge here, he's very young and he needs your guidance. I will be back as soon as I can to check on you."

Rachel left him at the front door of the church and then ran for Stormont. She dialed Simon as fast as she could.

"Simon, something is going wrong here. You know that little girl, Bonnie? Her parents killed her this morning. Not only that, a group of men are hunting people that they think classify as a waste of humanity."

"Rachel," Simon said at his end, "get out of there now. Drive if you have to, but leave. I've redirected funds and temporarily closed down all the rehab centers, but we have major problems still arising by the minute. We can't even get out from under this. No one will touch Arakun. Corporations aren't interested, no matter how much money is involved. Even if we just walk away, the terms of the will dictate that the charity continue as we set it up."

"Simon, I have to stay here. Turning my back on this doesn't make it go away. What about Millie and people like her? And Simon, there are two old people missing right now. Frankie Wakeland and a lady named Ida. I have Father Kessler taking people in at the church, and so far, one boy with one gun guarding it."

"Rachel, I'm sending help. Stay in the house. Please, please stay in the house."

"Simon, what you don't realize is that, basically, this is a town of old people. There are just a few of us that are young enough to do anything to try to stop this madness."

"Where is Charlie?"

"I don't know, I haven't seen him. I have to go now, Si. Do what you can at your end, and I'll call you again as soon as I see what else is going on here."

"Rachel, get my pistol, and there is a rifle locked up in the closet. And Rachel, don't let anything happen to you."

"I won't, my love. I'll be in touch."

Rachel ran upstairs two at a time and got the guns Simon had talked about. She laid the rifle on the table, put the pistol in her vest pocket, then hurried out the back door, locking it behind her. She ran back to the church to see how Father Kessler was holding up.

There were many people entering the church. She stopped one young mother. "How did you know to come here?"

"Father Kessler has been calling everyone and telling them to come to the church. Many of the people have guns, so we should be safe here."

Rachel called to Father and she saw him wave back that everything was all right. He looked like a benevolent scarecrow in his baggy black trousers and his white shirt. He was walking around the church organizing his flock. The gold cross, he still had not put down, cast rays of light across the people gathering within the old stone building with it's stained glass saints. Rachel left and went to the home of her cherished friend.

Millie answered the door at her first knock. Rachel went in and told her what was happening, as far as she knew.

"My dear!" Millie clutched her breast and sat down. She fiddled with a broach that held her blouse closed at her throat. "We were hearing strange things were going on, but we had no idea it was this bad! Laura was just here and told me to stay in, today. She didn't think there would be much trouble around here because the men have gathered around Charlie and made up a kind of posse.

Charlie and Nick have gotten out all of the Stormont horses and some of Nick's horses. They are going to form a circle around the town and keep it patrolled. He's called his old friends to try to get them to come back to Stormont, but they have their own problems where they are. Jake, you remember Jake, said that they are going to have to stay where they are right now, but he will stay in touch."

"Millie," Rachel said, "we never should have started this." She put her head in her hands.

"Nonsense," Millie said, with more conviction in her voice than Rachel had ever heard before. "Never, be one of those people that doesn't even try. Dilemmas don't get better by themselves. They don't get better, they just fester and grow. Now the problem is out. All you did was force an upwelling of the enigma."

She came over, sat next to Rachel, and held her. "Remember, how you and Clara use to go to the pond and sit and imagine all the things that were coming to the surface whenever the weather turned cold and the water temperature caused the water to shift? That's all you have done, Rachel. John and Clara knew it would happen and that it would be hard on you and Simon. They may not have known all that you would have to face, but they had an idea. Clara often talked about the tragedy of learning things the hard way."

Millie shifted so she could reach her Kleenex. "She never could understand why you can't just tell people what is going to happen and then have them change their lives accordingly for the good of all. It always has to be a big conflict. Even for a moral cause, many good lives are lost. Many innocent lives, like little Bonnie. Arakun didn't make her parents evil, they have been evil all along."

Rachel listened to Millie carefully. No one had known Clara as well as she had, and Rachel was forever fascinated with Clara and her ways. She looked around the small porch. "Millie," she asked, a little perplexed, "why is your bedding out here on the porch?"

Millie got up and, a little nervously, put away some of her things. "I thought the fresh air would be good for me, dear."

Rachel looked at her a little more closely, "It sounds like you are getting a cold, Millie. Maybe you should have Nancy put your things back in your room for you. The night air is a little damp, and it sounds like you have a little congestion in your chest."

"I will, dear. Thank you for being so concerned, but I thought it would do me some good, you know, the fresh air and all."

"O.K. Will you be all right if I go back and check on Mary Lee? I left her at the store, and she was really having a hard time of it.

She doesn't have any more idea what is going on than the rest of us. I need to tell Robert and Di, also, everyone seems a little isolated."

"You go ahead. Charlie is around with a lot of good men. I know that Mike, Russ, and Nick are with him, and a lot of other men they trust. Laura is next door, and Charlie left her well armed. Like I said earlier, their home base is right at my front door, so this is probably the last place Clyde McNiff and his bunch would come."

Rachel stood to go. "Where is Nancy by-the-way?"

"She is inside. She is thinking about getting married again, so she is looking through some travel brochures for some honeymoon ideas," Millie told her. In the silence that followed, she turned the ring on her finger over and over again.

Rachel leaned down and gave her a hug and kiss. "I'll not only be back later, I'll bring us enough cookies and coffee to really gorge ourselves. And then, I'll tell you everything I find out."

Millie looked happy with that thought, so Rachel left, making sure Millie locked the door behind her.

The streets were quiet. It seemed that everyone was where he or she wanted to be to feel safe. Rachel could see horsemen from time to time; they seemed to be keeping things in order. Good! Now, if it would just hold until Simon could work out the finances to suit everyone. As she walked, she thought about the back door that Si thought John would have left. Not only did it seem like there wasn't any intention of leaving a way out, it looked as if the whole idea was worked out to lock them in. John had certainly been determined to get this charity going and keep it going.

She had walked the three blocks to the restaurant before she knew it, but it was locked up. She looked in the windows, but there wasn't anyone in sight. Rachel felt Simon's gun in her vest pocket. It was awkward and heavy and was certainly something she wasn't used to carrying. She took it out and put it in the other pocket, but decided she couldn't reach it as quickly as she could before, so she put it back. She walked around to the rear entrance and knocked, but no one answered, so she returned to the front door.

"They went home!" someone yelled from across the street.

She looked up and saw Frankie Wakeland's son walking away from the hardware shop. "Mr. Wakeland!" she called. But he kept moving swiftly away from her, so she didn't get a chance to ask him about his dad.

Rachel looked down Main Street, long after the man disappeared from her sight. It had turned warm, and the flies buzzed against the cool glass of the stores. Faint mirages were being cast off the asphalt pavement. Most noticeable of all to Rachel, was the absence of children playing, the little humans whose young voices sing when they talk. No wonder animals often walk up to our young, she thought. They can hear the music born within them. She smiled and said out loud, "Children sing, Clara, children sing."

Rachel passed the closed hardware store and Town Hall and crossed Locust to the Boutique. She looked in the window and could see Mary Lee behind the counter, nervously having a cigarette. She looked up when Rachel came in. The little chimes she had above the door were more an indication of the state of her nerves than number of customers she was expecting.

"What's going on out there, Rachel?"

"I can only tell you what I have seen, I don't know the extent of the problems myself. I just know that things look pretty disorganized right now." She went around the corner and helped herself to some coffee while she told Mary Lee what she had learned up to that point. The air conditioner hummed in the window and everything seemed normal in the little shop. Rachel paused several times while she relayed the stories to her friend, wondering if she was telling the truth or if somehow she was the one confused.

"When things begin to happen that don't seem normal, it's easy to question your own judgment, not to mention sanity," Rachel told Mary Lee.

"I know the feeling," Mary Lee said, crushing out her cigarette and lighting another. "The longer I stay in here, the more ridiculous the whole thing seems. The only real part of it is that no one is on the streets as usual. It's time to close anyway," she said, moving around the counter to the door.

Halfway there, Grace Reecy ran in the door, her hair wild in her face. Her breath was in gasps, and she could only cling to a very shocked Mary Lee.

"Please!" she begged her, "Hide me!"

Rachel pulled out Simon's pistol, flicking off the safety as she ran to lock the door.

"Oh my God! They are trying to get me!" Grace screamed into Mary Lee's face.

"Mary Lee, do you have a gun here?" Rachel asked.

"I don't even own a gun," Mary Lee sobbed holding onto Grace's dress and trying to pull her closer to her.

Grace fell to her knees frozen with fear. The sound of her dress tearing on the way down, the crisp ripping sound made the other two women freeze momentarily. Mary Lee mashed out the cigarette that had fallen out of her mouth with the toe of her shoe. She picked up the fallen woman and held her close to her while she worked her way to the back door of the Boutique.

"Did anyone see you come in here?" Rachel asked Grace, as she followed the woman to the rear of the building.

"I don't know, I didn't even see them. They shot Vera and Lorraine while we were sitting at the kitchen table. I just ran."

Rachel and Mary Lee looked at each other. Here was their worst fear. Grace was slumped over some packing boxes trying to catch her breath. Several of the long, red, painted nails she had been so proud of were broken, and she only had one, of what appeared to be, a house slipper. A large wad of snot was hanging on one cheek. Mary Lee quickly found a tissue and tried to wipe it away while Rachel locked the back door.

"I feel safer back here, don't you?" Mary Lee asked Rachel.

"The walls do seem better than all that glass in the front," Rachel answered. "Do you have an attic or basement we could get into?"

Before Mary Lee could answer there was a horrible crashing at the back door and the hinges gave. The door was nearly opened on the first impact!

Grace started screaming, just screaming. So horrible was the noise Grace was making that it was hard for the other two women to get their wits about them. They began to drag Grace to the front of the shop. In her terror, Graces legs had completely given out on her. Rachel ran back around the counter and emptied the clip of Simon's 9mm pistol into the back door. Without waiting to estimate the extent of the damage she caused, she pocketed the gun and ran back to the front of the store. Mary Lee had the front door open and Grace was on her feet. All three women fled down the street. Rachel and Mary Lee kept Grace between them. Each one of them had one of her arms. The screaming had stopped, but she still emitted strange sobs of fear. A heavy shot sounded and Grace, screaming a scream of surprise and pain, fell headfirst onto the pavement. Another shot missed them. Mary Lee and Rachel grabbed Grace and tried to pull her up. A shotgun blast tore Grace's leg off below the knee. Most of the flesh was gone and white bleeding bone stuck out at raw shredded angles.

"Put her on my back!" Rachel screamed. "We're going to have to get between the buildings!"

Horsemen appeared at the far end of Main Street, and, for a second, Rachel thought they were saved. Mary Lee had managed to get the large woman on Rachel's back and was holding the bloody limb so Rachel could run. Together, they had gotten her to the end of the alley and were turning down it when a thunderous roar came from behind them. Rachel felt as if someone had hit her with enough force from behind to knock her for a block. All three women were swept to the ground.

Rachel reached behind her in an effort to drag Grace even further out of danger as the horsemen thundered by, showering bullets at their attackers. Mary Lee sat up and covered her mouth when she saw the older woman. The impact of the blast had blown Grace's brains out of her nose and mouth. Her eyes bulged and gray bits dripped down the front of her. Rachel got to her side first.

"Pick me up," Grace muttered. "I can take the pain. Pick me up."

Rachel tried to lift the woman to her feet. Grace put her weight on the broken fragments that were what was left of her leg, crumpled, and fell to the ground. More of the gray matter dripped from her nose and ears, it was mixing with blood from a place Rachel didn't know. She reached down to try to get her up again, but someone grabbed her and whispered in her ear, "Put her back down, Rachel, she's dead."

As she laid her on the grass, the puppet mouth with the oozing mixture was still saying, "Pick me up, I can take the pain, I can take the pain, I can --."

It was over. Those seconds it took for her body to acknowledge death seemed hours to the two women who had fought so hard to save her life.

Rachel looked up into the sad eyes of her dear friend Charlie. Once again, he was there, and once again, they shared a tragedy. "Charlie," she said, "we're always too late."

He nodded a slight understanding with her and took off his shirt. His fine chest was moist with sweat and dust. He covered Grace's face. His wife's fine stitch work fluttered, then settled and stuck to the bloody skin. Charlie went over to help Mary Lee.

Mary Lee was getting to her feet but still accepted his assistance when he leaned to help her. Both women were covered with bits of Grace. "What did they shoot at us with?" she asked him, shaking uncontrollably.

"The last one that got Grace was a bullet they make to explode on impact. It's used mainly for animals they consider pests. The explosion inside the body is so intense that the internal tissues don't have any place to exit except out of existing body canals to the outside. A shotgun took off her leg. It seems that they are all carrying their particular weapon of choice. Most of what they have, has been outlawed, it's a matter of ethics. Charlie looked back at Grace and said to himself, "nothing and no one should die like this.'

"They broke in the back door of the store," Rachel told Charlie. "I fired into the door as they were coming in, but I didn't check to see if any one was hit. We just ran. Grace said that a woman named Vera and a woman named Lorraine were killed in her kitchen."

Charlie looked at Rachel's innocent eyes and sighed heavily. If she had killed anyone, it would be the last time anyone would see that look.

"I'll take some men around back and have some one go over to Grace's house and see what's happened there," Nick said to him.

Mary Lee was standing and rubbing her arms. She looked down at the body and then at Rachel. "I'm going to go back to the shop and get some of the drapes we use to cover the dresses at night. I'll be right back."

Nick came back and reported his findings. "We have three dead men in the alley. They weren't expecting the women to have a gun, I would say. They must have all been in front of the door. One was Lewis Welch."

"Our old friend from the picnic," Charlie reminded Rachel.

"The other one was old Clyde McNiff, himself," Nick said. "Since he is the one that started this manhunt frenzy, maybe his death will end it all. It looks like the men have caught up with the ones that shot Grace." He pointed to the group headed toward the town hall. "I don't know the third man, but whoever it is deserves what he got."

Mary Lee came back and covered Grace completely with sheeting. People had come out of their homes, hesitantly at first, but were becoming braver as their numbers increased.

The sun was setting, and Rachel sat on the grass feeling the whole scene was very surrealistic. She had killed three men and hadn't even seen their faces. It was as if they hadn't existed and didn't exist now. She watched Mary Lee take great pains to make sure Grace was covered and kept her dignity in death. And the people gathered, they gathered like moths in the dim light of evening.

Mary Lee came over, took Rachel by the arm, and helped her up, much as Charlie had done for her. "They don't need us here, let's go to my house and clean up."

Rachel looked at her red, sticky hands and felt the dried blood that caked her hair. She only nodded as Mary Lee led her off to her little story book house with white shutters.

The inside of the house was as neat and clean as the Boutique had always been. The used ashtrays were the only sign of disorder. Rachel and Mary Lee showered together in a sisterly fashion. They washed each other's backs and hair, but mostly they just didn't want to be alone. Mary Lee gave Rachel some of her clothes to wear, baggy jeans and a light sweatshirt. She opened the window overlooking the back yard, and they threw all their clothes as near to the garbage can as they could get them from the upstairs window. Before she closed it again, Rachel thought she heard children playing, and it was a good sound. How easily they recovered from tragedy.

"I promised Millie that I would be back with cookies and coffee. I really want to check on her, so I must go."

She and Mary Lee hugged with earnest love for each other. Rachel went over to the chair, picked up Simon's gun, and put it back in her back pocket. She looked out of the window facing Main Street.

"It looks like everyone is out, Mary Lee, I even see lights on at Jacoby's. Want to tag along at least that far?"

Mary Lee came over and looked out of the window. "I think I will, it will be good to talk to people about what happened."

The women left the quaint, narrow house with their arms around each other and made their way to Jacoby's. The town had, more or less, gathered there to comfort each other. "Do you think this all happened because of Arakun?" Rachel asked Mary Lee.

"I hadn't really thought about what caused it," Mary Lee said. "I don't think it was Arakun itself. It just triggered feelings that have been smoldering for generations. It always boils down to the good guys and the bad guys if you ask me. In this instance, it came down to people that can easily take life and people that understand the meaning of life. And the way I see it, Rachel, we won."

Rachel stood in line at the counter listening to the relief in the mingled voices as they assessed the recent developments in their town. When it came to her turn, she ordered coffee and pie to go. Cookies were out of the question. The town was as near to a national disaster area as it was possible to be and still not have the National Guard on your doorstep.

"Thanks, Di," she said, accepting her white paper bag filled with goodies for Millie and herself. She pocketed the change and realized how very little money she had on her person. It frightened her, in a way, and made her think about Gib. He would probably finish his life as impoverished as he had come into it. She pressed through the waiting customers, waved good-bye to Mary Lee, and went down Spring Street to Millie's.

The lights from the screened-in porch looked warm and inviting. She hurried up the steps and knocked.

Millie answered right away. "Oh, thank God, you're all right! We've been listening to the radio, and I thought sure you must be injured or dead. Simon has been calling everywhere to try to find you." She ushered Rachel to a chair and sat down across from her.

Rachel pulled out the coffee and pie. "No cookies tonight, I'm afraid, Millie. I hope this will do." She smiled at Millie.

"Oh my, I can't eat a bite," she said, but eyed the coffee Rachel fixed for her.

"Your cold sounds worse, Millie," Rachel said with concern. "I can hear the congestion in your chest from here."

"Just a little phlegm," Millie assured her. "My daddy always said that a summer cold was the worst kind to get over."

"Here is your pie, Millie. If Nancy is here, she can have the other piece."

Millie shook her plastic fork, no, and finished chewing the bite of cherry pie. "She won't eat it," she said between bites. "She is on a diet again."

Rachel finished her pie and coffee very leisurely. "I should go call Simon and tell him that I'm fine," she told Millie.

"Charlie said he talked to Si and told him you would call him later," Millie said.

Rachel leaned back and listened to the frogs that she knew were on Stormont land. She told Millie what had happened but left out the abhorrent details.

Millie had already heard most of the news on the radio, so Rachel's rendition only confirmed what she had heard.

"Do you want to stay here, dear?" she asked Rachel, when the young woman stood up to go.

"No, I want to look over the notes that John left us, again, and see if I can understand what he might have been trying to do if he had been given enough time to finish working out the plans for this charity. Why don't you come and stay in Clara's room?"

"I think I would like to," Millie said. "Let me just get a few things, and I'll be right with you."

Together, they walked down the brick path to Stormont house. The evening was cool, and there was just that fresh scent in the air that it would soon be fall. Rachel opened the door and turned on all the coach lights that surrounded the house. Millie seemed to sigh with the remembered pleasures of times spent playing in the shadows of Stormont.

"I think I'll go to bed," she said to Rachel. "I am so tired, this has been such a long day."

Rachel helped Millie with her things and then said goodnight to her. As an afterthought, she went into the kitchen and got Gib's replica of Clara's music box. She went in and placed it on the dresser where Clara had always kept it and lifted the lid. The silken music filled the room, and Millie was asleep before it finished playing.

Rachel went upstairs and called Simon. He answered before the first ring was finished. "Rachel, I love you, Rachel, please don't put yourself in danger like that, ever again."

"Simon, it's all been like a dream, it's so unreal. I have actually shot and killed three human beings. I can't even cry over it, it's just beyond tears."

"It had to be done, Rachel, from what Charlie told me. If you hadn't weakened them by killing Clyde, all three of you would be dead right now."

"Grace wasn't that bad, she had her place in the world, she was as important as I am," Rachel said. She leaned back on the bed. She suddenly felt so tired.

"Everything and everyone is here for a purpose Rachel. That's the whole point of Arakun. They couldn't see Grace's value, and I can't say I could either, but it was there. It's there in every living thing. I can see your value perfectly, my love, the world would be very bleak without you."

Rachel smiled into the telephone. "Thank you, my love."

Simon cleared his throat at his end of the phone and then spoke again, "I should think, maybe, lawyers are fairly high on their list of useless people, also, Rachel."

Rachel laughed. "I hadn't thought about it, Simon. I see you as the future father of my children. How can I possibly do without you?"

"I'm taking the next plane that goes into the air back to Stormont, even if I have to hijack it."

Rachel sat up. "That reminds me, where are all the police, planes, military and government help?"

"Sent to the big cities. The smaller and more rural the area, the less help they are getting. After I talked to you earlier, I called the surrounding areas to send help, but they were already out handling similar problems. Clyde wasn't the only one who came up with the idea of extermination of the least valued people. It's an old story that just sits around waiting to be revived, from time to time. There are many Clyde McNiffs in the world. Animals, humans, who are we to judge who or what is useless."

"I wonder how many people live and die like Clyde that haven't lived during a time when circumstances let them show their true colors." Rachel said.

"It's not their true colors, anymore, Rachel, it's their true DNA." Simon laughed. "I think we will know a lot more about what a person is capable of, once we finish mapping the human genome."

"Speaking of what a person is capable of, have you looked at your copy of John's notes, again?" Rachel asked him.

Simon sighed at his end of the telephone. "Over and over again. I can't find the slightest hint as to how he expected us to get out of this horrible situation."

"I thought I would look them over again before I went to bed. There has to be an answer there, someplace," Rachel said, then added, "I don't suppose they have found Clara's killer yet, have they?"

"No, they are looking for Mary's nephew, Ben McNiff, for questioning. They had him for trespassing and trapping on Stormont, but he was only fined. Since he didn't have a gun in his possession, no one suspected he could have been the one we were looking for. It's interesting to know that he and Gib are the only ones in town unaccounted for. It look's as if they are both on the run."

"I hope they find him soon, but with everything else that is going on, they could dance in the town square and no one would pay any attention to them," Rachel said wearily. "I'll talk to you again tomorrow, Si my love, and if you can get a flight out and this mess settles down enough that you can come home, please bring Millie a suitcase full of cookies from every specialty shop you can find."

Simon thought about Millie for a moment. "I will, and I'll try to get a few packages sent. I think the mail is still going through, slower, but it's still going through. They used to have to worry just about dog bites, now it's every kind of bite you can think of. Many places are making residents pick up their mail at the post office."

Rachel laughed. "I imagine Arakun is paying enough to compensate?"

"Indeed. In fact, there haven't been any complaints from the postal department about the sums handed over for any kind of animal bites."

"That's good, I must say goodnight for now, my love. I wish you were here with me, and I hope to sec you soon."

Simon talked to Rachel a few more minutes and then Rachel hung up the telephone. She went over to Simon's desk and picked up the computer papers John had been working on. After an hour of reading, she took them downstairs with her and checked on Millie. Her breathing was slightly harder, but she was resting well and her cold didn't seem any worse.

Rachel closed the door and went in the kitchen to make some coffee. It wasn't yet two in the morning, but her metabolism had slowed enough that she felt chilled. She continued to read until about three. Poor Grace's image was on every page. The scene at the door of the Boutique was vague. She didn't even hear the men fall, but Grace, the true innocent victim, stayed fresh in her mind. She went over all the alternatives that might have saved her. But the fact remained that she and two other women were dead and two other people were missing.

Rachel put her papers down and took her coffee out to the back porch. There was lightning off in the distance, and the wind carried the smell of rain. She pondered a moment trying to describe to herself what exactly rain smelled like. She decided it was earth. Just another upwelling that turned everything around and gave our senses another look at what we were missing.

In the next lightning flash, she looked toward the little graves. She hadn't wanted to, she tried not to, but she did. She wasn't surprised to see two little forms tying to get over the fence. She sighed and put her coffee down. They still were there, putting her hands in her pockets she walked down the path to the cemetery. When she was very close, they disappeared back into the ground the same way they always did.

She sat down on the grass in front of the little crosses. "What do I have to do that will set you free?" she asked. She felt the ground above them with her hands trying to figure out the answer, the key that would fulfill her promise to Clara. She took one of the fresh wild flowers out of the vases and held it to her check, it's fragrances fresher than any perfume. "Why does Gib take care of this spot for Clara. What is it we are all waiting for to happen?"

She lay her head on the cool grass and for a time, she was free of the horrors of the afternoon. She felt Clara put a warm blanket over her and she heard her music box playing. She went to sleep and dreamed of the days when she and Clara would take her music box to the pond and let it play. There was always that one great big bullfrog that would come right up to the box and listen very carefully to the music. Then, when the music stopped he would wait for Clara to wind it up again for him to listen to. He would stay there as long as Clara would play it for him. Clara loved that frog, she called him Ryan."

Rachel woke up to big fat slow drops of rain falling on her face. She sat up and looked at the quilt she kept in the living room. It was tucked around her instead of lying on the back of the couch. She stood up, wrapped it around her Indian style, and went back to the house. From that day forward, she didn't hate Gib McNiff anymore and she knew that Clara hadn't either.

She went upstairs and slept until she smelled coffee and knew Millie was awake. She ran downstairs as fast as she could because she had a very important question to ask Millie.

"Millie," she asked as soon as she got to the kitchen door. She put a hand on each side of the door and leaned into the room and asked breathlessly, "what is Gib's middle name?"

Millie didn't seem surprised at the question, just at Rachel's entry into the kitchen. "Would you like eggs this morning?" she asked her.

"Are you going to tell me or not?"

"I can see you haven't had a chance to shower and get into some clothes of your own, so I'll fix breakfast while you clean up and then we'll have a nice chat over breakfast."

A nice chat over breakfast was all the incentive Rachel needed to hurry through the necessary rituals to be halfway presentable to the world.

Millie had laid her papers to the side of the table and had breakfast on the plates when Rachel came back down stairs. She was rummaging in the pantry for cookies.

"Check the freezer Millie, I remember us putting several packages in there the last time we baked."

The lid closed with a dull, swooshy thud and Millie emerged holding up a plastic bag. "Chocolate chip," she beamed at Rachel. She closed the pantry door and warmed several in the microwave before she sat down.

"Now what was that question you asked me dear?" she said.

"I said," Rachel refreshed her memory, knowing full well Millie was playing this for all it was worth, "what was Gib's middle name."

"His middle name was Ryan. Gibson Ryan McNiff.

Rachel stood up, gave a turn around the kitchen, and came around to Millie for a kiss, a hug, and a chocolate cookie. "I knew it, I knew it, I knew it!"

Millie dipped her cookie in her coffee and then took a bite before she said, "when she named that old frog I wondered how she decided on that name, so I checked the old school year books."

"Did she ever tell you why she named him after Gib?"

"She didn't have to," Millie told her. "I knew why. As much as she hated Gib's ways, she didn't hate Gib himself. Over the years, Gib mellowed; he came to understand some of Clara's ways. I think that for her he stopped doing a lot of the things he had thought were fun in his youth. Those baby raccoons are a perfect example. I never knew Gib to do anything like that again. But he never came over completely to Clara's side, in fact, not even close. He still killed the neighbor's dog if it got in his chickens and he shot every fox that came on his land. But Clara knew that if the dogs got his chickens, he wouldn't eat, and if the fox got his rabbits, he wouldn't have an income. She understood, but would never have been his friend."

"Did she ever try to help him out so he didn't have to live such a harsh existence?"

"She did," Millie said. "She would send anonymous gifts and he would send them back anonymously. The only thing he ever took was firewood. He was very sick one really nasty winter and she sent over a load of firewood and a blanket. He returned the blanket in the spring. Remember, after she married John she only came to Stormont twice a year."

Rachel leaned back in her chair and sipped her coffee. "Do you think that deep-down Gib is a nice person."

"No, I do not. I think that he can do horrible things in the name of what he thinks is right. I think he has a part of him that is good. But it's a small part. I don't think we should completely rule him out as the man who killed Clara. Didn't his brother just kill poor Grace?"

Rachel thought about that for a moment while Millie went in search of more Kleenex.

"I must be going now dear, I think Nancy is expecting company at dinner and I want to make sure everything is a great success. Remember that it's still not completely safe to go out by yourself. I wonder if there are going to be court trials that you will have to face over that business yesterday?"

"I'm sure there will be Millie, but I'm not too worried, I have a great lawyer and it was an obvious case of self defense."

As she went out the door Millie called back over her shoulder, "If you need me I'll be there, dear." She stepped off the porch holding a few belongings and the rest of the cookies. She held her ring up in the bright sunlight. The small stone sparkled to her satisfaction and she walked home whistling one of her lovely songs. The prairie wind pulled at her dress and golden rays of light flickered down on her through the leaves. Rachel watched Millie until she got home and then waved to her as she went in the door. She would recall that angelic scene to mind many times over the course of her life.

Rachel finished washing the breakfast dishes and sat down to look over the papers John had worked up. A knock at the door surprised her.

"Nick! This is a pleasant surprise, come in. Let me get you some coffee."

"Thank you, Rachel," he said politely.

"What brings you over to Stormont, Laddie's all right I hope?"

"He's very well, and no one knows he's with me, even yet. He stays out of sight of everyone, including the mailman."

"I thought he might do well at your house. I can't imagine anyone bothering him there."

"I thank you for your confidence in me."

She handed him his coffee and then he announced his reason for coming. "It's this check Rachel." He pulled out a check that was instantly recognizable as an Arakun check.

Rachel looked at it, and then at him. She did not say anything.

"It seems that there isn't a place to return the check if the money is not wanted. I don't mean to harm anyone's feelings but I do not wish to be paid for taking care of the animals that require my helping hand. It is enough of a gift to briefly share their world. To have the honor of being chosen to help them is all the gift any man could want. They give so much more than money to those that have the heart to listen." He pushed the check across the table and picked up his coffee.

Rachel looked at the humble man before her. She was learning something new about humans everyday here recently. "How did you know to return it to me?"

"Arakun, I remember talking to your husband about the Indian word for our bandit friends. I also remember the story surrounding the little graves. I didn't know Clara but I know the spirit of Clara. How or why you have the money to do this is not important."

"Well you can see how far our noble idea is getting us, Nick. So far, it has not been doing as well as John had intended. He would have aborted the idea if he had thought even one life would be lost."

Nick reached over and took her hand for a moment. "Do not give up little one. What you have been chosen to do is a very big task. It is going to make people who do not have a violent nature stand up for what they believe in against people who express violence and total disregard for life. This has been building for years. Arakun just pushed it over the top. It's the new learning, it is the age of enlightenment and compassion. God gave us a brain to figure out how this world we live in is put together. We are only on the fringe of what there is to know and we realize what we must do. We have to change in order to survive."

Nick went back to his coffee. Rachel noticed an old class ring on his finger, but she couldn't make out the name of the college. She looked at her own hand that held only her wedding ring. She suddenly wanted very much to know as much as she could learn. She would have to remember to talk this over with her husband. "I will tell Simon about the returned check, Nick. I wonder how many other people feel the same way you do about this?"

Nick shrugged his shoulders and said to her. "They wouldn't have had a chance to ask themselves that question if it weren't for Arakun." He stood up to leave and Rachel walked him to the door. He turned to her once again. "It's a good name you picked for John and Clara's charity. It suits them. I only wish I had known this Clara."

When he left, Rachel called Simon and told him about the recent events. He was aware that many of the checks were not being cashed and like Rachel, he had not considered that it was because some people might be offended. Rachel hung up and loaded Simon's pistol, then placed it in her shoulder bag. She locked up the house and crossed the street to the church.

"Father Kessler, how did you manage last night?"

"Rachel, how good of you to stop by." He walked around the inside of his church, straightening pictures and brushing away bits of dust. "I think the end of our suffering is near, I heard many people discuss the new learning with their children and I made the point very clear that the church would no longer tolerate this wanton killing for sport among it's parishioners." He stood up as tall as he could and pointed toward heaven. "They must choose Rachel, they must choose. And they must be responsible for themselves as well as their children."

"Did anyone approach the church Father or was the incident with Grace and her friends the only one?"

He took her aside and glanced at the cross before he spoke. "We still have some problems of a suspicious nature that are being investigated but nothing like the other night. It seems that we fought this evil to the ground the first night they tried to impose their wickedness on us. We are truly in the hands of angels my dear."

"Did Ida ever come to the church, Father?"

"No," he said, "she didn't. It is a bit of a puzzle, but it seems that her son sent her to her sister's to be safely out of danger. I didn't know Ida had a sister but we learn new things about people every day."

Rachel smiled and had to agree with his statement. "How about Frankie Wakeland, did you ever talk to his son about where he was?"

"No, I haven't, but I did notify the police about not seeing him around and his son's strange avoidance of the subject."

"That was a good idea, Father. I think that if Ida doesn't show up soon, we should tell them of our suspicions about her disappearance, also. Did you get a hold of the Sheriff, himself?"

"No, but I left the information with the dispatcher. I should think they would want to talk to us all about what happened here in this town."

"They will get to us, eventually, and then we will all be swamped with court appearances and paperwork. Well, I must go. I have to get some groceries in the house and see Mary Lee and the Jacoby's. Any messages I can relay to anyone, Father?"

"I wish them peace and love. I will be around to see everyone within the week. Right now, Terry and I have a lot of cleaning up to do, the altar guild can't do it all."

The day drifted into evening, and Rachel stopped her housekeeping chores and called Simon. After a long chat, she still didn't feel sleepy so she went to the pantry and took down a box of cookies and went over to Millie's. Much to her surprise, Nancy answered the door.

"Hello, Nancy," Rachel smiled at her. "Are you and your Mother ready to have some cookies and coffee?"

"Mother isn't here, Rachel," Nancy said without smiling.

Rachel was slightly surprised. Millie had certain programs she wouldn't miss for the world, and Rachel had timed her arrival for just after one of them and before Millie liked to go to bed. "Did she go to Laura's?"

"I'm really not sure, Rachel. Could you excuse me, I have a guest?"

Nancy closed the door in her face before Rachel could ask any more questions, but not before she saw what she thought were Millie's glasses on the floor of the porch.

Rachel felt uneasy and knocked again. This time a strange man answered her knock.

"Yes."

"Hello, I was asking for Millie a moment ago, and when Nancy opened the door I noticed my friend's glasses on the floor. I wonder if I might take them to her?"

From inside the house she heard Nancy coming. "So that's where they are. Mother had to use her old pair, and I told her I would look for these."

"Are you sure your mother's all right?" Rachel persisted.

"Everything is fine, Rachel. I will tell Mother you called, and perhaps if it isn't too late, she can call you," Nancy said.

Rachel waited until she was sure no one was watching her from the window and went next door to Charlie's.

Laura came to the door and welcomed her with a great deal of joy. "Rachel, you stay away too long at a time!"

"Charlie," she called over her shoulder, "Rachel's here to see us." She turned back to her friend. "I'm trying to can tomatoes this year."

Rachel looked around the kitchen. There were tomatoes everyplace and sparkling canning jars lay hot and steamy on the counters. Laura's favorite pattern was gingham and there was a lot of it in the kitchen. The windows were surrounded by yellow gingham and the dishtowels were a variety of colors of the familiar country checkerboard pattern. The tablecloth was the same pattern, and the rag rugs she had made were, of course, out of gingham.

"Please sit down Rachel, if you can find a chair in all this clutter," Laura said. She took a towel and dried her hands. When the twins came in, they were dressed alike in handmade blue gingham dresses with large matching bows. When Charlie came in, she half expected him to be in a gingham shirt, but he wasn't. It was, however, noticeable that his shirt was the same pale blue as Laura's apron. The general mood of the house made Rachel's fears wane and she accepted a glass of iced tea while the little girls put the cookies she had on a plate.

"I just came from Millie's, and she wasn't home," Rachel told them. "I just found it odd and wanted to see if you had seen her today."

"I saw her this morning, but I have been pretty busy in the kitchen." Laura said.

Charlie held the girls on his knees. "I haven't seen her either, but sometimes I don't for a couple of days at a time. I just got back myself. We've been checking the woods for old Frankie Wakeland. His son seems to think he might have wondered off. It doesn't seem like a thing he would do, but he hasn't been at home in some time."

Charlie leaned down and buckled one of the twin's shoes for her. "His heart may have given out, one never can tell."

The twins leaned against their dad's broad chest and ate their cookies in silence. They took turns staring at Rachel and then looking up at Charlie. They offered him bites of cookie.

He adjusted the girls on his lap so that he could reach the tea his wife had brought him. "You say her glasses were on the floor?"

Rachel had started helping Laura blanch the tomatoes. "Yes, on the floor of the porch by the door. Her daughter said she had worn another pair."

Laura dried her hands on a towel. "If she dropped them, she probably couldn't see them. She might have had another pair handy. Charlie can check around the house before he goes to bed tonight."

"I'll read the girls their bedtime story first," he said to her. He got up and took his daughters hands.

"Good night, Rachel!" they giggled and laughed from their daddy's shoulder as he picked up one in each arm and headed upstairs with them.

Rachel talked with Laura, and they canned until after midnight. Charlie had taken a flashlight and checked around Millie's house reporting that it looked as if everyone was asleep at their house and perhaps Laura and Rachel should think about the sandman themselves.

The two women finally called it a night and Rachel picked up the jars she had been given and went to the door. Laura helped hold the door.

"Thanks so much for the tomatoes, Laura," Rachel whispered. "Simon and I will have to put in a big garden next year so we can do this."

"It was great to have the help and the company," Laura told her. "I'll see you tomorrow."

Rachel agreed and then made her way back to Stormont. Alone, and in the dark, all of her fears came back to her. When was Simon going to be able to come home? Where was Gib? In the house? Did they catch all the men that killed Grace or did they miss someone who was lurking in the shadows? Why were Millie's glasses on the floor and why wasn't she home? Most of all, who killed Clara, and where was he now? Rachel unlocked the back door and turned on most of the lights. She set her jars of tomatoes on the table and took Simon's gun out of her shoulder bag. She checked it and took it upstairs with her. The gun was steady in her hand. When she was reasonably satisfied that the house was safe, she turned off some of the lights and went up to her bed. She sat awake many more hours looking over John's papers. She was determined to spend the next day with the computer. He had to have left an answer for them. Even if it were just a thought in his head, it would come through somehow in what he was writing. She tried to fall asleep, but couldn't, so she tiptoed down and got Clara's music box. She put it on the nightstand beside her dresser and let it play while she drifted off to sleep. Thinking about Clara always was peaceful.

The next day was rainy and slightly cool. Rachel sat at the computer for hours, finding nothing she went downstairs to fix some coffee. After it had warmed her, she opened the back door and stepped out on the porch. The prairie was washed a vivid green in the misty drizzle. All the waxy leaves on the foliage were shining in the dim light the sun had managed to impart. It was also one of those days when Rachel wished she were anyplace else doing anything else. She went back in the house and called Simon.

"Simon, when can you come back to Stormont?"

"I have a ticket for the day after tomorrow. It was the first opening they had. Everett is back, and we are training a new man to give us a backup person in case of emergencies. I think he will work out just fine. Arakun is still having its problems, but I think I can work on it from Stormont. Are you getting lonely, Rachel?"

"Yes, it's raining off and on here and I feel very isolated. Sometimes I like the peace and quiet, but today I want to do something different."

Simon smiled at his end of the telephone. "I think you miss me," he said.

"Of course I do, Simon, but I want to do more than just wait for you to come home."

Simon leaned back in his chair. This was the old Rachel talking, the one who wanted to set the world on fire with her ideas. He understood the drive she had and hoped to help her nurture it. "What are your thoughts for today, Rachel, do you have anything specific in your mind you want to do?"

"No, I guess I'm just restless."

"Why don't you go get Millie and walk down to Jacoby's in the rain and have lunch. You know that talking to Millie always stimulates your brain. She usually manages to put her finger on the pulse of the problem. Maybe you will wind up telling her enough that she can help you out."

"You're right," Rachel perked up a little. "There are some big black umbrellas in the old umbrella stand. I'll get them and go over to her house before she has a chance to fix lunch and we'll walk down. I'll bet she has dozens of stories about those umbrella's."

Simon could hear the joy come back into her voice and felt relieved. Actually, he needed more time to look into the matters involving Arakun. There were some very sinister accusations being leveled at their charity, and he had to legally deal with all of them. He had hired several other attorneys and was appraising Everett of the situation. He wanted to be with his new bride, but he had serious matters that demanded his time and attention.

"I will let you go for now, Rachel. Call me later and let me know how your lunch went."

"I will, Simon, take care of yourself, I love you."

Rachel hung up and ran into the living room. There in the corner were the umbrellas. Rachel opened two of them to make sure the material would still hold up. They looked as good as new. She didn't see any need for Simon's gun, so she unloaded it and put it away in the closet. It wasn't exactly as easy to carry around as a lipstick and everything seemed back to normal. She stepped off the back porch and tried to whistle a tune as she made her way to Millie's.

Rachel knocked several times on the door, no one answered. She left one of the umbrellas on the front steps and went around to the back door. The house was unusually quiet. Millie liked to keep the radio on for company during the day. If the radio wasn't on, she would be talking to Nancy or running the washing machine. She had her favorite soaps to watch. Rachel couldn't keep track of which ones, but she watched them with her sometimes. Nancy's car was in the garage so she must be home. Rachel tried calling out.

"Millie!" "Nancy!" "Are you all right!"

She returned to the front door, and shading her eyes, she peeked in. She could see Millie's glasses still on the floor. No one had picked them up. It was the deciding factor she used to justify her next move. She went around to all the doors and windows trying to get in. She went next door to get Charlie and Laura, but they weren't home. She left a note on Laura's little note pad indicating she was trying to get into Millie's house and to assist if they came home in the near future. She then returned to Millie's and went around to the garage. She found an old, rusty crowbar hanging on some nails and took it to the kitchen door. She couldn't pry it open, but managed to do a lot of damage to the door jam. She finally shrugged her shoulders and smashed in a glass window just off the porch. She dragged a metal garbage can over and climbed up on it. She reached in, unlocked the window, and then tried to raise it without cutting herself.

The drizzle of rain had soaked the back of her shirt. She felt slightly chilled but left the black umbrella on the ground where she had thrown it earlier. With an increased feeling of urgency, she returned to the garage and brought back an old piece of hammock material she had found. She laid that over the broken glass of the sill and went through the kitchen window on her belly. Small scratches went unnoticed.

The house was so still that it frightened Rachel. She looked at the back door and thought about going back for Simon's gun. Her mouth had gone so dry and she felt so dizzy she had to hold the sink for a moment. When the feeling passed, she went over, unlocked the back door, and then opened it wide. It was still cloudy, and the rain still was misting down.

She went to the kitchen door and looked into the living room. The room was gloomy because the shades had been drawn. When Rachel's eyes adjusted to the light, she saw Nancy huddled on the couch. She wasn't moving, she was just holding her knees. Nancy was a pampered Dresden beauty, and that's all she was. Rachel didn't move when she saw the familiar figure because she wasn't acting in a way that Rachel recognized as Nancy. She looked around the room for other clues, and seeing nothing out of the ordinary, she walked slowly over to the distraught women.

"Nancy, do you hear me? It's me, Rachel. Aren't you feeling well?"

Rachel tried to move her, but she was like a person dazed. The only thing Rachel could tell for sure was that she wasn't dead. Rachel took one of Millie's hand made afghans from the back of the couch and put it around her

"What is that funny smell in the house, Nancy?"

When Nancy didn't answer, Rachel went down the hall to the room she knew to be Millie's. The carpet was thick and blue. Her fingers trailed along the raised wallpaper. The door was closed. She stood outside the door for a moment and absentmindedly traced the pattern on the wall with her fingertips. Something was wrong and Rachel knew she was about to discover what it was. The skeleton key was in the keyhole so Rachel unlocked and opened the door slightly. Inside, and lying on Millie's bed, was the biggest raccoon she had ever seen. Rachel gasped in surprise and closed the door. She leaned her head against the dark wood for a moment and then went down the hall checking the rest of the rooms. The bathroom with its shiny white porcelain was spotless. Nancy's room with its huge walk in closet looked untouched. Nothing was out of place. She went past Nancy and up the stairs to the dormer that Millie had turned into a library. Nothing was out of the ordinary, and Millie wasn't there either. Rachel went back downstairs.

"Nancy honey, where is your mother? Why is there a raccoon in her room? Did Millie tell you to put it there?"

Nancy still didn't move, but she had started to cry. It managed to frighten Rachel more than being shot at.

Rachel went out to the kitchen and down the basement stairs. Maybe Millie had fallen. A quick examination of the concrete rooms told her the same story. Nothing was amiss. She went back to Millie's room and opened the door slightly. The animal watched her with some interest but stayed where he was. Rachel made herself look at every corner of the room. There was a small box of cat sand near the window that hadn't been used. The animal had obviously not been trained to the litter. Judging from the amount of waste throughout the room, Rachel felt he had been there about a week. Everything had been torn off the walls, and he had begun to try to chew his way out. Blood on the window showed clearly where he had banged his head in a frantic attempt to get out. His back arched and for a moment it looked as if he might try to run past her. Rachel closed the door and went back to the living room.

"Nancy, we are going to have to let the raccoon go. There isn't anything wrong with him. Then we'll get all of Millie's personal effects out of the room and have the rest of her belongings hauled away. She will like getting new things anyway, don't you think?"

Rachel left her and went back to Millie's room. She let herself in slowly and closed the door behind her. The big animal growled, but Rachel just talked to him softly and slowly and made her way to the window. He stood up and arched his back in a threatening posture but stayed where he was. Rachel unlocked the window and opened it. Millie's screens were the old fashion kind that hung on hooks on the outside of the house. Rachel got up on a desk and very quietly and slowly pushed it out as far as it would go and then lifted it off its hinges. One came off easily, but the other one caught so Rachel just let it swing to the side. She slowly walked backwards out of the room, never looking the raccoon in the eye but keeping him in her peripheral vision.

It took many minutes but finally she was out of the room and looking through the crack in the door. The agile animal moved silently to the window and sniffed the air. He looked out through the opening Rachel had made and carefully pushed his nose through it. When he could see that it wasn't another barrier, he disappeared through it and was gone. Rachel closed the door and locked it again. She would ask Millie what she wanted to do now.

Rachel sat on the couch and spoke gently to the weeping woman. "Nancy, where is Millie spending the nights? And where is that man that was here? Is that who you are going to marry?"

Nancy was alert to her last question. "I can't believe I was so wrong about a man."

Rachel felt a little more comfortable with the familiar statement and leaned back against the couch. "There will be other gentlemen, you are a very attractive person."

"He said the raccoon would be an extra income for us and Mother agreed to let me keep him in her room. She said she needed the fresh air anyway." She turned to Rachel and emphasized again, "Mother said it was all right to keep him in her room. I didn't know Mother already had so much money."

Rachel leaned forward, now she was getting someplace. "How did you know she had so much money?"

Nancy's face turned ugly when she cried, she was crying now. "Wayne went through her papers, and he said she had a lot of money."

Rachel found herself incensed that anyone would touch Millie's things without asking. She would have to advise her friend to put her private papers in a safe place. She went over and picked up Millie's glasses. "Tell me where she is so I can return these glasses to her, Nancy."

Nancy turned away and started to wail. Rachel had had enough. She went over to her and pulled her up by her shoulders. "You tell me where she is, right now, Nancy!"

"I didn't know what it meant, Rachel, she was old anyway you know."

Rachel's heart skipped a beat. Where had she heard those words before, and why did she find them so ominous?

She shook Nancy. Rachel found she was quite a bit stronger than the woman who sat around and painted her nails all day for exercise. "What are you saying about your mother!" Rachel was beginning to shout.

"I thought he was just going to put her to sleep for a while, I didn't know he meant to put her down."

Rachel literally threw the woman away from her. She suddenly had a clear picture of a large dog in a young boy's arms. She stood over Nancy and slapped her as hard as she could. Then she pulled her to her feet and yelled in her face. "Where is she! Tell me where she is!"

Nancy was visible frightened. "She was suffering, Rachel, she wasn't enjoying life anymore."

Rachel slapped her again. "You little bitch!" Rachel hung onto the terrified woman who was now beginning to fight back. She pushed Rachel as hard as she could and Rachel staggered slightly backward.

Rage made her keep her balance and she grabbed Nancy again and screamed at her, "I'm going to kill you right here and now if you don't tell me where he has taken her!"

Nancy didn't answer. She started to slap Rachel and kick her just as hard as she could. Rachel managed to push her over a footstool, a trick she had seen as a child and thought she had forgotten, clicked into her memory. She sat on Nancy's chest and held her arms with her knees. She put her hands on Nancy's wrists and leaned into her face. She was breathing too hard to speak. Fist fighting was not a sport she had learned.

Nancy spoke in gasps, "He said I would get over it in a couple of days and then I would see I had done the right thing. She would have wanted it that way. She didn't want to linger."

Rachel turned her face away and buried it in her shirtsleeve to control the nausea and overwhelming sense of loss.

"Get off me, Rachel, I can't breathe," Nancy whined. "He took care of everything, I don't know where Wayne took her." She started crying again. "He was suppose to come back but he didn't, and now the money is gone too."

Rachel got off her. She didn't want to touch her any more. She pushed herself away from Nancy until she was pressing against a chair. She clung to it as if it were a life raft. She tried to think, three old people were missing, and no one could find them. Where would a con man put them in a hurry? She sat straight up, surely not. Rachel got to her feet and went into the kitchen to wash her face in the sink. Then she walked out the back door of Millie's house and started walking down Spring Street. She would run when she got her breath back.

She alternated walking and running all the way to Main Street. She crossed over to the town hall and then down the block to the tavern. She ran down the alley staying well to one side to avoid the puddles of old tobacco and urine that had formed in the steady drizzling rain. The smell was intense; there wasn't enough water to wash away the filth. It had saturated into the ground for years and there wasn't anyplace for it to go.

She reached the old wooded lot and slowed down. She passed the old abandoned house with its sad windows and didn't even look at it. Rachel looked beyond it to the large oak trees that she knew were bending over the old death pit. She began to wring her hands the way a small child does when they are frightened of their parent's wrath. The rain dripped off the ends of her hair and gathered on her eyelashes before they ran down her cheeks like tears.

Rachel went over to the oak, she looked only in the direction she had come from. She embraced the tree and held onto it until the rough bark had made an imprint on her face. She had to make herself look into the pit. Slowly, she turned around and looked at the edge, she saw a strange little hat with a soaking wet feather still protruding from its band.

A sob escaped Rachel and she knelt down on the edge of the pit and looked at what lay near the hat. She covered her mouth. An old woman with curly gray hair and her face buried in the wet mud was reaching up as if for her lost hat. Rachel made herself look further. Frankie Wakeland lay looking up at the rain with his mouth strangely drawn and open. Partially laid across him was dear sweet Millie.

Rachel could see from her wet dress the depression in her hip. Rain filled the hole in her flesh as if it were part of the earth that had weathered out. Rachel didn't cry, she just let out strangled sobs as she let herself slide down the side of the hole. She made her way through the remains of many dead animals to her dear, dear friend. She lifted her up and tried to pull her up the side of the pit. The skin on Millie's arm gave and came away like a parchment glove in Rachel's hand. She slid back into the pit. The rain had washed away all of her makeup and the freckles stood out like a young child's. Her china eyes were warm and soft even in death.

Rachel put her arms around her and tried pulling herself and her burden up by roots that protruded from the slick clay banks. The stinking hole was hardly six-foot deep but Rachel couldn't get the leverage to pull them both up, so she lay against the bank and held Millie against her and out of the mud of her common grave. She regained some strength and tried again to get them both out of the pit. Rachel pressed Millie against the bank and lay on her while she held onto the protruding roots.

Millie's head fell against her shoulder like a sleeping child. Rachel told her, "I won't let you fall Millie, I won't let you fall, dear, sweet, Millie." She lay her head on Millie's shoulder and smelled perfume in the flowered fabric. The cool rain kept the smell of death at bay.

Millie's body began to move and Rachel looked up. Gib McNiff was leaning over the edge and had a hold of Millie's arm. Rachel began to push her towards him. When he had Millie completely over the edge he put her down and he reached for Rachel. He had just managed to pull her out when a voice shouted loud and clear.

"So, Uncle Gib, you finally put your gun down." They both looked across the pit and down the barrel of Ben McNiff's rifle. Rachel grabbed Millie and moved against the oak pulling the dead woman onto her lap and holding her tightly. Ben didn't give her a second glance.

"You aren't going to dog me anymore, old man. Clara was just a stupid old woman that got in my way. It was an accident but you just won't let go of it will you?"

Gib didn't say anything to Ben. He just stared at him. Rachel could see Gib's rifle but it was too far away. It was leaning against an oak on the other side of where Gib was standing. He had not meant for it to be there long because the barrel was pointed upward letting in all the water that was running off the leaves.

Ben relaxed and toyed a little longer with Gib now that he had the upper hand. "You know I have to kill you, Uncle Gib, and you too, Rachel," he said. "Then I can have some peace, I'm tired of spending my nights running through these woods. All for one stupid old woman. You're good Uncle Gib, we were a team once, us against the world! You had a soft spot for her didn't you Uncle Gib? Well, it's going to be what brings you down." He raised his gun to fire at Gib, and a single rifle shot pierced the air. Young Ben stood for only a moment and then pitched headfirst into the death pit.

Charlie walked out of the bushes and over to the edge of the pit. He took his pistol out of his shoulder holster and methodically fired six shots into Ben's head. Then he walked around the edge of the death hole towards Rachel. He surveyed the contents of the pit as he walked.

Rachel's teeth chattered with cold and shock at what she was witness to. She held Millie tightly and, as if talking to her, she said, "He was just a boy, he was just a child, was he even eighteen?" She directed this last question to Gib.

Gib came over and knelt down in front of her. He reached over, closed Millie's eyes, and then turned his attention to Rachel. "A child doesn't carry a gun," he said. He put his hand under her chin, and when she was looking straight into his eyes, he said quietly, "If you're going to continue to spy on me little Clara, don't wear perfume." He stood up, gave a brief farewell wave to Charlie, and retrieved his rifle. He disappeared toward his house and Rachel could hear him laugh. Rachel knew it was at her expense, but she also knew she was as much of a survivor as he was. Clara's killer was dead, let him laugh.

Charlie reached her side and evaluated the situation. Millie was obviously gone so there was not a need to hurry. He sat down beside her and put his arm around her.

"How did you know where to find me, Charlie?"

"I didn't. I got what I could out of Nancy and then I could see that your footprints had headed towards town. This was the only place I hadn't looked when we were searching for old Frankie. I didn't know euthanasia was the new game in town. I thought he had gone fishing and maybe had a heart attack or stroke. I stopped on the way here at Jacoby's and told Robert to send an ambulance this way and to keep it quiet until he heard back from me. They should be here any time now."

Rachel held Millie closer when she saw the vehicle coming across the grass to the edge of the trees. She looked down at her friend for one last time and then reached to hold her hand. It was then that she started to cry. She pried open Millie's fist and found that her ring was gone. She took off her own wedding rings and placed them on Millie's cold finger. She turned them until they were straight and had caught a little of the gray light. She let go, and Millie's fist closed solid and forever around the golden bands.

Stretchers were brought. Within minutes, the bodies were gone. There wasn't a siren, only a few flashing blue lights signaled these good people had passed this way.

Charlie and Rachel went back the way Rachel had come. Rachel sloshed through the puddles in the alley near the tavern and said good-bye to Charlie when they reached Main Street.

"Are you going to be all right, Rachel?" Charlie asked.

"Yes, I'll be fine. You should go on to Jacoby's and let people know what's happening. I have a few things to do."

It was still drizzling and both Charlie and Rachel were soaked to the skin and muddy.

Charlie persisted, "If you wait for me, I can take you to Laura and she will stay with you for a while."

Rachel had an incredible need to be alone. She didn't care about anything else except being completely alone so she could respond honestly to her grief. "Honestly, Charlie, I'm fine. I just want to be alone for a while."

Charlie nodded that he understood, but he watched her until she was out of sight before he went about the dreary business of relating the past hour to the police, and making people aware of this new threat at their back door.

Rachel went straight to the old family cemetery on the Stormont estate. She sat long hours at the foot of the graves of John and Clara. She had seen so much death lately that she was beginning to feel more at ease with dead people than live ones. Nearly everyone she loved was on the other side.

She sensed the sadness over the graves, and she idly patted mud up over the mounds. "John, what could you have been thinking when you started this? The sorrow that touches us is becoming so commonplace that I can't even remember what life is like without it."

Rachel looked up and listened to the pines while she let the rain run slowly down her face. She tried to find a key to her problems in the prairie wind that brushed the graves of these dear people. She bent her head again and continued the hopeless task of filling in the rivulets of water that kept forming on the serene resting-place.

Rachel's head snapped up. "That's it!" she cried. "That's the back door we couldn't find! Of course, of course, of course!" Rachel got to her feet and waved her hands around wildly in no particular pattern, her wet sleeves sticking to her arms and dripping water. "How could I have missed it." She plopped down on the grass and laughed up at the sky. "How could Simon have missed it!" Rachel got to her feet, and with the energy she had left, she went back to Clara's homestead.

What she had to tell Simon could wait. She tiptoed across the kitchen to the shower room. She spent a very long time in hot soapy water putting her emotions in perspective. She gathered up all her soiled clothes in a bag and threw them out the back door. She knew it was for the last time.

She called Simon and found that he had already been told what had happened and was frantic because he hadn't been able to reach her. There would be time enough to tell him the events that had led up to her discovery of what had happened to Millie, but for now, they had urgent business to attend to.

"Simon, I know what the back door is that John left us."

There was a slight silence at the other end and then he asked her excitedly, "Where did you find it. What did I overlook?"

"You didn't overlook anything, my love, it wasn't there. It just came to me when I visited the old cemetery. The grass hasn't had a chance to grow in very thick and so the water was making rivulets in the dirt."

"I'm lost, Rachel, help me out."

"I read John's papers until I was blind, and I went through everything on the computer. The answer isn't in what's there, it's in what's not there. Is it true, Si, that you can liquidate John and Clara's assets that are supporting Arakun?"

"I think it's true, Rachel, I think you are on to the answer," Simon said. "If we liquidate them, when the money runs out, it's over. The charity will fold. The question is, do we want to do it? There won't be any turning back if we do. We couldn't possibly run it on our income if, in the future, we find we have made a mistake."

Rachel sat down with her freshly brewed coffee. She enjoyed the smell of it lingering with her body lotions and perfume. She took a sip and gave herself a chance to contemplate the enormity of their decision. It would wipe out the estate of John and Clara Rossi.

She spoke with certainty, "It has caused so much turmoil and unhappiness, Simon that I don't feel that it should go on. Millie's death was the ultimate sacrifice, and there isn't any way to tell how much worse it can get."

Simon listened at his end of the telephone and agreed with her. The decision was made. "I've been looking for a way to stop this since I got here. I have done everything I can to prevent tragedy and it happened anyway. I will consult the other lawyers, and if they can't find a clause preventing us from liquidating, then, that is what we will do."

Rachel sat alone at the table for a long time. She was too tired to go to bed. When she finally went upstairs, she didn't bother to take off her jeans and Simon's flannel shirt. She just pulled up the covers and went to sleep.

Waking up was hard. All of her body ached and she could hardly stand. The sound of voices drifted up the stairs and Rachel tried to orient her thoughts and figure out who was in her house. The delicious smell of food and coffee drove her to get up. She cleaned up quickly and went downstairs. The closer she got, the more voices she recognized. One voice in particular made her run the minute she got to the bottom of the stairs.

"Simon!" she cried, when she saw him in the kitchen. She ran to his arms, hugged him, and bathed his face with kisses.

"O.K., you two," Robert laughed. "Let's break it up."

Rachel looked around the kitchen at all of her friends; Mary Lee, Charlie and Laura, Father Kessler, Terry the alter boy, Robert and Di who had obviously brought dinner, Nick and even Michael and his new wife. But the biggest surprise of all was old Gib McNiff standing with a coffee cup talking to Charlie. He had an arm slung loosely around a young boy. Rachel thought she recognized him. Then she remembered who he was, the boy with the dog.

Simon took her over for a formal introduction, "Rachel, I would like you to meet Laundy McNiff, our new gardener."

"Welcome to Stormont, Laundy," she said, shaking his hand.

"Thank you, Rachel," the boy said shyly.

Simon leaned over Rachel and took a closer look at her face. "You have a black eye."

Rachel let him examine her face in the light and took the opportunity to glance at Charlie. She saw him shrug and then smile. He obviously hadn't told Simon everything he knew.

"It's nothing, Si, really, I just must have bumped into something and don't remember it. How did you get home so fast, anyway?" she whispered.

He took her slightly aside from the main group and poured her some coffee. "After you called last night, I went straight to work. We were able to liquidate everything, there isn't any clause put in there to stop it. Within hours of putting everything on the market, it was sold to the highest bidder. The money was divided equally by area and a lump sum sent out explaining that Arakun had gone broke. The money was to be used to pay any outstanding debts and to notify all charity participants of the financial circumstances involving Arakun."

"It's over, then?" Rachel asked.

"It's over. I put Everett in charge of our finances and told him I would be in touch. We have to stay here for a while until all the legal situations are cleaned up that you, my love, have been involved in, and then I would like a vacation."

He kissed her and then went around the table to congratulate the Jacoby's on the fine food.

Rachel looked around at her friends, Gib had left without bringing any notice to himself, and some of the men had joined Simon in the living room.

The kitchen at Stormont was, once again, alive with people. She could hear the twins talking in Clara's room and then she heard the music box play. She went in to join them. They were sitting on the bed like two little angels. Rachel sat down beside them to listen to it. She thought about the one upstairs on her dresser that resembled Clara's in every way. She would return it to Gib, someday.

Fall had come to Stormont, the leaves had turned and the hot sticky days were over. Simon and Rachel found the cool days of September a joy and lived happily in their little country house. They had spent a great deal of time redecorating the interior and bringing some of their own things out of storage to the farm. They had gone for a lovely walk and had just picked wild flowers for the graves in the family cemetery.

"Si," Rachel said, "are there any more court appearances I have to make?"

Simon took her hand. "No, none, it's finally over. And with Charlie as our new sheriff, you will have to keep your nose clean."

Rachel laughed. "Everyone will."

"We haven't been to Jacoby's in over a month," Simon said to her, as he lay some wild flowers on the graves. "Let's say we go over and have something to eat?"

"Robert missed you while you were gone, Si," Rachel laughed. "He knows you have a weakness for his homemade pies."

"I have to eat sometime. You don't eat enough for a mouse, and don't seem to think anyone else should either."

They passed the house and went across LaDue instead of walking past Millie's. The house was boarded up for the time being. Millie's estate was far from being settled, but it was known that Simon and Rachel were going to buy it when it came up for sale. No one else really wanted it.

"Simon," Rachel asked, "what are you going to do with Millie's house?"

Her husband took a deep breath and held her hand with both of his. "I don't know, yet. Sometimes I want to tear it down and burn it, and other times I want to restore it and pretend Millie is still in there eating cookies and whistling a tune that carries all over the neighborhood. I just don't know."

He looked down at her ringless hand. His eyes filled with tears, and he said softly to Rachel, "I'm proud that she has our rings to wear. I'll get you a new set, soon." He leaned down to kiss her.

Jacoby's was warm and smelled wonderful. It was a combination of homemade bread and hot soup simmering on the stove. Robert and Di had their hands full with all the customers on these fall evenings. It seemed everyone wanted to spend as much time outside as possible, before the winter snows. And no one wanted to cook on a Friday night. Robert took their order, and they sat down in a big corner booth overlooking Main Street. Mary Lee came in, and a delighted Rachel insisted she sit with them. The two had become like sisters. This new development delighted Simon because he still liked to spend time discussing the stock market with friends, and Rachel hated it.

"I have ordered a new dress that is simply you," she was telling Rachel.

"I'll be over to see it," Rachel said happily.

"What on earth is that pin you are wearing?" Simon suddenly asked Mary Lee.

He startled both of the women when he grabbed the lapel of Mary Lee's jacket.

Mary Lee looked down at her coat and then took it off and showed it to him. "It's an Arakun button, don't you have one yet?"

Both Rachel and Simon felt ill at the same time. Surely, the nightmare wasn't about to begin again.

"I don't have one," Rachel finally ventured to say. "Where did you get it?"

"Well," Mary Lee went on, "it's because you two have been so busy at Stormont that you don't have time to keep up on what's going on in the world. It's even been in all the papers."

Simon and Rachel were baffled. They knew that Arakun was finished, the funds dried up, and here Mary Lee was telling them it wasn't.

"Well, it seems that the old people on that island that started the whole thing? Well, they couldn't manage their money well enough to keep it going. I hear they went bankrupt. Well, they had just enough saved to give everyone a little start on their own charity and the most freaky thing happened." She leaned forward for the best part of her story. "Everyone chose the name Arakun. And this was all without anyone knowing what name the others were choosing. Isn't that weird?" She leaned back while the waitress set down her dinner.

"When did all this happen?" Simon asked her.

"Last week sometime. Everyone is excited about it. After seeing how it was to be treated like animals ourselves, everyone has a new outlook." She looked knowingly at Rachel. "It's not funny to be stalked, and I'm sure that if Grace was here she could add a little more to that story."

They were silent at the table for a few minutes as each of them remembered the ones that had been lost.

"Anyway," Mary Lee went on, "towns all over are starting up their own Arakun charity. They are being run by volunteers and everyone chips in what money they can. It belongs to the people. Everything and everyone is welcome there. Especially kids. No one and nothing is turned away. We kept the same basic rules but added a few things of our own, like this pin. At the store, I have Arakun shirts and cups; the little handles are raccoons, and dishes with little raccoons or little possums on them. It depends on what you like. They have other designs, but I like those two. A certain percent of the sales goes to Arakun and then it's used to help anyone or anything in true need in our own community.

"Does anyone else know very much about this?" Simon asked.

Mary Lee set her coffee down and looked at him. In general, her look often let him know how dense she thought he must be. "Simon," she said, leaning over Rachel, "you have apparently missed the ten foot sign that says, A-R-A-K-U-N."

Mary Lee went back to sipping her coffee and watching the other customers. She looked very smug. She knew what the next question had to be and was willing to give out more of her wisdom.

"Where is it?" Rachel said. "I haven't seen it." She didn't care if she had to beg for the answer, she had to know.

"We got together at the town meeting and bought the old hardware store and all the lots behind it. We'll add on as we get funds. There is a volunteer list just inside the door, but I'll save you the trouble of going over there. It's filled for the next year."

Simon smiled at her, he didn't mind her teasing. "You can count on Rachel and I for anything."

"Good," she said, bringing out a list. "I'll put you down for one cage and four bags of old, white material. We make bandages and roll them up for the visiting vets to use."

Rachel was thrilled, she could think of all kinds of things to do to help. She suddenly had a bad thought.

"What about that death pit?" she asked her friend.

Mary Lee gave her a small hug. "Filled in. We are going on into the future, and we are going to make it better for the children. Places like that pit don't exist anymore."

A handsome man approached the table and Mary Lee became slightly nervous, "I see a friend of mine has just come in," she whispered to Rachel, "I'll talk to you later."

Simon and Rachel went to the counter to pay their bill, and there was a can that said Arakun. Simon dropped his change into the can, and they left the restaurant. They walked over to Frankie Wakeland's old hardware store, and sure enough, there was a ten-foot sign that read, ARAKUN.

Rachel leaned closer to him in the dark and gazed at the sign. "Do you think we should make an anonymous, generous offering?"

Simon took her hand and started walking home. "I definitely do not. Arakun isn't run on money. It's run on love."

"You know, Simon," Rachel said, "once you told me no one would fault me if I wanted to have a life of my own, and I thought I did have one. But now I see there is even more. But I wouldn't have seen it or been ready for it if it weren't for Clara."

They walked the rest of the way to Stormont in a happy silence. The crisp air made them hurry in anticipation of that warm fire in the fireplace. Laundy had taken up residence with them. He slept in a spare room off the kitchen that had been used for storage for a long time. Rachel had helped him pick out furniture and clothes, and he was as happy to be with them as they were to have him. He refused to spend all his time with them though. He liked being independent and spent his days learning to run Stormont. Looking at Laundy was like looking at the future. Stormont would go on, Stormont was the sweet an-ces-te-ry that Clara had left for those that followed in her footsteps.

"Simon," Rachel said. She leaned against his arm. "I think Millie would approve if we eventually set Laundy up in her house. I think he is the one who belongs there."

Simon kissed her on the top of her head and held her closely as they walked. He didn't need to answer, it was just so right.

Laddie barked once at the window when he heard the little squeak of the old iron gate. Then he was gone, they knew he would be waiting at the back door for them. He spent half of his time with Nick and the other half at Stormont. He had a nice big family to take care of him. He was particularly fond of Laundy.

"You're just in time for the movie," Laundy said, when they came in. "It's going to be a good one and it starts in about fifteen minutes."

"I'll take Laddie out if you make the popcorn, Simon," Rachel said.

"That's a fair deal," he said, as he headed for the pantry.

Rachel stood on the porch and waited for the dog. She casually glanced around the estate.

"Oh no," she said under her breath. She looked past the barn at the place she knew the little white crosses to be, and as had happened before, she could see two little images. The light from the house was blurring her view. There seemed to be something else out there. With a sigh, Rachel stepped out on the path and went toward the barn. As she drew near, she saw the two little forms trying to get over the fence. Then they disappeared. Rachel moved a little closer and then cried out with joy. She wept as one weeps with too much happiness. The two little raccoons were running, playing, and slowly making their way toward the trees in the distance. She watched them for as long as she could see them.

"Clara, I mean, Rachel, Simon said to bring you a jacket and tell you the popcorn is ready." Laundy handed her the coat and took her hand. Laddie bounced happily beside them.

"Watch your step here," he said, and then let go of her hand. "You know, Rachel, when I was little I used to see Clara stand in that same spot, you reminded me of her just then."

Rachel put her arm around his shoulder as she walked back to the house. "I want you to do me a favor, Laundy. The next time you see your Uncle Gib, tell him he doesn't need to bring flowers anymore, the little raccoons are with Clara."

THE END

□

ORDER FORM

Telephone Orders: **Toll Free 1-877-405-4255**

On Line Orders: **www.wildwindspublishing.com**

Postal Orders: **Wild Winds Publishing**
Post Office Box 83
Mt Sterling, IL 62353

Please send ______ copy(s) of Possums Sing to the address below:

Name:____

Address:____

City:____________________________State:__________Zip:________

Telephone: (____)________________________

Payment per book is $ 11.95 plus shipping of $2.50 per book.

Payment:
□ Check
□ Credit Card: □ Visa □ MasterCard
Card Number: ____

Name on Card:

____

Exp.Date: ____/____

Please call for pricing on orders over 10 books.